Long Way Home

by
Melissa Hart Romero

Windstorm Creative Limited
Port Orchard, WA

The Long Way Home
copyright © 2000 by Melissa Hart Romero
published by Windstorm Creative Limited

ISBN 1-883573-15-7

9 8 7 6 5 4 3 2
First Edition October 2000

Cover Design by CKD for Blue Artisans
Interior Design by CKD for Blue Artisans
Series Design by Windstorm Creative Limited
Edited by Beth Mitchum
Author Photo by Joey Romero

Windstorm Creative Limited is a six imprint, international
organization involved in publishing books in all genres,
including electronic publications; producing games, toys,
videos and audio cassettes as well as producing theatre,
film and visual arts events.

Windstorm Creative Limited
7419 Ebbert Drive Southeast
Port Orchard WA 98367
360-769-7174
home@windstormcreative.com
www.windstormcreative.com

Acknowledgements

I would like to thank Nicola Morris, Jacqueline Woodson, Jane Wohl and Mariana Romo-Carmona for continuously inspiring me during the writing of this novel. My deepest gratitude to Jennifer DiMarco, Cris Newport and Natalie Brown at Windstorm Creative for believing in this story and putting it out into the world. Most of all, I thank my family for their tremendous love, support and humor.

Dedication

I dedicate this novel to the countless children who have been unjustly separated from loving parents. May you find peace . . . and laughter.

Long Way Home

by
Melissa Hart Romero

Windstorm Creative Limited
Port Orchard, WA

Chapter 1

Two weeks before I was supposed to begin junior high school, my mother put my little brother, sister, and me in her newly-purchased red Volkswagen bus and drove us away from the middle-class suburban life I'd always known. Earlier in the day, she had tossed books and records into paper bags. She had flown through our closets and dresser drawers, packing what she felt was necessary to keep, discarding the rest without a word. We stood open-mouthed in doorways watching her and got into the bus without being asked. Katie and I even let Tim sit in the front seat. We buckled our seatbelts behind him, and Mother stacked paper bags on top of each other at the back of the bus. She locked the front door of our house and backed the bus out of the garage. As the automatic garage door lowered back down, Mother rolled down the window and tossed the back door key and the garage door opener into the clipped hedge beside the driveway.

She slowed at the stop sign at the end of our street, then thought the better of it and gunned the engine, jolting the bus forward. A thick white book with a picture of a frog on its dust jacket fell out of a box, hit me on the shoulder, and then landed on the floor of the bus with a thud. I picked it up and clutched it as tightly as Mother was clutching the steering wheel. I knew this book. It was a collection of short stories by Mark Twain. Mother liked to say that he was the funniest writer in the world. Whenever Katie, Tim and I argued, she would cuddle us to her and say, "Against the assault of laughter, nothing can stand," which is something Mark Twain used to say, too.

The book had stood at my eye-level on the oak bookshelf in the hall of our house in Newbury Park. The frog on the spine matched the frog on the cover— both were green and spread out as if they had been pressed there like the four-leaf clovers my friends and I hunted for in the schoolyard during lunchtime.

Next to the oak bookshelf was a closet with

mirrored doors. Last night, Mother had asked me to wait in the hall for the baby-sitter while she and my father got dressed to go out to dinner. Even though I was twelve, Mother liked to have a baby-sitter at home when she and Daddy went out, in case Tim did anything weird. The one time I'd stayed alone with my little brother, he'd tried to fly down the stairs using a bath towel for a cape. He sprained his ankle.

"We know you're responsible," Mother assured me, "but with Tim's disability, I feel better having Mrs. Carter here."

So last night, I'd hung out in the hallway waiting for Mrs. Carter and staring at my reflection, pretending that I was looking at a stranger. The girl in the mirror was short and thin, with blue eyes so big that she looked like a bug. She had a long brown ponytail, and her smile revealed crooked front teeth. Standing sideways in her blue tank top, it was evident that she still didn't need the cotton training bra her mother had just bought her.

Quickly, I had turned away from the mirror and sat on the stairs to wait for the baby-sitter. No matter how much I pretended otherwise, the girl in the mirror was definitely me, Veronica Davis. I didn't look like a girl boys would ask to dance with at the junior high dances, but Mother promised me that boys would fall all over me this year because I was nice and funny. Besides, Daddy had agreed to pay for braces to straighten my teeth.

Now, I clenched my teeth together as Mother rounded the corner by the Burger King, tires screeching against the pavement. The bus rocked like a boat. I was terrified that it would tip over. Mother had traded in her blue mini-van for the bus a few weeks ago. Clearly she wasn't used to driving it yet. Beside me, Katie held on to her seat with both hands and began to sing. We always sang in the car. Mother had taught us rounds — songs sung in two or more parts — like "Frere Jacques." We knew all the songs from the musicals *Cats* and *The Sound of Music*, too. Katie was singing "My Favorite Things" and getting the words all messed up on purpose.

"Dogs in white dresses with goose hats and rashes . . . "

"Be quiet, Katie," Mother said. Her voice sounded tight, as if her vocal cords might snap at any moment like the strings on a guitar. She pulled onto the freeway and glanced into the rear view mirror.

"Quiet!" Tim echoed, turning around in the front seat beside Mother. He stuck his tongue out at Katie and rolled his eyes back in his head so that only the whites showed.

"Make me!" Katie's blond curls were plastered to her forehead from the summer heat. Ordinarily she was adorable, with downward tilted blue eyes and two front teeth missing out of her wide grin. At the moment she looked like an apple left to shrivel in the sun.

I looked down at my clothes, packed in paper bags by my feet. Mother had just bought me two flowered dresses and a pair of green corduroy overalls for the first week of school. I could never decide which I liked better— overalls and T-shirts or pretty dresses— so she bought me both.

"Are we going hiking?" I asked, bending down to retie the laces on my green high-top tennis shoes. Mother liked to load us all in the car to go on picnics by the lake or on hikes up in the mountains, particularly after she and Daddy had stayed up all night yelling, but she'd packed too many clothes for just a picnic. And there were the books and her box of jazz records piled high behind me.

"We're going to a friend's house."

Mother hunched over the steering wheel, glaring at the freeway ahead of her. I wanted to remind her of the time she was driving Trisha, Dolores, and me home from gymnastics, and we were all singing "Señor Don Gato," a song about a cat who falls off a roof while reading a love letter. A policeman had pulled Mother over and given her a ticket for speeding. After he drove off, she said "Dammit!" but then she laughed and gave the ticket to Tim so he could pretend *he* was a policeman.

I scanned the freeway for police cars now and didn't say anything about how fast Mother was driving. She pulled her hair into a loose ponytail and held it with one hand off her neck, which was shiny with sweat.

When I first remember noticing Mother's hair, it was blond and teased high up on her head with hairspray. Once, when I'd shown Trisha a picture of Mother with her tall hairdo, she told me that she knew of a woman with hair just like that— when she died they found a nest of spiders in her hair. I was glad Mother didn't wear her hair like that anymore. Lately, she'd let it go back to its original brown. She wore it loose around her face. A photographer had taken her picture with Tim at last month's County Fair, and it had been in the newspaper. She didn't like the photograph because her tongue was sticking out, licking the candy apple Tim held. I thought she looked beautiful. But today, a frown line cut deep between her eyebrows, and her cheeks were red with heat or anger— I wasn't sure which. Her face scared me.

I traced the flattened frog on Mark Twain's book with one finger, wondering why the fight my parents had last night had felt so different from all the fights before.

When Daddy and Mother had returned from dinner last night, I was outside on the lighted patio helping Katie and Tim make people out of rose petals on the warm cement. The whole August night smelled of roses, and the sky was thick with stars. When Daddy went out to say hello to us, he found the sliding glass door locked.

"Why was the goddamn door locked?" he yelled. I smelled garlic and wine as he bent to pick up Tim. He stepped on a pink and yellow face and crushed the petals into the ground.

Tim shrieked and pushed his lower lip out in a pout. "You crazy, Dad!" he said.

"*Why was the door locked*?" Daddy's thin lips tightened under his mustache and he glared at Mrs. Carter.

Our baby-sitter was an older woman with black hair knotted into a tight bun. She didn't talk much. She served us our dinner from the oven where Mother had put it and left us to play while she read *People* magazine on the couch. When Daddy asked her about the locked door, her dark eyes got black and swallowed their pupils. It was the only time I could remember seeing an expression on her face.

"Honestly, Mr. Davis, I had no idea the door was locked," she stammered.

Daddy's voice rose higher with each word until he sounded like a woman. The yellow circles in his eyes glowed with fury. "You locked my children outside in the dark!"

Mother put her hand on his arm. "Zach, I'm sure it was an accident. Carol would never . . ."

Daddy jerked his arm away. My heart began to pound. "Stay out of this, Maggie!" He turned back to Mrs. Carter. "I'd just like to know where you get off locking my children outside, while your fat ass sits on the phone all night!"

I wanted to tell Daddy that the back door locks by itself sometimes if you slam it hard enough. Mother herself knew this. Just last weekend, Katie had locked herself outside, and Mother had to let her back in. I opened my mouth to tell Daddy this, but now his face was so red that I was afraid he would explode. I imagined little pieces of him flying all over the room— his mustache stuck to the chandelier, his terrible yellow-rimmed eyes bouncing into separate corners.

Mother took Tim by the hand. "I'm going to put the kids to bed," she said quietly. She led us up the stairs and into the bedroom Katie and I shared. But instead of tucking us into our twin beds and sitting in the rocking chair with Tim to tell us a bedtime story, she said, "Ronnie, Katie, you girls stay here and be quiet," and took Tim to his room.

Tears began to drop from Katie's eyes. "I'm scared," she whispered. She huddled up on her bed and hugged her pillow to her chest. "Daddy's so loud."

I tiptoed into the bathroom to get her a tissue and peeked in at Mother. She was putting Tim's pajamas on for him. Usually, she waited patiently for his stubby fingers to fumble with the buttons, but Daddy was still yelling at Mrs. Carter. As I walked back to my room, Mother rushed past me and down the stairs.

I handed the box of tissues to Katie. She had wrapped her ragged, grayish-white security blanket around her shoulders like a shawl. She'd had that blanket since she was a baby, and even though she was nine years old, she refused to let anyone throw it away. She called it Seymour and slept with it even after Daddy told her it was full of germs.

I lay down with my ear pressed to the carpet and listened to Daddy's voice thundering below me. Then I heard quick footsteps and a door slamming. I crept to the top stair and looked down through the railing at my parents. They were standing on either side of the dining room table with their fists clenched, glaring at each other like the boxers in the fights Daddy watched on TV on Sunday afternoons.

"You chose the sitter!" Daddy yelled. "Aren't you a better judge of character than that?"

"Carol has been watching the kids for three years. It was an *accident*, Zach. You're over-reacting, as usual." Mother's voice was gentle and slow, the way it sounded when she was working on shapes and colors with Tim.

As she spoke, Daddy's hand lashed out and snatched an apple from the crystal bowl of fruit in the center of the table. He threw it hard at Mother. It bounced off her shoulder and rolled into the kitchen.

Mother clutched her shoulder. "Fuck you," she said in a low voice that frightened me more than Daddy's yelling. I scrambled into my room and shut the door. Katie looked up at me with her face all splotchy from crying. I put my finger to my lips and got into bed. I reached for the copy of *Little Women* that Mother's mother, Grandma Hammond, had bought me for my birthday in July. I tried to read the first page, even though I'd just finished the book yesterday. The words swam in front of my eyes.

Daddy and Mother kept yelling and swearing at

each other all night. Once, I heard the sound of glass breaking, but I didn't come out of my room again. I wondered if I should call the police or Mrs. Jackson from next door, but the phone was downstairs. I hated myself for being such a coward. *Mother might be hurt downstairs, and you don't even have the courage to see if she's okay*, I thought. I glanced at Katie. She had finally fallen asleep with Seymour draped over her head. I wished I could sleep.

I knew that one time Daddy had broken Mother's nose. I didn't know how or when. She had a pretty nose that reddened and freckled in the sun. Sometimes I caught her examining the crooked part in the hallway mirror. Mother had hit Daddy once, too, with her wedding ring hand. He had a little white scar under his right eye that I could see when he bent down to kiss me good night.

Tonight, when Daddy came in to kiss us, we'd be gone — vanished up the freeway. I wondered if he would realize that our clothes and even our toothbrushes were missing and come looking for us.

"Is Daddy meeting us somewhere?" I asked Mother.

"*Absolutely not!*" Mother spat out the words as if Daddy were a gross taste in her mouth. We'd left the city now. The bus fled past cactus-covered hills down the grade to Camarillo.

"Are we going to our new house?" Katie asked.

I almost smiled with relief. Of course we were going to our new house. Mother couldn't wait to move in. Neither could I.

"There is no new house," Mother told Katie.

I stared at the back of Mother's head in disbelief. "But Daddy bought it, didn't he?" I cried. "He said it was my birthday house! What about the horses? What about the grapes and the acre with a view?"

After months of house hunting, Katie and I knew almost as much about real estate as Mother's realtor. We followed Mother into the realty office and soberly looked over her shoulder at the color photos of houses, as we sucked on peppermints from a bowl on the desk. We sat in the back seat of the realtor's car and ran our hands over the velvety green upholstery, struggling to understand words like fixer-upper and square feet. At each house, Katie and I examined the rooms, opening closets and imagining what our new bedroom would look like.

Mother didn't care about the houses themselves. She wanted land and animals and a complete change from the elegant two-story house she and Daddy had bought in Newbury Park thirteen years ago. Daddy had grown up in a rural part of Vermont, so he was glad to move, even though it meant he'd still have to commute an hour to his job at the insurance company in Los Angeles every day. "The kids need room to run around in," he'd agreed with Mother.

Mother almost decided on a three-bedroom house with a large yard full of animal pens. "The rabbits will go here," she told us, "and the chickens will go there, because there's a shelf for roosting. And look!" Her eyes shone bright blue. "That pen is big enough for a goat!"

"But no room for horses," Daddy said after he'd gone with her to look at the house. "The girls want horses."

Katie and I had crossed our fingers and even our toes for luck. Mother smiled at us and promised to keep on looking until she found the perfect yard and house.

In July, she found it— three bedrooms on an acre of grassy fields that sloped gradually into a hill. Katie, Tim, and I rolled down the hill and discovered a grapevine hanging over a wooden fence. The grapes were hard and green, but we stuffed them into our mouths and winced happily at their sourness. I'd never seen grapes growing on a vine before.

"Horse property," Daddy said that night. "We'll take it."

But a man had already made a bid on the property, higher than Daddy could afford. We waited, thinking up terrible things to do to the man if he bought our property. Then the realtor called, the day before my birthday. The man had decided to buy a bigger house. The grassy hill, horses, and grapes were ours.

"Well, happy birthday, Veronica," Daddy had said. "Some kids get a bike . . . you get a house."

"We'll fix it so that you can still go to junior high

with your friends," Mother said. "I'll have to drive you to school, since the bus doesn't come out to Ojai." When she said that, I felt a shiver of happiness across my back. I imagined bringing Trisha and Dolores home from school on the weekends to ride my horse and eat grapes in our field.

Three weeks later, Daddy threw the apple at Mother.

Now, imprisoned in the back seat of the VW bus, I felt as angry as Daddy had been last night. "What do you mean we aren't moving!" I shouted at Mother.

Tim covered his ears with his thick, square hands. "Shut up!"

Mother ran her hand over Tim's blond hair, letting it rest on the flat part at the back of his head. "Don't say 'shut up,' Timmy — you sound like your father," she said softly.

I wondered if Tim was the reason we weren't moving. Daddy was so protective of him. Maybe he was afraid Tim would break his neck rolling down the hill or that he'd get stepped on by a horse.

When Mother had Tim, everyone whispered that he was a strange baby with a big head that he couldn't lift from his thin, pale body, even after he was several months old. Mother put him in a special school for disabled kids when he was only a year old, so he could learn how to move his body and react to lights and sounds. His teacher, Ms. Whitney, said that Tim was making terrific progress and that he needed to be encouraged to do things on his own, but Daddy wouldn't let Tim play in the backyard on the weekends without Mother or me outside with him. He still cut Tim's meat at the dinner table and tied his shoes for him, even though Mother said that wasn't doing Tim any favors.

Mother took her hand off of Tim's head and drove the bus up the six-lane freeway bordered by fields of some sort of leafy vegetable. A horrible smell seeped into the car.

"Eew! Tim farted," Katie said.

"Did not!" Tim stuck his tongue out so far that it touched the tip of his chin.

"That's just fertilizer," Mother sighed.

"Tim isn't really our brother," Katie whispered to me. "Some people from outer-space stole our real brother and gave us Tim instead."

I ignored her. The fertilizer smell was making me feel sick. I didn't know where Mother was taking us, but I knew I wasn't going to like it. I wanted to go home and try on the new pink nail polish I'd bought for the first day of school with part of the allowance Daddy gave me for keeping my room clean. I pictured the bottle sitting unopened in my nightstand drawer and wished I had brought it with me.

"We *are* moving, girls," Mother said suddenly. "We're moving in with a friend of mine at the beach."

"Who?" I demanded.

"You know Ms. Whitney."

"Tim's teacher?" Katie squeaked.

Mother nodded. "Her oldest daughter just moved out. She's got an extra room. We'll stay there until we find our own house. It's only temporary."

"Our *own* house?" I cried. "What's wrong with the one Daddy just bought, or the one in Newbury Park!" The fields blurred green and gold through my tears. We'd already been driving for a long time, far away from my junior high and our new house. "I can't believe you're doing this!" I yelled. "You can't just take us out of our lives!"

"It'll all work out," Mother said grimly. "It has to."

Katie watched me, her blond eyebrows drawn together ferociously. I kept on yelling.

"We have a good life! What about my friends? What about school? What about Daddy?"

Katie reached over and put her hand on my arm. For just a moment, she seemed like the big sister, and I felt like the little one. "You know why we have to leave," she whispered. "Mother was getting hurt, and she was scared Daddy might hurt us."

Mother met my eyes in the mirror. She reached over and behind the seat to take my hand. "I know it's . . . it's *horrible* to take you away from your friends and your school. But your father hurts me, Ronnie. I don't know why he does, but he does." Her own eyes filled with tears. "And that's *not* a good life."

I swallowed hard and sniffled. "Okay," I muttered. I turned away from everyone to stare out the window. "Fine."

But it wasn't fine. Since when had Mother become friends with Ms. Whitney? Tim's teacher wore ugly button-down shirts and no make-up. She had a raspy voice and lines all over her face as if she'd smoked too many cigarettes. Mother's friends had always been the mothers of Katie's and my friends— they helped with the Girl Scout troop and sat around having Tupperware parties. I couldn't imagine Ms. Whitney at a Tupperware party. She didn't look like she even *owned* Tupperware.

I'd wondered what Mother and Ms. Whitney had been talking about so seriously all those afternoons that Mother stood in front of Tim's school, while Katie and I waited in the car. I figured they'd been discussing Tim's progress, laughing about his big head, but now I knew they'd been talking about ruining my life.

Until this afternoon, I thought Mother was the best mother in the world. She was our school's Girl Scout leader. She spent every Monday afternoon in the school cafeteria, teaching us camping skills and helping us make Valentine and Easter cards for elderly people in retirement homes. Katie and I had the best birthday parties in the neighborhood, because Mother put out all sorts of decorations for cupcake decorating contests and invented games like who could spoon the most cotton balls from one bowl to another blindfolded. She had her faults, like cooking liver and onions, which I hated, but I never imagined she'd just rip me away from my life.

Katie wrapped Seymour around her head like a dirty white turban. "How many kids does Ms. Whitney have?" she said.

"Four," Mother replied. "Three of them still live with her. They're older than you, but they're nice. You'll like them." Her hand trembled as she reached for a piece of paper on the dashboard and examined it. The ring Daddy had bought for us to give her last Mother's Day sparkled in the late afternoon sun. It was called a "Mother's Ring" because it had each of our birthstones — a red stone for me, and two green ones, one for Katie and one for Tim, both born in May.

Just as I had finally gotten used to the horrible smell from the fields, the freeway curved to the left, and there was the ocean — deep blue the color of Tim's eyes — stretched out perfectly straight against the sky.

"The beach!" Katie and Tim cried, rolling down the windows all the way. A breeze blew through the car, cooling my hot face.

Tim propped his feet up on the dashboard. "I surf!" he said and gave the thumbs-up sign to an old man in the car next to us. Katie sat up on her knees to see better. Mother consulted the piece of paper again.

There was no ocean in Newbury Park. We drove to the beach in Carpinteria every few months to camp under eucalyptus trees with their sharp smell that got into the eggs and bacon Mother cooked, and made breakfast, each time, the best I'd ever eaten. I wanted to jump out of the car and run to the beach now, to bury myself in the soft, damp sand the way we'd buried Daddy one time. Katie and I had piled sand on him up to his neck, and Mother ran over from the bacon she was frying and sat on him, laughing, until he stood up all sandy and chased her into the ocean.

"You girls can walk to the beach," Mother said absently as we left Ventura and headed up the coast. "Ms. Whitney said she'll teach you how to fish."

I thought of Ms. Whitney with her chopped-off, curly black hair and deep, scratching voice. "I don't like her," I muttered. "And I hate fish."

Mother ignored me. She drove until we came to Carpinteria, and then she pulled the bus into a driveway on a short street across from the beach. She turned off the motor and just sat there for a moment. "Here we are." She pointed to a house that looked like a dirty gray shoebox up-ended. A volleyball net sagged in the sand beside the house. Katie and I got out of the car. My knees popped from sitting for what seemed like hours. I kicked at the sand with one shoe, and a grain flew into my eye. I rubbed at it furiously and followed Mother up to the house with red eyes, hot and aching.

I wanted to go home and call my friends. Trisha and I were supposed to go for a bike ride this afternoon. Last weekend, both of our mothers had let us ride bikes to the mall. A group of boys whistled at us from the music store and told us to meet them at the food court next week. Now Trisha would be mad at me, and she'd go with Dolores instead, even though she said Dolores rode too slow on her bike.

Mother knocked on the front door of the gray house twice, then reached up into the cobwebs behind the porch light and pulled out a key. I eyed her suspiciously as she unlocked the door, wondering how she'd known where the key was. We followed her into a room with three beds in three different corners on a cracked cement floor. A TV balanced on a blue plastic milk crate in the fourth corner. In the middle of the room stood a refrigerator, a stereo with a record player, and a square table hidden by piles of socks and towels and a bunch of black bananas. The walls were also cement, covered with pictures of tattooed men dripping with sweat and scowling over electric guitars.

"This used to be a garage," Mother murmured. "Liz . . . Ms. Whitney turned it into a bedroom when her kids got older." She peered at the stairs in the corner, hesitating.

"Do we get to sleep in here?" Katie asked.

Mother started up the stairs. She held Tim's hand while he climbed each step slowly, one at a time. "There's a bedroom for you girls upstairs." She opened the door, and we walked into a carpeted living room full of couches. I counted five, all different colors and sizes. A woman's voice wailed a country western song from the stereo in the corner. Ms. Whitney stood with her back to us in a tiny kitchen, reaching into the refrigerator.

"Liz," Mother said, the name expelled as if someone had just sat on her and squeezed out all the air in her body.

Ms. Whitney turned around with a bottle of beer in her hand. "Maggie. You're here." She walked over, and Mother crumpled on her shoulder.

"Iss my teacher!" Tim exclaimed, poking me in the side.

"I know," I muttered. Ms. Whitney had a face just like her cracked leather boots, and her T-shirt was full of holes. Smoke drifted across the room from a cigarette lying in a glass ashtray on the kitchen counter. I coughed loudly.

"Eating time," Tim said, looking at the kitchen. "Pizza, maybe?"

I reached for Tim and hugged him. It felt good to hold on to someone the way Mother was holding on to Ms. Whitney.

Everything was happening way too fast. I knew Daddy and Mother hadn't been getting along. Katie and I agreed that lately, we both hated weekends because Daddy was home, and he'd yell about every little thing, like the garbage disposal not working because Tim dropped a toy car down inside it. Mother could yell just as loud as Daddy, but he was stronger. Once, he'd backed her up against a wall and just held her there with one hand against her chest.

On the weekdays, though, everything was okay. I'd almost gotten used to being afraid of Daddy when he was home, and I figured Mother had, too. But watching her cling to Ms. Whitney in the living room that looked like a graveyard for dead couches, I knew then that Mother couldn't stay with Daddy even one more night.

But she was holding onto Ms. Whitney for too long, I thought. What about us? I coughed again and waved imaginary smoke out of my face.

Mother looked up and saw my frown. "These are my girls," she said, pulling away from Ms. Whitney. Katie and I had already met Ms. Whitney once at an open house for Tim's school and once at a parent-teacher conference we'd had to go to because our baby-sitter was sick. I raised one eyebrow at Ms. Whitney, then stared down at my green high-tops.

This is only temporary— I repeated in my head. I could stand the idea of moving somewhere else with Mother, but if I had to live with Ms. Whitney for long, I'd run away.

Ms. Whitney pointed down the hall. "Your room's in there," she croaked. The room she showed us looked like a jail cell, with two foldout cots and bare, dirty walls full of thumbtack holes. Mother put her arms around Katie and me. "We'll go out tomorrow and buy pretty bedspreads and posters." I knew then that she, too, was thinking of our bedroom at home, with its matching yellow-and-white-checked bedspreads, curtains, and lampshades.

"Why don't you bring your things upstairs," Ms. Whitney suggested. "Your room'll look more like home."

"It's not *my* room," I muttered under my breath. "And it's not *home*."

"I like it," Katie said, twirling around like a ballerina on the stained brown carpet. "It's empty."

"I'll be down in a minute to help you," Mother said. Her red cheeks had grown pale, and the corners of her mouth hung down. She dug a coloring book and some crayons out of Tim's backpack. He stretched out happily on one of the cots. "I've gotta get out of these jeans," Mother sighed, reaching down to pull off her white tennis shoes. Ms. Whitney led her down the hall and into another room.

Katie and I found our way downstairs and outside to the bus. We struggled to lift the crate with Katie's and Tim's toys. "It's too heavy," Katie wailed and dropped her end of the crate.

As we knelt down in the sand to pick up Tim's toy cars and boats, a deep voice behind us said, "Here, let me help you with that." A man, or almost a man, reached down and lifted the crate up onto one shoulder. "Welcome to Carpinteria. I'm Max."

Katie and I traded wide-eyed looks. Max grinned at us and headed upstairs. He was at least six feet tall, skinny, with pale, freckled skin and bushy black hair— the most handsome man I'd ever seen.

"Maybe he's Ms. Whitney's husband," Katie whispered to me.

I shook my head. "She's too old for him."

Max walked straight into our new room and set the crate down beside Tim. "Hi. You're Tim, right?"

Tim looked up from his coloring book. "Hi. You tall."

Ms. Whitney stood in the doorway. "Your mom's lying down, girls. I'll take care of her. Max'll help you with your stuff."

I didn't like the way Ms. Whitney talked about Mother as if she owned her. I'd known Mother a lot longer than she had, and I could take care of her just fine. One day last winter when she was sick, I'd made her oatmeal and orange juice and played with Katie and Tim all day so she could lie on the couch and read.

"There's just a few more boxes, Ma," Max said, striding back down the hall.

Katie pinched my arm as we followed him down to the bus. I pinched her back. *Max is Ms. Whitney's son*— I thought, surprised. When Mother had said that Ms. Whitney had kids, I'd imagined they'd be in grammar school or junior high, ready to make our lives miserable because we were invading their house. Max looked as old as Dolores' brother who went to the community college. He gave me a paper bag full of clothes and handed Katie two jackets. He carried three bags of clothes up the stairs, along with Mother's brown leather suitcase. "My sisters'll be home from school in a while," he said.

"Why did your other sister move out?" I asked shyly.

"Claire? Oh, she decided to go live with this loser. She's pregnant, so there's not much Ma can do about it." Upstairs, he looked around our new bedroom. "She sure didn't leave you much, but you can come hang out downstairs with us. One more bag, okay?"

Max slid a bag of books to the back of the car. I grabbed *Little Women* off the top of the stack and smoothed the bent cover. "You can take more books than that, can't you, Ronnie?" Max said, smiling down at me. My name sounded strange in Max's deep voice. When he said it, I felt older and sad, because we were leaving Daddy, and Max seemed to know more about it than I did.

"Of course I can take more," I said, picking up an armful of books.

We started towards the door just as two older girls were going inside. Both girls were very pale, with frizzy red hair that stuck out from their heads. "Hey, Pam, Sage, these are Maggie's girls," Max said. The girls regarded us with icy eyes.

"I'm Veronica . . . Ronnie, I mean, and this is Katie." My face flushed hot with humiliation at being caught moving into their house, even if it was only temporary. I felt like one of the homeless people I saw on the streets when Mother drove us into Los Angeles to see a musical.

Katie had Seymour wrapped like a sling over one shoulder, carrying two books in her blanket. "Can we see your room?" she asked.

The taller girl, Sage, shrugged. "Yeah, I guess." She had a gold hoop earring in one nostril and a tiny diamond earring in her chin.

I opened my mouth to remind Katie that we'd already seen their room, but I didn't feel like arguing. I took Seymour and the books and said, "I'll be down in a minute, if it's okay."

"Of course it's okay!" Max exclaimed. "We're all family now!"

I laughed — a weak, silly sound — and he rumpled my hair with one big hand as if I was a pet dog. "This has got to be pretty rough on you," he said.

"Yeah," Pam nodded, some of the ice melting from her eyes. "Why don'tcha hang out down here with us — we can watch TV or something."

It seemed that everyone knew what was going on in

my life except me. I needed to be alone for a few minutes, to think things through. "I have to put my clothes away," I lied. I didn't even have a dresser to put them in.

"Come down when you're done, then. We have chips, sodas, and there's a little store down the street," Max said. He climbed up the stairs and set the bag of books on the living room floor.

I walked into the bedroom and sat on one hard cot, watching Tim scribble across the pictures in his coloring books. I liked Max. He was the only thing that made sense about this messed up day, until he mentioned that we were all family now. Didn't he know that we were moving just as soon as Mother found us another house?

Parents were supposed to be stable, predictable as the graham crackers and milk Mother set out for us every afternoon. But she'd been acting strange all summer. She'd decided to go to college, and the dining room table was covered with thick books on art and literature. Daddy always spent part of every weekend over the summer building her an office in the attic. Sometimes, I'd come home from swimming or playing at the park to find Mother sitting up there among the boards and strips of yellow insulation, studying her textbooks next to a lamp she'd taken from Tim's bedroom.

I glanced over at Tim. His head was bent in concentration over a picture of a green cat. "We're never going home again, Timmy," I said to hear how the words sounded.

"So?" Tim said looked up with his happiest smile, the one that showed all of his small white teeth. "This place cool. Other one hurts my ears."

I got up from the cot and walked down the hall. I wanted to see Mother, to make sure this was all temporary, like she said. The door to the other room was shut. I tapped on it, and it swung half-open. Mother stood by a double bed in a T-shirt and underwear with a pair of green shorts in one hand. Ms. Whitney had her arms around her. Mother was crying quietly.

Ms. Whitney glanced up and saw me. The muscles

in her face didn't move, but she said "Maggie," in a way that made Mother look up abruptly. Mother bent down and pulled on the green shorts. "Veronica, wait in your room," she said firmly. "I need to talk to you." Her mascara had run down to half circles under her eyes, and for the first time I could remember, my beautiful mother looked ugly.

"It's not *my* room!" I yelled. I ran out of the room and stomped down the stairs to find Max. Katie sat on one of the beds watching cartoons. In one hand, she held a Coke, in the other, a bag of cheese puffs. "Want some?" She grinned at me with orange teeth. I sat down beside her.

Pam and Sage lay on their beds. Pam was flipping through a magazine and chewing on a long red rope of licorice. Sage pursed her lips, concentrating on painting her fingernails with glittery purple polish.

"Where's Max?" I asked.

Pam looked up from her magazine and smoothed down her wild red hair with one hand. "He went to the market with Sally," she said.

"Sally's Max's girlfriend," Katie said importantly. "She's got big tits."

I reached for a cheese puff and crunched it without tasting. "Where's your father?" I asked Sage, who began to paint her toenails. "Does he live here?"

"Ha! He left us. He was an asshole. He smacked us around and used the grocery money to buy cocaine." Sage's voice came out flat, as if she were reciting words she had learned by heart.

I looked away to avoid staring at the diamond earring in her chin. Daddy never hit me, and we always had groceries. *He could've been a lot worse* — I thought.

I wondered if he was home yet, and if he was worried about us. Maybe he thought we'd been kidnapped. I knew that sometimes when kids got lost, their parents put their pictures on posters in the library or on milk cartons. I hoped that if Daddy did that, none of my friends would see the pictures.

Pam braided her hair and tied it with a rubber band she slipped off a newspaper on the table. "Ma says men are jerks except for Max. She thought he might turn out gay 'cause he's so sweet, but he's definitely straight."

"So what if he *was* gay!" Sage snapped. She lifted up her shirt a little. "Hey kids, you wanna see something cool?" She pointed to a silver ring, stuck through her belly button.

"Did it hurt?" I asked.

"Like hell," she said.

Pam sat back down on her bed and snorted. "You loved it. And by the way, her name's really Christy, but she changed it."

"Shut up!" Sage threw a pillow at Pam and knocked a statue of a duck off the milk crate next to Pam's bed.

"Bitch!" Pam picked up the pieces of white porcelain and tried to fit them back together.

I felt like crying again. I dragged myself back upstairs to the living room and flopped down on a red velvet couch beside the box of books, then reached for *Little Women*. Meg, Jo, Beth, and Amy had been pretty happy without their father, but he was away at war, and they were happier when he got home. I put *Little Women* down and picked up the Mark Twain book. On the second page, I saw Daddy's sharp black handwriting. "To Maggie. Forever yours, Zachary."

Forever. Until today, I'd understood that word, believed in it. Now, I felt as cheated as I had the day Trisha told me there was no such thing as Santa Claus, and Mother had reluctantly agreed. I felt the sting of tears in my eyes, but I pushed them back and turned to the first short story in the book. "The Jumping Frog of Calaveras County," I murmured to myself and began to read.

"Ronnie, are you okay?" Mother's voice cut through the story. I looked up to find her standing in the living room.

"Do you . . . d'you want to help me make spaghetti for dinner?" She had wiped the mascara off her face and brushed her hair into a ponytail. Beneath the fringe of her bangs, I could see a large purple bruise near her left eye.

I shut the book with a bang. "Yeah, I guess I'll help."

Tim trotted out to the kitchen. "I help?"

"Ms. Whitney's coming out to work on your reading," Mother told him.

"Cool," Tim said. "She my best friend."

"Everyone's his best friend," I muttered, following Mother into the kitchen.

"Will you open this, honey?" Mother handed me a package of noodles and looked closely at me.

I took them from her silently, not sure of what to say. I wasn't really angry with her anymore. I just felt lost.

Mother bent down and pulled a jar of spaghetti sauce out of a cupboard. The lid wouldn't come off, so she hit it with a knife. It popped off when she tried it again. Usually, she made sauce from scratch. At home, I liked to sit on the counter, watching her chop up onions, tomatoes, and basil. But I knew without even looking that there wasn't any fresh basil in Ms. Whitney's refrigerator. Mother poured the sauce into a pot. "We need to talk," she said. She filled another pot with water for the noodles. "I'm leaving your father."

I wanted to say "no shit," the way Daddy said it when he was being sarcastic, but I knew Mother would get mad. "*Really*?" I said instead, making my voice high with pretended amazement.

Mother looked at me, and her jaw tightened. Even without mascara all over her eyes, she still looked miserable. "Your father is an . . . *impossible* man to live with, Ronnie. Do you understand?"

I thought about the apple he'd thrown as if it were a baseball and Mother's shoulder a catcher's mitt. I nodded, but I didn't say anything.

"Ms. Whitney is a nice woman, Ronnie. She's helped me to find a little confidence . . . she's given me the strength to take you kids and get out."

I broke the noodles over the pot of boiling water with a sharp snap. "You could've asked, or at least prepared me," I said. "Then maybe *I* would've had the strength to get out, too."

"I didn't want you to tell him," Mother replied. She leaned on the counter, looking out the window toward the ocean. "I had to leave. I know you and your father are close, Ronnie. If you . . . if you want to go back and live with him, I'll understand."

I thought about that. Daddy and I weren't *that* close. We'd been jogging on Sunday mornings lately, out at the high school track, but we never really talked. He asked me about math, which I'd gotten a "C" in, and he talked about how I was fast enough to make the high school track team in a few years, but that was all. I was nervous around him even when we were running. His feet pounded the dirt track, and he spat at the ground in hard, white bullets.

"I don't want to live with him," I said. I dumped the noodles into the pot of boiling water. "I want to live with you."

Mother turned and hugged me hard. Finally, I was able to hug her back. My head brushed the purple bruise, and she winced.

"I'm sorry he hurt you," I whispered. Sudden tears rolled down my cheeks.

We stood there for a while, both of us crying, and then Max walked in. "Hey, is dinner ready? Oh. Sorry, Maggie, I though Ma was cooking."

"It's ready," Mother said, letting go of me to dump the noodles in a strainer. "We'll talk more later," she promised. I quickly wiped away my tears in front of Max.

Ms. Whitney came in with Tim and hollered downstairs for Pam, Sage, and Katie. She lit different colored candles in glass candleholders all over the living room and turned on the stereo low to a country-western station. We all sat down on the couches with our mismatched plates of spaghetti. I looked at Ms. Whitney out of the corner of my eye. She chewed with her mouth closed and used her paper napkin often. Somehow, I hadn't expected her to have manners. I wondered what Trisha and Dolores would say if they saw me having dinner with all these strange people in a room full of candles and incense that smelled like a forest.

Thinking about my friends made me sad. Trisha, Dolores, and I had waited for so many years to go to junior high together. We planned to study at the library every afternoon after school. I had promised to help Trisha in English if she helped me in math. Dolores was good at everything.

I forced my brain to stop thinking about school and my friends so that I wouldn't cry again. I thought about how I didn't miss Daddy yet, and I chewed twenty times on each bite of spaghetti the way Dolores told me you're supposed to for good digestion. I figured good digestion would be important tonight. Otherwise, what with my life completely turned upside down, I was sure I'd throw up.

Chapter 2

Tim's year-round school was on a different track than Katie's and mine, so the Monday after we left Newbury Park, he rode off with Ms. Whitney in her white pickup truck, grinning and giving us the thumbs-up sign. The local grammar school and junior high didn't start for another week, so Katie and I wandered around Carpinteria every day, while Mother circled Help Wanted ads in the newspaper.

Carpinteria seemed a lot smaller than Newbury Park. Kids and dogs played in the streets, and people walked to the market, or rode bicycles. The street Ms. Whitney and her kids lived on ran right into the beach. Mother gave me permission to walk down and wade in the ocean by myself because there were hardly any waves. "This house *is* pretty crowded," she said the day after we had invaded Ms. Whitney's house. "I know you're going to need some time alone."

I went wading in the ocean every day that week. Sharp shells scraped against my legs, and the cold salt water stung as it sloshed against the scrapes. In the early mornings, I was usually the only person on the beach besides a few fishermen in thick jackets and high rubber boots. Pam told me about a beach further down the road where the local kids went to surf and lay out in the sun, but

Mother was right — I didn't feel like being around people. A gang of neighborhood dogs trotted beside me as I waded, waiting for me to throw driftwood for them to fetch. I stuffed my ponytail holder into the pocket of my shorts and ran with the dogs the length of the beach with my hair whipping across my face and the sand cold between my toes.

Running helped me think. Or rather, it helped me *not* think. When I ran, I concentrated on my breathing and on my legs aching from the pull of the soft sand. But somewhere in the back of my head, I was also thinking about Mother and Daddy getting a divorce and about how different my life had become in just a few days.

Mother took Katie and me shopping for flowered bedspreads and pillow-covers that first week. She bought two framed prints of flower gardens by an artist named Monet and hung one above each of our cots. Our room looked pretty and comfortable then, even though the stains wouldn't come out of the brown carpet, and our curtains were sheets Mother stitched on the old sewing machine she'd brought with her from Newbury Park. As I lay in bed at night, I could hear the splash of the waves breaking on the shore. Listening to the low call of the foghorn in the dark, I felt almost happy on the narrow, hard cot in a house that wasn't my own.

When school began the next week, Katie and I stood without speaking at the bus stop on our street corner, while the neighborhood kids laughed and whispered in tight little groups. My bus arrived first. I climbed on and watched Katie from the window. She gave me a tiny, sad wave, but when I looked again, she was already talking to two little girls and grinning her missing-teeth grin.

The junior high was ugly, painted mustard yellow with a barbed wire fence all around it. My homeroom teacher — a tall, skinny man with greased-back black hair and glasses — said, "Welcome to seventh grade, class. Oh, this is Veronica. She just moved here." He never looked at me again. I struggled to catch up to the other kids in math and hid my disappointment in English class when I discovered we were going to read *The House on Mango Street*, which I'd read twice on my own last year.

That first Sunday afternoon after school began, I was trying to do my math homework when Mother came in and sat on my bed. She smoothed my bedspread even though it was already straight, and plumped up my pillow. "Ronnie," she said finally, "your father's here and he wants to take you out to dinner."

I jumped up, knocking my math book to the floor. "Daddy's *here*, right now?" I ran out to the living room and found him standing in the doorway, with one arm around Katie and one around Tim.

"Hello, Veronica, how are you?" he asked me quietly. There was more gray in his dark hair than I remembered, and he looked small and thin in his jeans and a purple polo shirt.

"I'm okay," I said, hugging him. Tim hugged him, too, then Katie joined in, and we were all standing there hugging each other while Mother watched us. I broke away first, with my stomach churning. I had been so sure that Daddy had forgotten all about us. Since we'd left, he hadn't even called, but now I guessed that it had probably taken him a while to find us at Ms. Whitney's if Mother didn't leave him a note.

"Want to go out to dinner?" Daddy asked me. "I thought we'd go grab a hamburger."

I looked at Mother. She folded her arms tightly across her chest and walked into the kitchen, where Ms. Whitney stood drinking from a bottle of beer and glaring at Daddy out of angry black eyes.

Daddy glanced toward the kitchen, then looked away. "I'll have the girls back by seven," he said to the floor.

"I go too?" Tim asked.

Ms. Whitney stalked into the living room, rolling up the sleeves of her red flannel shirt. "Tim, you're gonna stay here and have hot dogs," she said sharply. She and Daddy looked each other up and down. I realized then that they'd never met because Tim's parent-teacher conferences were always while Daddy was at work.

Tim threw his arms around Ms. Whitney's legs. "I haff peanut butter on my hot dog?"

"You can have whatever you want, Tim," Mother said from the kitchen.

It didn't surprise me that Daddy wasn't inviting Tim to go with us. He never seemed to know what to do with Tim. Most of the time, he left him to Mother, who had read all sorts of books about kids with developmental disabilities and treated Tim just like Katie and me.

"Let's go, girls." Daddy's voice sounded too loud in the small living room. As Mother walked over to kiss us goodbye, he frowned at her torn T-shirt and her blue jeans with a hole in one knee. "Who sleeps here?" he asked as we walked through the empty downstairs bedroom. He wrinkled his nose at the smell of tar and dead fish blowing in off the ocean through the open window.

Katie chattered about Pam, Sage, and Max all the way to Carrow's, but Daddy didn't even seem to hear her. We walked into the restaurant and sat in a big, cushioned booth facing the ocean. Daddy ordered us all cheeseburgers and French-fries.

"Do the worm trick, Ronnie!" Katie said when the waitress brought us our Cokes. I slid the paper off my straw in a tight, pleated bundle and put drops of Coke on it so that it grew and wiggled on the table. "Do mine, too!" Katie said. "Do Daddy's!"

I glanced up at Daddy. He was looking at us and crying. He had a powerful, jutting chin, but when he cried, it wobbled and wrinkled — a sad, weak thing. "I miss you girls so much," he said in a voice like a cassette player when the tape spills out. Katie slid closer to him and patted his hand.

"We miss you, too," I said, hoping he'd stop crying. The waitress came over with our food and I smiled up at her, as if it were the most normal thing in the world for Daddy to be crying in a Carrow's.

My father's crying had a sort of power over me. He could be terrible and loud and angry, and I would be so scared of him that my teeth would chatter. But after he calmed down, he always cried and I felt sorry for him.

I could forgive Daddy for anything when he cried.

He blew his nose on a white paper napkin. "I'm sorry," he said to us. "Your mother . . . she's just very confused. And that *woman*, if you can call her a woman . . . " He stopped in the middle of his sentence and reached over to cut Katie's hamburger in half for her. "Next weekend, I'll take you back home, and we'll go to a party," he said. "This'll all work out somehow."

"Daddy's gonna take us to a party!" Katie cried to Mother as soon as we got upstairs in Ms. Whitney's house.

Mother looked at Daddy out of sharp blue eyes. "Whose party, Zach?" she demanded. "Is it really appropriate for the girls to go?"

"It's a party my friend Marty is having, but there'll be other children there."

Their words sounded stiff and formal, as though they were two strangers talking— two strangers who didn't like each other, instead of my parents who had slept in the same bed just a few weeks ago.

Daddy knelt down and kissed my cheek. "I'll see you next Friday," he said.

"Okay." It felt weird to be saying goodbye to him, knowing he was going back to our old house. I could still smell his spicy aftershave when I got into my nightgown, and for just a moment, I wished I could've gone back home to Newbury Park with him. *Home.* It felt like a long time since I'd been home. I hadn't forgotten what my bedroom or the rosebushes in the backyard looked like, but I couldn't remember if the carpet in the living room was brown or green.

Mother came in to tell us good night. She bent down to kiss me, and I could see that the bruise beside her eye had almost disappeared. "Good night, you two," she said. She tucked Seymour in beside Katie. "Have a good sleep." At the door, she turned. "I don't remember your father having a friend named Marty. What's his last name?"

"He didn't say," I said through a yawn.

"I can't imagine why he's taking you to this party," Mother murmured.

I wondered if she was remembering the nights when she and Daddy would dress up in beautiful clothes and go out to parties themselves. She leaned her head against the doorway, and I thought that perhaps she was missing Daddy just a little. She didn't say anything else, though— just turned and walked off to the other bedroom.

I spent the week half in anticipation of seeing Daddy again, and half not wanting to see him at all. Dolores once told me that in the Catholic religion, there's a place called "limbo," where you're neither in Heaven nor Hell, but you're just hanging around dead somewhere in between. I felt as if I was in limbo that week. I hated eating lunch by myself at school, but I didn't want to make new friends, in case Mother decided to pack us all up and go back to Daddy.

But on Friday, she picked us up from school and handed Katie and me each a small, gold foil-wrapped box. "I got a job," she announced, her eyes shining. I knew then that we wouldn't be moving back to Newbury Park.

Katie and I unwrapped pairs of identical gold hoop earrings while Mother told us about the small newspaper she'd be writing for. "I used to do some freelance writing." She shrugged off the light blue jacket that matched her skirt. "But I gave it up to be a full-time mother. Don't look like that, Ronnie," she said, catching my scowl in the rear view mirror. "I loved being a mother full-time, but now I have to make a living, too. Pam said she'd come home early on the days I have to work late or go to school."

I pretended to look for a book in my backpack, so Mother wouldn't see my face. I was used to her being home every day when I got home from school, waiting with graham crackers and milk to hear about my day. I liked Pam a lot better than I liked Sage, but it wouldn't be the same to come home to her. Mother seemed really happy for the first time in weeks, though, and I didn't want to spoil it.

"What time is Daddy coming tonight?" Katie asked, adjusting the rear-view mirror so she could see her earrings.

"Seven," Mother said. "He promised to have you home by midnight." The white pickup truck was outside when we got to her house, and Mother flew upstairs and kissed Ms. Whitney on the cheek. "I'm back in the newspaper business!" she cried. Ms. Whitney grinned her cracked grin and opened a bottle of beer for Mother.

I went into my room to change clothes for the party Daddy was taking us to. I didn't like Mother and Ms. Whitney being so friendly. They were always hugging and whispering to each other like they had some big secret. I hated sharing Mother. If she liked Ms. Whitney enough to start smoking cigarettes with her out on the upstairs porch after dinner every night, then maybe we wouldn't move into our own house after all.

And Ms. Whitney's house was too small. Katie and I had our room, but Mother slept on the floor of the other bedroom so Tim could have the bed, and Ms. Whitney slept on one of the living room couches, since she got up the earliest. There was only one bathroom, and all six of us kids fought over who was in there the longest every morning until Ms. Whitney and Mother threatened to limit us to five minutes each.

I'm glad I have the beach — I thought, as I put on a tie-dyed sundress and pink sandals for the party — *it's like another room all to myself.*

Daddy knocked on the door in the middle of dinner. Katie jumped up to open it. He stood in the doorway, looking at all of us spread out on the couches eating baked beans and hot dogs in the light from a dozen candles. His glance stayed on Max longer than on Pam and Sage. *Maybe he thinks Mother's having an affair with Max* — I thought, choking back a giggle.

"Do you mind if Tim stays here?" Daddy said.

Mother and Ms. Whitney rolled their eyes at each other. Tim groaned and slapped his hand against his forehead. "Not again!"

"Of course I don't mind if Tim stays here," Mother said, her voice flat and cold. "We're all going to watch movies and have popcorn." That sounded like more fun than some party. For a moment, I thought about asking if *I* could stay, but I didn't want to hurt Daddy's feelings.

Katie and I carried our half-eaten dinner into the kitchen. "You two be good at the party," Mother said, kneeling down to wipe Katie's mouth with a paper napkin. "Be sure you say please and thank you."

"Mother, I'm *nine*," Katie said in a disgusted voice that managed to sound cute. I wished Ms. Whitney and her kids would laugh and stop glaring at Daddy — maybe even invite him to have beans and hot dogs so the tension in the room would disappear, and I could breathe again. But no one laughed, and Max cleared his throat loudly.

"Sorry. Too much incense," he muttered.

"They'll be home by midnight," Daddy said, not looking at Mother.

We followed him down to his silver Lexus. "Who are all those people?" he asked us when we were on the freeway.

"Ms. Whitney and her kids," I said. "They're nice, but that one with all the earrings, Sage, is pretty freaky."

"She got a tattoo of a spider on her ankle last week," Katie said. "It was so cool!"

Daddy shook his head. He didn't talk on the drive to Newbury Park, so Katie and I sang along with the oldies on the radio station. When we got to our old town, I looked out the window at the grammar school, the park, and all the places my friends and I had hung out at only a few weeks before. I wished we could drive by our old house, but Daddy turned down a different street and parked in front of a house with lit-up windows and music drifting out of the open front door.

The party turned out to be more of an adult get-together, with drinks in tall glasses and unappetizing appetizers, but there was a girl Katie's age and a high school girl standing in the kitchen drinking sodas.

"That's our stepmother." The younger girl, Deanna, pointed out the hostess — a tall woman with long black hair and a cream-colored dress that clung to her thin body. She walked up to Daddy and handed him a drink. "She's from England," Deanna said.

Daddy walked over to us with a blond-haired man in a gray suit. "This is Mr. Martin," he told us. "Marty, these are my girls."

Mr. Martin had a very red face, and he chuckled as he shook my hand. "Delighted you could come, girls," he said in a booming voice. "They look just like you, Zach."

Katie wrinkled her nose. I knew what she was thinking. *I* looked like Daddy — we both had the same sharp jaw line and high forehead, which I hid behind brown bangs. But Katie had Mother's light, curly hair and her soft, round face.

Mr. Martin and Daddy carried their drinks into the living room and sat down on a blue and white striped couch.

"Wanna play Twister?" Deanna chewed on the end of one of her blond braids and blinked at Katie and me. We nodded and followed her into her bedroom.

Deanna's older sister, Donna, sat on the bed and watched us from behind a curtain of thick, dirty-blond hair. I was usually shy around new kids, but it was hard to be shy around Deanna. She had a loud voice like her father's, and she kept telling jokes and snorting, falling on top of Katie and me as we tried to keep our hands on the colored dots in the game. The three of us were shrieking and laughing, collapsed on top of each other, when Daddy came in.

"Get off her right *now*!" he commanded, pointing at Katie who was sprawled on top of Deanna.

Katie stood up with her mouth open in surprise. "We're just playing," she told Daddy.

"Well, *don't*," he snapped. "It doesn't look good."

His voice became instantly quiet and kind. "How'd you like to spend the night here?" he asked me.

"We have to be home by midnight," I reminded

him.

Daddy nodded impatiently. "I called your mother. She said it's fine."

Katie and Deanna clapped their hands and hugged each other. I was silent. If we were going to spend the night, I wished we could spend it in our old house.

"I don't have a nightgown," I said.

"You can borrow one of mine," Donna said. She disappeared into her room and returned with a red and black plaid flannel nightgown.

"Then it's settled." Daddy's shoulder smacked into the doorway as he walked out of the room. "Shit," he muttered, but then he turned toward us and grinned broadly so that Katie and Deanna laughed.

"Donna, let's play the flying game!" Deanna cried. Donna obediently lay down on the floor with her legs bent. "Watch this!" Deanna sat on the balls of her sister's bare feet, and Donna pushed her legs up, sending Deanna flying into the air.

Katie rushed over. "I wanna try!"

I watched them for a while, wishing I were back home with Mother. She would've been in bed hours ago, falling asleep to the sad moan of the foghorn. I was surprised that she'd said we could spend the night in this strange house. I wondered if Daddy had really asked her.

Katie went flying through the air, screaming with laughter. "Ronnie, you have to try this!" she said.

"Can I?" I asked Donna.

She looked doubtful. "You're kind of tall, but I guess it'll work."

I sat on her feet, and she pushed me so that I flew up into the air, but I came down flat on my back. I lay on the carpet, stunned and unable to breathe. My stomach contracted in sharp jerks. I wanted to cry, but no sound would come out.

Deanna rushed into the living room. "Mom, come quick! Donna's killed Ronnie!"

The adults gathered in the doorway, looking down at me. Mrs. Martin pushed through them. She knelt down and put my head in her lap. "You're all right, Veronica. You just knocked the wind out of yourself." She smelled expensive, like perfume and delicate lotions. Her words came out precise and elegant in her English accent. I felt like a huge, gasping fish in her arms.

At last, I was able to breathe and to talk. "It was my fault," I whispered. "Donna said I was too tall."

Mrs. Martin stood up and straightened her dress. "Even so, I think it's time for three little girls to go to bed." She smiled brightly at the adults in the hall. "If you stay up past midnight, you'll turn into pumpkins, or something like that." She laughed — a beautiful, musical sound — and the adults smiled back and her and moved into the living room.

Mrs. Martin laid out sleeping bags for Katie and me on the carpet in Deanna's room. "Try to get some sleep," she said, and turned out the light. Donna followed her out, pausing at the door. "I'm sorry you got hurt," she said to me, but before I could say anything, she'd gone.

"Your mom's beautiful," Katie whispered to Deanna in the dark. "I love her accent."

I thought about how, in a few hours, Mother would wake up, and she and Tim would walk across the street to the beach to look for sand dollars. My eyes ached with homesickness. I smashed the pillow over my head so I wouldn't hear Katie and Deanna giggling, and went to sleep.

In the morning, Mrs. Martin made us pancakes with strawberry syrup. She wore a pair of short green shorts, and with her long, tanned legs, she looked like nobody's mother I'd ever seen. Daddy had slept on the couch. His hair stuck up on one side of his head. Mrs. Martin laughed and tried to smooth it down with her hand. "You look like Donald Duck," she said. Then Daddy talked in his best Donald Duck voice, making Katie and Deanna giggle.

Mr. Martin buried his head in the sports section of the newspaper and drank black coffee. He didn't even touch the plate of pancakes Mrs. Martin set in front of him.

"Tim and I missed you," Mother said when Daddy brought us home a few hours later. She closed the door in his face before we could even say goodbye.

"Can we have strawberry pancakes for dinner?" Katie asked.

Mother sat on the red velvet couch and pulled us to her. "Where did you have strawberry pancakes?" She propped her bare feet up on the coffee table.

Katie snuggled against Mother. "A really pretty lady gave them to us. She was nice, wasn't she, Ronnie?"

I shrugged. "She was all right.

Mother smoothed my hair. "Have you done your homework? I can help you with it this afternoon."

"I hate school," Katie said. "It *sucks*."

"Katie, please don't use that word." Mother frowned.

I wanted to laugh. "Sucks" was the perfect word to describe the mustard-yellow junior high and the fraction exercises I still had to do for Monday morning.

Daddy picked us up again the following Saturday afternoon. He drove straight to the Martins' house without going home. "I'm going to leave you here for a while," he told Katie and me. "I've got a meeting at work. You can play with the girls, okay?"

But Donna and Deanna were at soccer practice.

"Let's go see a friend of mine," Mrs. Martin suggested after we had eaten several of her big oatmeal cookies and drank tall glasses of milk. "His name is Dr. Chichester."

Katie and I got into her clean white car. Mrs. Martin stuck a tape in the tape player. "Do you like Supertramp?" she asked me. "They're my favorite band."

"I've never heard of them," I said. I listened to the singer's high, British voice. He sounded almost like a woman instead of a man. Mrs. Martin sang along with him in a lower voice. I thought she sounded better than the band.

Dr. Chichester's office sat three stories up in a tall,

mirror-paneled building. Katie and I jumped in the elevator as it rose, to feel the floor hit our feet. "What's he a doctor of?" I asked Mrs. Martin.

"Oh . . . the mind," she said. She tucked her long black hair behind her ears. Her pearl earrings glowed softly in the fluorescent light as we stepped out of the elevator. "He wants to ask you a few questions, so please be as honest as you can." She sat down on a chair in what looked like a waiting room. Katie sat next to her.

"Mrs. Martin?" a receptionist said, looking up from a notebook. "Dr. Chichester is ready. He'd prefer to see one child at a time."

"You go in first, Ronnie, since you're the oldest," Mrs. Martin said, pointing. "Right through that door."

I didn't like doctors, but to please Mrs. Martin, I walked in and sat down in a chair across from a bald man seated behind the desk. Dr. Chichester had a shiny black rock on his desk with a hollow in it that just fit my thumb. "It's called a worry stone," he said, running his hand over his head. "You can play with it if you want." I rubbed my thumb once in the smooth hollow and put down the rock.

Dr. Chichester leaned his folded arms on his desk and smiled at me. "Do you miss your father?" he asked me curiously, almost as if he were Trisha or Dolores, and we were hanging out at home.

I blinked at the silver-rimmed glasses perched on his nose. "Sometimes."

"Hmmm. Do you love your dad?"

"Of course!" I tried to sit up very straight in the deep, soft chair, but I kept sinking into it. *It's none of his business whether or not I love Daddy* — I thought— *how could any friend of Mrs. Martin's be so rude?*

"Interesting," Dr. Chichester said, drawing the word out as long and smooth as a snake. He wrote something on a pad of paper on his desk, then asked me a lot of questions about Mother. I thought he was even ruder to be writing while I was talking. "Where does your mother sleep?" he asked me. "And what can you tell me about . . . er, this Ms. Whitney person?"

"I don't know," I replied to everything he asked. I hoped Mrs. Martin wouldn't be offended that I didn't like her friend.

When I walked out of the office, Katie was sitting on Mrs. Martin's lap, waving her feet in new blue sandals.

"We found a shoe sale right down the street while you were gone," Mrs. Martin said, handing me a brown box. "I bought you a pair, too, Veronica."

I tried them on while she took Katie into Dr. Chichester's office. The sandals had a half-inch heel, and I felt tall and sophisticated as I walked around the waiting room. "They fit pretty good," I said shyly to Mrs. Martin when she came out of the office. "Thanks."

Katie was only gone a few minutes. Mrs. Martin and I sat and looked at *People* magazine. She stopped at a picture of Elizabeth Taylor from one of her old black and white movies. "You remind me of her when she was young, Veronica," Mrs. Martin said. "You have the same big eyes and beautiful, clear skin."

"Oh," I said, blushing. I watched *National Velvet* every time it was a Sunday afternoon movie on TV, and I didn't think I looked anything like Elizabeth Taylor.

Katie came out, followed by Dr. Chichester. "Just what we thought," he said to Mrs. Martin. His bald head gleamed under the ceiling lights. I raised my eyebrows at Katie. She shrugged and bent down to adjust the strap on her new sandals. Mrs. Martin handed her friend a check. It slipped out of his hand and floated down to my feet. When I picked it up to hand it to him, I saw that it was signed with Daddy's signature.

"Nice to have met you, girls," Dr. Chichester said, smiling again. His smile reminded me of the sticky black tar I had to scrape off the bottom of my feet every time I ran barefoot on the beach in Carpinteria.

In the elevator, Katie stuck her tongue out and rolled her eyes while Mrs. Martin searched for her car keys in her purse. I could tell that Katie thought Dr. Chichester was dumb, too.

Mrs. Martin drove us back to her house. We spent

the afternoon playing hide and seek with Donna and Deanna. Mr. Martin came home carrying a bag of golf clubs and fixed himself a drink, which Deanna immediately bumped into and spilled.

"Deanna, go to your room!" Mr. Martin yelled, picking ice cubes off his pants.

Mrs. Martin hurried over with a towel. "I'll fix you another one, Marty."

Katie and I shrank behind a chair in the living room. I wondered if Mrs. Martin and Mr. Martin were going to argue the way Mother and Daddy did. I wanted to go home to Carpinteria right then.

Donna crawled out from underneath the coffee table, murmured something about having to use the bathroom, and disappeared. Mr. Martin finished his drink and walked into the kitchen to make himself another one. Katie and I crawled out from behind the chair and stood near the front door.

"Where's your father, ladies?" Mr. Martin asked, returning to the living room.

"I don't know," I said, almost ready to cry.

"He's a good man, your dad," Mr. Martin said, opening a magazine. Katie and I sat down beside the coffee table. We looked at a book full of weird pictures by a man named Salvador Dalí and didn't talk. The doorbell rang, jangling through the silence.

Daddy walked in grinning. Mr. Martin walked into the hall. "The meeting went really well," I heard Daddy say. "Chichester's sending her the test, but he says he's already got all the information he needs."

"Hi, Daddy," Katie said in a small voice.

His dark eyebrows jumped in surprise. "What're you doing, girls?"

"We were playing hide and seek," I said.

"I guess!" Daddy looked at Mr. Martin, who chuckled and took another sip from his glass. When Mrs. Martin invited us to stay for dinner, Daddy agreed, even though Mother had asked us to be home for dinner. Donna and Deanna came out, and Mr. Martin put an arm around each of them. We sat around the dinner table and ate beef stew and homemade apple pie with vanilla ice cream, and the adults laughed and joked. Mrs. Martin's brown eyes glowed happily. My father flashed her his nicest smile, including us all in its confusing warmth.

"Who is this Mrs. Martin Katie keeps talking about?" Mother asked that night, when she tucked me into bed. "Is she your father's new girlfriend?"

"She's Daddy's friend's wife."

I remembered that I'd left my new sandals under Deanna's bed. "She's nice."

I wondered if I should tell Mother about talking, or rather, *not* talking to Dr. Chichester. She was already pretty upset about Daddy bringing us home late when she'd cooked a whole ham and sweet potatoes for dinner. I decided to tell her later.

Mother bent down and kissed me. "Have a good sleep. I'll be in the next room if you need me." I listened to her voice, low and troubled through the wall, and then to Ms. Whitney's deep, soothing croak, until I fell asleep.

The next Saturday, we didn't see Daddy. Instead, we played on the beach all day with Mother. Sunday after breakfast, Katie and I went outside and tossed the volleyball around. Pam and Sage had gone camping with some friends, but Max had promised to take us to the movies when he got home from work. Even though it was nearly October, the sun had already warmed the sand until it was almost too hot to stand in barefooted.

"I'm going for a run on the beach," I said, tossing the volleyball to Katie.

"No fair!" she cried. "You said you'd play with me!"

I tried to think of a way to explain to Katie that my insides felt all knotted up, and if I ran for a while, the knots would untie themselves.

"Look!" Katie said, dropping the volleyball. "The fuzz!"

A police car pulled up in front of our house, and a

short, muscular policeman with a handsome face stepped out. "Is this Twelve Seaborn Place?" he asked us.

"Yeah." My heart started to pound, and my knees felt shaky. I thought maybe I should go in and get Mother, who was inside with Ms. Whitney teaching Tim the alphabet. Another police car drove up, and then my father drove up in his Lexus with someone in the front seat whose face was hidden by an open newspaper.

"Hello, girls. Where's Tim?" Daddy said calmly. He got out of the car and smoothed down the jacket of his black suit. My heart pounded faster, and I couldn't answer him.

"He's upstairs," Katie said. "What're you doing here, Daddy?"

Daddy had a funny, blank look on his face. He ignored Katie and walked up to ring the doorbell.

Ms. Whitney opened the door. "What do you want?" she said.

"I need to see Maggie," Daddy said. "*Now.*"

"What for?"

Mother pushed past Ms. Whitney, Tim at her side. "What's going on, Zach?"

"Yo, Dad," Tim said, waving a red cardboard "T." "Whass up?"

Daddy ignored Tim and looked straight at Mother, who was staring at the police cars. "I'm taking the kids, Maggie."

"Like hell you are." Ms. Whitney stepped down to the porch and crossed her big, freckled arms in front of her. "Katie, Ronnie, come inside."

From the street, the mustached policeman held up a piece of paper with typing all over it. "Mr. Davis has a written court order giving him temporary custody of the children," he said loudly.

"On what grounds?" Ms. Whitney demanded. She put one arm around Mother's waist. I thought that this was not the time to be getting all friendly, but then I looked at Mother's wide, frightened eyes, and I was glad Ms. Whitney was holding on to her.

"The court feels that Mrs. Davis is emotionally unstable," the policeman said.

"Why?" Ms. Whitney snapped, matching his cold tone. "Because of some ridiculous questionnaire your so-called psychologist forced her to take?"

"He didn't even talk to me in person . . . " Mother said in a faint, faraway voice. "He just sent me a test to fill out."

The policeman looked at Ms. Whitney and Mother standing in the doorway with their arms around each other. I saw something hateful flash in his eyes — something mean that I didn't understand at all.

My mind raced. If I went with Daddy, I could go home and see my friends. I hated the ugly junior high at Carpinteria and fighting five other kids for the bathroom all the time. But then I thought about the nights we all had dinner together with candles and music and we collapsed on the couches to watch movies for hours.

And I realized that in the month since we'd moved there, the house in Carpinteria had become home.

I ran over to Mother and clutched her hand as if I were Tim's age. "I'm staying with Mother," I said to Daddy.

The policeman moved closer. Sand slipped over his shiny black shoes. He held up the paper again, but Mother made no move to examine it. Ms. Whitney snatched it from him and looked at it.

"I'm sorry, Miss," the policeman said to me, "but you have to go with your father."

I looked at Mother. She stared at Ms. Whitney, who looked up from the paper and nodded shortly.

My mother's face dissolved into tears. Someone— Ms. Whitney— I guess, gathered up our clothes and put them in my father's car. Katie cried, Ms. Whitney yelled, and the lights above the police car flashed blue and yellow across Daddy's stern face. The policeman put a hand on my shoulder, guiding me in the direction of Daddy's car. I yanked my shoulder out of his grasp and turned to Mother. Tears rushed down her face, and she pressed her fist hard against her mouth.

I thought of all the times in the last month that I'd seen my mother cry. This was the worst. "'Bye, Mother, " I whispered.

And suddenly we were being driven away, waving frantically at Mother from the back window of Daddy's car. She leaned sobbing against Ms. Whitney. "I'll see you soon, kids!" she cried. "We'll be together soon!"

"We'll be back!" I cried through my tears. I waved until Daddy turned the corner, and then she was gone.

Chapter 3

I turned from the back window of the car to glare at Daddy. Tears ran down my cheeks and slid off my nose. Beside me, Katie whimpered. "Daddy, I forgot Seymour!"

"Who the hell is Seymour?" Daddy snapped.

"Katie's blanket," I muttered under my breath. "I can't believe you don't remember *that*."

Daddy looked sideways at the man behind the newspaper. The man folded up his newspaper and turned around. It was Mr. Martin.

"What are *you* doing here?" I cried.

Mr. Martin loosened his red and blue striped tie with one hand and smoothed his blond hair away from his face with the other. "I'm a social worker, Veronica."

I thought that if I didn't hit something right then, I'd explode. "What's he need a social worker for!" I yelled, banging my fist against the seat beside me. It was soft brown leather, and it absorbed my punch as if I had no strength at all.

"Cool it, Ronnie," Daddy cautioned.

"Your father needs a social worker to assist him in obtaining legal custody of you children," Mr. Martin said, pronouncing each syllable of each word in a cold, clipped voice.

"We play baseball, Pop?" Tim asked. He sat on the front seat between Mr. Martin and Daddy, eating animal crackers from a box Daddy had handed him.

"Sure, we can play baseball when we get home,"

Daddy said. "Maybe the girls would like to play, too."

"Daddy, we have to get Seymour!" Katie wailed. Snot dripped down her chin. She wiped it off on the sleeve of her T-shirt.

"That blanket's full of germs. I'll get you a teddy bear," Daddy said.

"I don't want a teddy bear! I wanna go back to live with Mother and Seymour at the beach! *Please*, Daddy!"

My father swung the car onto the freeway and began the long drive back down the coast. I took Katie's hand— something I don't usually do— and squeezed it. "It's okay. We'll get back somehow," I whispered. "I hate you!" I said louder, in the direction of the front seat.

"That's understandable," Mr. Martin said calmly.

This time I hit the window with my fist, so hard that I felt the shock like fire all up my arm and into my shoulder. "You can't take us away. She's our *mother*!"

"Enough, Ronnie!" Daddy said. His voice was dangerously quiet.

He turned on the radio to a football game. The commentator's droning voice filled the car. Once in a while, he or Mr. Martin would say, "Make the touchdown!" or "All right!" and Tim would applaud.

In spite of the noise, Katie fell asleep, breathing in little, sobbing hiccups and clutching the front of her T-shirt in one hand as if it were Seymour. I kept holding her other hand as I stared out the window. Daddy drove up the grade bordered on both sides with dusty cactuses, and then we were in Newbury Park in front of Mr. Martin's house.

"Sure you don't want to come in for a drink?" Mr. Martin asked Daddy. "Elsa's out with the girls, I guess. Her car's gone."

My father jerked his head toward the back seat. "Maybe tomorrow. I've gotta get the kids home. Thanks for your help."

"Thanks for nothing," I muttered.

Daddy eyes flashed a warning at me. He pulled the car out of the driveway so fast that the tires skidded sharply against the pavement. Tim slid into Mr. Martin's seat and began playing with his animal crackers. "Roar!" he said, biting the head off a lion.

"We're going home, Timmy," Daddy said brightly, looking at me in the rear view mirror.

I closed my eyes and thought hard. At home, I could see Trisha and Dolores. Maybe I could move in with one of them and never have to see Daddy again. Or maybe I could get one of their mothers to take me back to Carpinteria. The thought almost made me smile. I opened my eyes to find that Daddy had pulled the Lexus onto the freeway. He was heading out of Newbury Park. "Where're you taking us?" I demanded, but he only turned up the radio louder.

An hour later, he pulled off the freeway. We passed a green sign that read "Welcome to Torrance" in white letters beneath black graffiti. Daddy drove along a street lined with stores that looked faded and old under the gray sky. Some of the names of the stores were written in English, some in Spanish, and one neon sign said "Chuy's Chinese House" in English with Asian letters below it. Daddy turned down several more streets until we came to one on which all the houses looked identical, painted brown with tan shutters. The lawns were all neatly clipped rectangles. He pulled into the driveway of one of the houses and stopped the car.

"We're home," he announced.

Katie woke up and her eyes widened at the one-story house with its closely trimmed lawn.

"Where *are* we?" I cried. Two girls on bicycles rode by and stared at us.

"This is a town called Torrance." Daddy's eyes pleaded with me suddenly as he turned around in his seat. "Ronnie, you know I can't go back to our old house in Newbury Park. Not with all those memories of happy times, of all the fun we had."

"I can't believe you took us away from Mother!" I yelled. I didn't care if the neighbors heard me. Anyhow, I didn't see how they could help hearing even if I whispered— the houses were so close together on this street.

Daddy's jaw tightened, and the sadness disappeared from his eyes. He bent toward me, so close that I could see the yellow circles around his pupils, and raised his hand. I slid away from him, terrified. He'd never hit me before. I squeezed my eyes shut and waited, wondering how hard he'd have to hit me to make a bruise like the one Mother had beside her eye when she left him.

"Bring in your things," Daddy commanded. Then he got out of the car and walked up to the house. I wiped my palms on my shorts and breathed deeply, trying to get my heartbeat to slow down.

Katie and Tim ran up the cement walkway to the front door where a woman stood with her arms stretched out. "Welcome home!" Mrs. Martin said. "You must be Tim."

Tim threw his arms around her. "Roar!" he said, pretending to attack her with another cookie lion.

"Roar!" she said back to him.

"What're *you* doing here?" Katie grinned. "Wow!"

I stayed in the car. My shoulders began to shake with sobs. Two hours ago, I was living at the beach with Mother. Now, I had no idea where I was living, and I hated my father.

I felt like the seaweed Katie liked to drag home from the beach in Carpinteria. Sometimes, it got flung around in the ocean, and other times it ended up stretched out on the beach, depending on what the ocean felt like doing that day. I imagined myself brown and limp, helpless against the tide.

"I thought I'd come over to help you get settled in." Mrs. Martin stood outside the car, shivering a little in her thin, rose-patterned dress. "Come out, Veronica, please."

I got out of the car and stood there, brown and limp. Mrs. Martin put an arm around my shoulders and led me to the door. "This house is bigger than it looks from the outside. You each get your own bedroom!" She pointed to a half-open door at the front of the hall. "That's yours. I fixed it up for you a bit."

Katie did a pirouette on the shiny wood floor in the

hall, then smiled up at Mrs. Martin with all traces of her tears erased. She seemed even to have forgotten about Seymour. "Can we have strawberry pancakes?" she asked.

Mrs. Martin pushed her long black hair off her shoulders and smiled down at Katie. "I don't see why not. It's past lunchtime. Would you girls like to help me make them?"

I scowled at the bare white walls in the empty living room and said nothing.

"Relax, Ronnie. We're only renting," Daddy said, brushing past me with a box of Tim's toys.

I walked into the bedroom Mrs. Martin had pointed out to me and closed the door. There were the pretty yellow and white checked curtains and the bedspread I'd picked out from the J.C. Penny catalog with Mother years ago. I sat on the bed and hugged my old, lumpy pillow to my chest. My head ached, and there was a sharp pain in my ear. I wanted to scream until my throat was red and raw. I wanted to climb out the window above the bed and run back to Mother's house, but I didn't know how to get there. I didn't have a car, and I only had a dollar and a dime left over from the allowance Mother had given me last week. That didn't seem like enough to take a bus two hours back to Carpinteria. I sat and stared numbly at the pale blue carpet on the floor.

In my mind, I pictured myself running out to the front of the house, standing in front of Daddy as he unpacked the car. *Take me back to my mother!* I'd yell so that all the neighbors on the street would hear me. *I hate your guts!*

Then Daddy would see that I was strong and brave, and he'd take me right back to Carpinteria.

But I wasn't strong and brave. I was afraid of Daddy — too afraid to yell. Too afraid to move.

The next day, Mrs. Martin dropped Katie off at the grammar school and took Tim to a school she'd found for disabled kids. Daddy drove me over to the junior high school. My head felt stuffy from crying all night. Life didn't even seem real this morning.

"This is my second junior high in a month," I muttered as we walked up to the school office. My voice sounded far away and strange to my plugged-up ears.

"That's your mother's fault, not mine," Daddy replied. Inside the school office, he showed the secretary his rental agreement as proof that he lived in Torrance.

I stood in the brightly-lit school office feeling ugly and awkward in a pink T-shirt and a green skirt with pink hippos on it. I hadn't worn the skirt in years, but Mother had sewed it herself, and wearing it made me feel closer to her.

"Come with me, Veronica." The secretary beckoned to me with one long red fingernail that matched her lipstick. "I'm sure she'll be fine, Mr. Davis," she told Daddy as if I were five years old.

"Of course she will. Ronnie's a highly intelligent girl." Daddy patted me on the shoulder. "She's just at that difficult age, you know." He and the secretary exchanged amused smiles.

I wanted to kick him. Instead, I turned away without telling him goodbye and followed the secretary down an outdoor hall. At least this school was painted a nice, decent brown, instead of mustard yellow. The secretary opened a door with a brass "8" on it. Her fingernail summoned a heavy woman in a lavender dress and white, low-heeled shoes. "This is Veronica Davis," the secretary explained as the teacher walked outside. "She just moved here yesterday."

The teacher smiled at me— a real, welcoming smile that shone out from her round blue eyes. I almost burst into tears right there outside the classroom. "I'm happy to meet you, Veronica," she said. "I'm Mrs. Ellis, your homeroom and English teacher."

"I'm Ronnie," I whispered.

"I'm sorry?" Mrs. Ellis bent toward me. Her curling brown hair smelled like flowers.

"You can call me Ronnie."

"Ronnie. I like that name," she said. "Shall we go

in?"

I walked into the classroom, feeling thirty kids' eyes on me.

"This is Ronnie Davis," Mrs. Ellis told them. "Where are you from, Ronnie?"

"Newbury . . . I mean, Carpinteria," I stammered. My face burned, and I sat down quickly in the empty seat Mrs. Ellis pointed out to me.

"Nice hippos." A short, dark boy with almond-shaped brown eyes grinned from the seat beside me.

I folded my arms across my chest and pretended to listen to Mrs. Ellis as she began talking about how to use a comma. Another boy behind me hissed, "It's the hippo girl!"

I clasped my knees tightly together under the thin cotton skirt, remembering the day Mother had sewed it.

She'd made the skirt two years before, out of fabric I'd picked out. Katie got a skirt, too, only hers had pink flamingos. I sat with Mother at the dining room table, watching her cut out pieces and stitch them together on her sewing machine. She showed me how to sew the scraps into a skirt for Katie's doll, and we talked the way I imagined Laura Ingalls Wilder and her friends had talked when they had big quilting parties. I remember asking Mother if she and Daddy got married in a church.

"No," she'd replied. "We got married in Las Vegas a year before we had you. We were driving from Vermont to California, and we just pulled over to some horrible place with plastic flowers and the wedding march on a tape recorder and got married. I was wearing a purple bikini top and shorts and no shoes."

"That's it?" I'd said, shocked. "That's all the wedding you and Daddy had?"

"That's it," she'd laughed. "A big wedding wasn't important to us. We'd both been married before."

Now, staring down at the hearts and initials carved in the blond wood of my new school desk, I decided that the informality of the purple bikini top and the plastic flowers had jinxed my parents' wedding.

"Hey, hippo girl," the short boy beside me whispered. "Didn't you hear Mrs. Ellis say to get out your grammar book?"

I leaned down to pick up the grammar book in the wire basket under my desk.

"Nice hippos," the boy said again, looking right down my blouse.

I straightened up quickly and stared at the exercise on commas, telling myself over and over in my head that I would not cry.

Daddy had told me to pick up Katie at the grammar school down the street in the afternoon. I walked down the sidewalk past stores with names like "Christy's Casualwear" and "Bill's Pawn Shop." Cars sped by me spurting exhaust, and there was a sudden, sharp squeal of brakes. I whirled around to see a man in a blue pickup giving the finger to an old woman in a Chevy.

Torrance is completely different from Carpinteria— I thought— *different in an* awful *way.*

Right before the grammar school, I saw a pay phone in a gas station parking lot. I fished four dimes out of my backpack, then froze, horrified. I couldn't remember Ms. Whitney's phone number.

I tried to picture the piece of paper with her phone number on it in my school backpack in Carpinteria. I'd looked at it just last week when I'd forgotten my lunch. I imagined myself pushing the buttons on the phone in the office of the mustard-colored junior high. I couldn't see the numbers in my head.

"Darn!" I hit the plastic wall of the phone booth with my fist. A gas station attendant in a blue shirt glanced over at me. I turned my back to him and pushed "0."

"May I help you?" the operator's male voice asked me.

"I need a phone number," I said, choking back tears. "Maggie Davis in Carpinteria."

"I'll transfer you to information," the voice said.

"Carpinteria," I repeated to the woman who

answered. "Maggie Davis."

"I'm sorry. That name isn't listed."

"Could you . . . could you look up Liz . . . um . . . Elizabeth Whitney?" I asked in a small voice.

There was a pause, and then the woman said, "I'm not showing any listing for that name, either."

"What about Max Whitney?" I asked, but the woman had hung up. I slammed the phone into the receiver and went to look for Katie. I found her in the grammar school yard, playing hopscotch by herself. "What's up?" I sighed, rubbing the tears out of my eyes.

"Nothing!" Her blond eyebrows were bunched together. She threw a rock so hard that it bounced far out of the last yellow-painted square.

"You miss Mother, don't you?" If I hadn't seen two boys playing basketball across the playground, I would've hugged Katie right there.

Katie shook her head. "Uh-uh. Mrs. Martin said Mother's real sick, and we shouldn't be around her right now." She picked up another rock and threw it. It broke, and gray pieces of it scattered over the blacktop. "This stupid boy in my class, Ricky, didn't invite me to his birthday party tomorrow. He invited everyone else, and they were all talking about it. I felt left out."

Then I wanted to smack Katie instead of hugging her.

In the weeks that followed, it seemed like my little sister and brother didn't even miss Mother. Katie made friends with a girl across the street, and they rode bikes together and sold See's candy so that their school could buy a new jungle gym. Tim ran in from the school bus every day full of news about the pet guinea pig in his classroom and his teacher, Miss Rosa.

Daddy hired a housekeeper so that someone was home when we returned from school. Her name was Mrs. Anson, and it was her job to get Tim off the bus and stay with him in the afternoons while she cleaned the house. Her arms and legs were bony, and she smelled like Comet cleanser. She insisted on teaching me to make up my bed with stiff hospital corners that I had to undo every night because my feet got hot.

I tried to argue with Daddy that I could watch Tim by myself. I didn't do anything after school but sit in my room and read, anyhow. As soon as I finished one book, I picked up another. I pretended that I was the main character in each one, until I began to wonder if Ronnie Davis really even existed at all.

One afternoon, I looked for Ms. Whitney's number in the stack of phone books at the public library. There was one Whitney listed in the Carpinteria phone book, but his name was George. I closed the phone book and wondered why Mother didn't call us.

I began to wonder if what Mrs. Martin had told Katie was true. Maybe Mother really was sick. Maybe she was in the hospital with some contagious disease. I couldn't sleep at night, now, wondering if Mother was going to die.

Then one afternoon, the phone rang.

"Ronnie, telephone!" Mrs. Martin called through the crack in my door. She'd been over at the house every afternoon for a week, making Katie's and Tim's Halloween costumes.

I went out to the kitchen, where Mrs. Anson stood glaring at the scraps of black fabric all over the dining room floor.

"Hello?" I said into the phone.

"Is this Veronica?"

"Yeah." My heart jumped. The high, soft voice on the other end of the line sounded like Mother. But when the woman continued talking, I knew it wasn't her.

"I'm Julia Goldberg's mother," the woman said. Julia Goldberg was a girl in my new math class. She had curly black hair and red cheeks that got redder when she had to do long division problems up at the chalkboard. "Julia mentioned your name," the woman continued, "and I recognized it from the Newbury Park Girl Scout roster. Isn't your mother the leader of that troop?"

"She moved," I said.

"Oh." Mrs. Goldberg paused. "Well, I'm the troop leader for the junior high here, and we were wondering if you'd like to join our troop."

I almost said yes. If I joined the troop, I'd be out of the house. I wouldn't have to listen to Mrs. Anson's vacuum or make my bed correctly. I pictured myself working on badges with Julia Goldberg, learning how to build a fire and mark a trail. Mother had been just about to teach our troop those things when she left.

Mother. How could I be in Girl Scouts without her?

"I'm sorry," I said into the phone. "I have to watch my brother after school. And anyway, I'm moving back in with my mother in a few weeks, and she's going to lead the troop in Carpinteria."

"That's too bad for us," Mrs. Goldberg said, sounding disappointed. "Julia's having a sleep-over in two weeks. It's kind of a combination Halloween party and birthday party. Would you like to come to that, if you're still in Torrance?"

"Sure," I said to get her off the phone. Mrs. Martin and Katie were giving me curious glances, probably wondering why I'd told that lie about having to watch Tim.

"Okay, I'll tell Julia. Bye, Veronica."

"Bye." I hung up and went back to my room. *How embarrassing—* I thought. There was no way I was going to some party Julia's *mother* invited me to, no matter how much I wanted to get out of the house. It didn't matter what junior high I went to; rules were you didn't go to a party unless the *kid* having the party invited you. *Not* the mother.

"Can we go back to Carpinteria to see Mother?" I asked Daddy almost every day.

"No," he said. "Your mother is not in a stable frame of mind right now. When she's back to normal, you can see her."

I got up all my nerve one night and said, "She's in the hospital, isn't she?"

"No, but she should be." Daddy's hands clenched into fists, his knuckles big and faintly purple. "Don't ask me about her again, Veronica. I *mean* it!"

After Daddy said that, I chewed off all my fingernails worrying. Maybe the operator couldn't find Ms. Whitney because she'd moved. Maybe Mother had decided to move with her, to adopt Pam, Sage, and Max because Daddy had taken us away. Or maybe she was dying.

On Halloween night, Mrs. Martin came over with her stepdaughters, Donna and Deanna. She and Daddy took Tim, Katie, and Deanna out trick-or-treating. Last year, I had been an octopus with eight purple sock legs Mother had sewn to a purple leotard. This year, I didn't feel like dressing up. Donna and I watched *The Blob* on TV and ate the miniature Hershey bars we were supposed to be handing out to trick-or-treaters. I missed a lot of the movie because I had to keep jumping up to answer the door. Donna didn't take her eyes off the screen.

I was surprised when, at a commercial, she gathered her blond hair up into a ponytail at the top of her head and sighed heavily. "I hate my life," she said.

I looked at her from the doorway. She was bigger and taller than me, with the most beautiful ankles I'd ever seen. I liked to look at them when she wasn't watching me. Her ankles were slim and tanned between the tapered hem of her blue jeans and her white, cuffed sock. I wanted ankles like that when I was in high school. But I could never tell Donna that. Girls weren't allowed to say that kind of stuff to other girls. It sounded weird.

"I hate my life, too," I offered. Donna didn't answer.

The Blob came back on. Silently, we unwrapped candy bars, dropping the foil on the carpet. At the next commercial, Donna stood up. "There's some more kids coming," she said, glancing out the window.

I got up to answer the door as she walked to the bathroom. "It's just that my dad drinks all the time," she said and shut the door.

The trick-or-treaters turned out to be Tim, Katie,

and Deanna. Tim thought he was really smart to be knocking at the door of his own house.

"Who are you? I don't know you," I said, pretending to shut the door on him.

"Iss your brother!" he cried, ripping off his plastic Superman mask. "I trick you!"

Mrs. Martin and Daddy walked in and made the kids dump their candy on the floor, so they could check it for razor blades and rat poison, just like Mother used to do. Donna came out of the bathroom. We knelt on the floor beside the little kids, trying to steal their packages of M&M's while they were busy trading candy. Donna winked at me when I slid her a Milky Way bar behind Deanna's back, and it was as if she'd never said that thing about Mr. Martin drinking all the time.

One evening in early November, the doorbell rang during dinner. Mrs. Anson had made meatloaf before she left, so we were sitting around the table with Daddy, eating meatloaf with frozen French fries he'd heated in the oven.

"I'll get it. Can I go bike riding with Maria if it's her?" Katie yelled over her shoulder on the way to the door.

"It's too dark." Daddy reached over to cut up Tim's meatloaf. He stood up abruptly as Katie led Mrs. Martin into the dining room, and his chair fell over backwards.

Mrs. Martin was crying. Her mascara had clumped together on her long lashes, but her hair hung about her shoulders like a smooth black velvet cape.

"I left him," she said, looking straight at Daddy. He walked over and put his arms around her, then led her into the living room.

"Finish dinner and do the dishes, girls," he said as if nothing were out of the ordinary. "Then you can come in with us."

I washed and Katie dried, standing on a chair so that she could put the dishes away in the cupboard. Tim sat at the table trying to stack his French fries on top of each other. "All fall down!" he chanted, then stuffed all his fries into his mouth at once.

"Shh, Tim, I wanna listen," Katie whispered.

I pretended like I didn't care what was going on in the living room, but I washed the dishes as quietly as I could, turning the water on low to hear over it. All I could hear was Mrs. Martin's muffled crying, and Daddy saying over and over, "It'll be okay."

As soon as the last dish was put away, Katie jumped off the chair and ran into the living room. Tim trailed behind her. I folded the damp dishtowel and hung it on the refrigerator door before I went in to see what was going on.

Mrs. Martin sat on Daddy's lap on the couch, one arm draped around his shoulder. He reached up and wiped her eyes with a tissue, something I've never even seen him do for Tim. He nodded at the empty spot on the couch when I walked in. "Sit down, Ronnie," he said.

I sat down on the beige carpet near the fireplace and waited. Katie giggled in the strange silence, and Tim pretended to read the front page of the *Los Angeles Times* on the coffee table.

Finally, Daddy spoke. "Mrs. Martin is going to stay with us for a while," he announced. "I don't think the housekeeper is working out, anyhow."

"All right! No more housekeeper!" Katie and Tim slapped each other five and danced around the living room singing "Ding Dong, the Witch is Dead." I sat very still. *Mrs. Martin is going to leave Donna and Deanna to come live with us, just like Mother has probably left us to live with Ms. Whitney and her kids—* I thought.

I jumped up from the floor and ran into my bedroom. "Doesn't anyone keep their kids anymore?" I yelled and slammed my door shut.

The next day, Mrs. Martin brought over three suitcases and two small gold and white dogs. "They're called Shelties," she explained to us as she led them out to the back porch. "I used to breed them in England. They are named Sweetie and King." She let the dogs out off their leashes, and they raced around, sniffing at the grass and the ivy-covered wall with long, prim noses.

From Daddy's bedroom doorway, I watched Mrs. Martin unpack her clothes and put them in Daddy's dresser drawers. Katie sat on the carpet, sorting Mrs. Martin's earrings. "Are you getting a divorce?" she asked, holding a pair of pearls up to her ears.

Mrs. Martin was silent a long time. She continued putting blue jeans and shorts away, and I wondered if she'd even heard Katie. "Yes," she said at last. "I *am* getting a divorce."

Her voice sounded so sad. I didn't ask what I was thinking, but then Katie asked it for me. "Are you going to marry Daddy?"

Mrs. Martin pressed her lips into a tiny smile. She clipped her hair into a ponytail with a gold barrette and said, "He hasn't asked me to, Katie-Cat."

"But how can you be our new mother if you don't marry Daddy?"

Mrs. Martin hugged Katie to her. "You can think of me as your mother while I'm here. I'll take care of you." She looked up at me. "Would you like that, Veronica?"

"I already have a mother," I said stiffly.

But I did miss someone taking care of me. Since we'd moved to Torrance, I fixed cereal for Katie and Tim every morning and took them to the park on weekends, when Daddy was busy washing his car or mowing the lawn. Some of the kids had started talking to me at school, and Julia Goldberg had invited me to go horseback riding next month. I hoped Mrs. Martin would start taking care of Tim and Katie, so that I could have something like a normal life again.

But Mrs. Martin and Daddy slept until noon on the gray November weekends. I poured pancake batter into rabbit shapes for Katie, and space creatures for Tim, and we all watched cartoons in the living room until Daddy and Mrs. Martin woke up.

"What were you *doing* in there?" Katie demanded one Sunday, when they finally emerged at twelve thirty in their robes and slippers.

"Oh, just screwing around," Daddy said, winking

at me.

I bit my lip and stared down at the puzzle Tim and I were working on. It was a brightly-colored picture of a tropical forest that Mother had given me last Christmas. I wondered grimly what we were going to do about Christmas this year. Maybe Daddy would forget all about it. Since Mrs. Martin had arrived, he'd forgotten a lot of things. He'd promised to help me with my math homework, but every night after dinner, he and Mrs. Martin poured themselves a glass of wine and watched some boring movie on the VCR or played backgammon and checkers, as though they didn't have any kids at all.

In mid-November, Mrs. Martin went to England for a week to visit her parents. Daddy cooked hamburgers out on the grill and let us put as much salt as we wanted to on our French fries, even though Mrs. Martin always said, "Salt's a killer."

"We all have to die sometime," Daddy laughed as he shook salt on his fries.

That week, he left work early in the afternoon. He took all three of us miniature golfing and walked over to the neighborhood park with us to play softball. "You girls should be on a team," he said, when Katie and I had caught ten pop-ups each.

"Yeah!" Katie said. "When?"

"I'll find out when the Little League season begins," Daddy promised. "Probably in the spring." He tossed me the ball. "Would you like to play on a team, Ronnie? You're a good pitcher."

I started to say no. I wanted to tell him that I had every intention of going back to Mother in Carpinteria as soon as he'd let me. But I wasn't even sure she was alive. I squinted up at Daddy in the late afternoon sun and gripped the grass-stained white softball. "Maybe I'll check it out," I said.

The night before Mrs. Martin was due to come back from England, the telephone's shrill ring split the two a.m. silence wide open. I sat up in bed terrified, and tiptoed to

Daddy's door. His low, serious voice broke suddenly. I heard him begin to cry.

"Mother's dead," I thought and walked into his room without knocking.

He sat on the edge of the bed in his white boxer shorts and a light blue T-shirt, cradling the phone on his lap. When he saw me, he reached out and held my hand tightly. "Oh, Ronnie, your grandpa's sick," he choked.

I sat down beside him, and he put his arms around me. I patted his back awkwardly, as if he were the child and I were the adult, the responsible one. Then I stood up and handed him a sweatshirt from the dresser. He put it on, still crying. "I'll go get you some orange juice," I said, hoping he'd put on a pair of sweatpants while I was gone. I stood in the dark kitchen and listened as Daddy made another phone call. He spoke so quietly that I couldn't hear his words.

I didn't know my grandpa, Daddy's father, very well. He'd visited a few years ago, but he and Daddy had an argument over who got to drive to Disneyland, and Grandpa Davis left sooner than he'd planned. He was a tall, stocky man with white hair and white stubble that scraped my face when he kissed me goodbye at the airport. "Come visit me in Vermont, Ronnie," he'd said. "Come in the fall, when the leaves are pretty."

I walked back into Daddy's room and handed him the glass of orange juice. He looked up at me and said thickly, "Ronnie, I can't deal with this by myself. Your mother isn't here . . . God, I miss her."

"I'm here, Daddy," I said firmly.

He lay a hand against my cheek. "I know it's not right . . . but you've always been my favorite child. You're the oldest, the only one I saw being born."

The phone rang again. Daddy reached to answer it. He spoke in a voice so broken and low that it was almost not a voice at all, but just a shadow, like the shadow of his bent head against the wall. I sat down on the bed, hugging a pillow to my chest and watched the thin sliver of white moon outside the window. *I have to take care of him*— I repeated in my head until I fell asleep.

Daddy shook me awake in the gray, early morning. Outside the window, clouds hovered, dark and full of rain. "Ronnie," he said, his face drooping with sadness. "Can you get your brother and sister dressed?"

"Sure," I said.

I woke Katie and Tim and made them pancakes. I was helping Katie button her denim dress when Daddy walked in wearing slacks and a button-down shirt.

"Katie," he said slowly, "your mother will be here in an hour to pick you and Tim up. Ronnie . . . "

Katie and I stared at Daddy, waiting.

"Ronnie, how would you like to go to Vermont with me? We're going to go visit your grandpa, but we'll stay with your grandma, and we can make a little vacation of it."

"Is Mother better?" I cried. "Is she out of the hospital?"

"What're you talking about?" Daddy said. "She's fine."

"Does Ronnie get to go on a plane?" Katie wanted to know.

"Yes, because she'd the oldest," Daddy said. "Will you go with me, Ronnie?"

Any other time, I would've chosen to see Mother a hundred times over some airplane ride. But Daddy needed me now. "I guess I'll go with you," I said slowly.

"Lucky," Katie said as she watched me put sweaters and socks into my blue suitcase.

"I'll bring you some pretty leaves off the trees," I said.

"Gee, thanks." Katie wandered off to the front porch to wait for Mother.

I had just finished packing when I heard the red VW bus chugging up the street. I stayed in my room, folding and refolding shirts and jeans. Finally, Daddy came to the door. "Your mother wants to see you."

I walked to the door, and Mother was there, gathering me up in her arms. "Honey, how are you?" she cried.

My body stiffened against the tears that threatened to pour out. "I'm fine."

Mother stepped back and looked at me. She'd gained weight since I'd seen her two months ago. She looked healthy and normal. It made me mad to see her looking okay. For weeks, I'd pictured her skinny and pale. I'd even pictured her dead. I'd sobbed in the middle of the night over the thought of it, and now, here she was, just fine. Tears deepened the blue of her eyes, and she didn't try to hug me again. "He wouldn't give me your phone number," she whispered. "And he wouldn't tell me the address until this morning."

I shrugged, not trusting myself to say anything. There had to be ways to find your missing kids. She could've put pictures of us on milk cartons or something.

"So. You're going with him to Vermont," she said quietly.

"Yeah."

"I understand. It'll be nice for you to see Grandma Davis. Tell her . . . tell her I said hello."

"I will."

She pressed her hand against her mouth, then whispered, "I wish you'd come home with me instead. I miss you so much, Ronnie. Ms. Whitney misses you. Even Sage . . ." A tear pooled in the corner of her eye. "Even Sage asked when you'd be back."

"I have to take care of Daddy."

My voice came out cold, surprising both Mother and me. "You have Katie and Tim." I turned to go inside. I knew I was being horrible. I wanted to rush out to Mother, to beg her to take me back to Carpinteria, but Daddy needed me.

"G'bye, honey," Mother called after me. "I'll see you soon."

I didn't answer her, but I watched from my bedroom window as the red bus rolled slowly down the street. Katie waved Seymour triumphantly out the window. My throat ached from not being able to cry.

That morning, Daddy and I flew to Vermont. I'd

never been on an airplane before. He let me have the window seat, and I watched the cement buildings in Los Angeles disappear as the plane rose above clouds as white and fluffy as whipped cream. A bell chimed, and the seat belt sign above us flashed off.

"That means you can get up and use the bathroom if you want," Daddy said. He looked handsome in a maroon sweater that faded the yellow circles in his eyes. He smiled down at me and patted my knee. "I like those pants," he said. I was wearing a pair of soft tan chinos Mother had bought me for school in Carpinteria and a green cardigan over a white T-shirt.

"Thanks," I said. I watched as the stewardess began to roll a large silver cart down the aisle. She handed each passenger a small cardboard box.

"What would you like to drink?" an Asian stewardess with black, silky hair like Mrs. Martin's smiled at us.

"I don't suppose you have a piña colada in there," Daddy said.

She shook her head. "No, but I can make you a gin and tonic or a Bloody Mary."

"A gin and tonic would be great. Ronnie, what do you want?"

"A 7-UP, please," I said. My stomach felt funny from being up in the air. Mostly, flying felt like being in a car with a few hundred people, but whenever the plane bounced through a cloud, my stomach turned over. I opened my cardboard box and found a sandwich, an apple, blocks of cheese and crackers, and a miniature candy bar. All I really wanted was the candy bar, but I unwrapped the plastic around my sandwich.

Daddy unhooked the tray from the back of the seat in front of him and opened his box. "Airplane food is usually bad," he said, taking a big swallow of his drink, "but it's hard to ruin a roast beef sandwich."

After we'd eaten, the stewardess took away our boxes. Daddy sighed heavily, reminding me of why were going to Vermont. "I'm going to take a nap," he said. "I don't think either of us got much sleep last night." He reached under his seat for a flat, paper-covered pillow and tilted his seat back. "Wake me up if you need something," he said and closed his eyes.

I pulled my jacket over me and looked out the window. Below me, I could see fields and mountains. The fields lay below me in perfect brown and green squares like a quilt. I wondered how the farmers had made them so straight.

I woke up at the chime of the seat belt sign. "We'll be arriving shortly," the pilot said. "The time is seven P.M."

I massaged my stiff neck with one hand and looked sideways at Daddy's watch. "It's only four," I told him.

He rubbed his eyes. His face had red creases from the pillow, and he looked sleepier than he had before he'd slept. "There's a three hour time difference on the East Coast," he explained. "It really is seven at night here."

The plane began to drop through the clouds. Lights from the cars below stretched out into bright lines of red and white. Squares of light shone from the windows of people's houses. The plane hit the runway with a gentle bump, and finally, I felt my shoulders relax.

"I think I thought it was going to crash the whole time," I confessed to Daddy.

He stood up and reached for our carry-on bags. We had to wait a long time for the first class passengers to get off the plane. "They get top sirloin and champagne," Daddy said absently, "but they pay a fortune for it." He put a hand on my shoulder. "Ronnie, I'm glad you wanted to come with me. I feel better knowing you're here." He looked down at me with tears in his eyes and took me by the hand. "My father and I were never close like you and I are . . ." he began, and then stopped as the people in front of us began to shuffle toward the front of the plane. I stood very straight and held his hand firmly as we walked down the aisle.

"What beautiful eyes," I heard one of the stewardesses say as we passed her on our way out the door.

"They must be father and daughter," another

stewardess said.

Daddy and I walked along a tunnel that led to the waiting room of the airport. "We're going to rent a car and drive to your grandma's," he explained. We stepped out into the airport, and I saw a crowd of people in heavy jackets and scarves hugging and kissing each other, grabbing suitcases and laughing.

"Zach! Over here!"

I looked around, wondering who could possibly know my father in an airport in Vermont. I found myself face to face with Mrs. Martin, who looked exactly like a model in a black leather jacket and a black angora beret.

"What . . . what is *she* doing here?" I cried to Daddy.

My father didn't answer me. He dropped his suitcase, and Mrs. Martin put her arms around him and held him in a long, long embrace.

Chapter 4

My father took Mrs. Martin's hand and walked with her down the airport stairs, not even looking around to see if I was following him. At the baggage claim area, they held hands and kissed until suitcases began sliding down the ramp and onto the metal carousel. Daddy swung our suitcases to the floor and turned to me. "We're going across the road to get the rental car," he said. "Why don't you wait in the airport with the suitcases, and we'll pick you up."

"Okay." Numbly, I watched them walk out the sliding glass door together. Cold air rushed in from outside, pulling at my cheeks and at my earlobes below the blue wool ski hat that used to be Mother's. I shivered in my turquoise jacket and black mittens. Or were they gloves? I wasn't sure of the difference. One had fingers and the other didn't. Either way, the cold came right through them. I stuffed my hands down into my pockets and sat down on my suitcase as Mrs. Martin and Daddy walked off toward the parking lot.

I wondered how Mrs. Martin had flown from

England to Vermont so fast. Daddy must have called her last night, so that she was able to rush across the world to get here. *Did he call her before or after he told me he needed me—* I thought bitterly, and then I had another, sadder thought. *I could be with Mother right now.*

My anger warmed me in spite of the chill wind that blew in every time the door slid open in front of me. People in heavy coats and scarves hurried past me, anxious to get into their warm cars and drive off into the night. By the time Daddy drove the rental car over to me, my cheeks were hot with fury.

Mrs. Martin got out of the car and put a cold hand against my cheek. "Veronica, you're frozen," she said. "Don't you have a winter coat?"

"This *is* my winter coat," I said stiffly. I got into the back seat of the car and zipped my coat up over my chin.

"We'll have to find you something warmer," Mrs. Martin said. "Winter in Vermont is much different than winter in California." She helped Daddy put the suitcases in the trunk, then got in the car and turned up the heat as far as it would go.

"Cold enough for you, Ronnie?" Daddy asked. I stared out the window at the stark, leafless trees lining the parking lot and didn't answer him.

"Zach," Mrs. Martin said, "we have to go straight to the hotel and find Veronica a bowl of soup. She's not used to this weather."

"I thought we were staying with Grandma Davis," I muttered.

Daddy grunted and pulled cautiously onto the road. His knuckles were clenched white around the steering wheel. "Been a long time since I've driven in a real winter," he said to Mrs. Martin. He drove much more slowly than he did at home and put on the brakes every few seconds. I pulled my hands up inside my jacket sleeves. We drove past dark mountains covered with naked, spidery black trees. I thought miserably of the endless stretch of ocean in Carpinteria.

"Too bad you couldn't have seen this place a few months ago, Ronnie," Daddy said. "Autumn in Vermont is incredible."

Again, I didn't reply. Daddy looked at Mrs. Martin and raised his eyebrows. She put one hand on his leg and shook her head slightly. I closed my eyes so I wouldn't have to see them together in the front seat. Now I hated Daddy more than I had hated him the day he'd taken us away from Mother. He'd just taken me away from her again— only now, I was stranded on the other side of the United States with him and Mrs. Martin.

In my mind, I saw myself unbuckling my seatbelt and rising up in the car behind Daddy, strong and angry. *You said you needed me to take care of you!* I'd yell. *You lied to me, Daddy! I hate you!*

Then he would fly me straight back to Carpinteria, impressed by how brave I was.

Suddenly, a red car cut in front of Daddy, and he had to brake so quickly that we all lurched forward.

"*Asshole!*" Daddy yelled at the driver. He urged the rental car forward so he could give the man in the red car the finger. I bit my lip and shrank into the corner of the back seat. I knew I could never stand up to Daddy— he was too terrifying.

I stared out the window and tried to imagine what Mother was doing right now 4:45 P.M. California-time meant it was almost time for dinner with candles and incense and Max making jokes. Mother would cook tacos or pizza to celebrate the family being together again, and everyone would sit warm and comfortable on all the couches in the living room listening to Ms. Whitney's country music tapes. I choked back a sob. It made a strangling sound in my throat.

"Are you all right, Veronica?" Mrs. Martin turned around.

"No," I whispered and buried my head in my arm.

I woke up with my neck bent at an uncomfortable angle against the car window. Blue neon light from a hotel sign lit up the car. Mrs. Martin shook my shoulder gently. "Wake up, Veronica. We're here," she said.

I stumbled behind her up a flight of stone stairs.

"We got you your own room," she explained. She unlocked a door and led me into a small room with a single bed and a TV. "Your father and I will be right next door." She opened the door to what I thought was a closet, and I saw a room with a wide bed covered in the same rough green bedspread as mine. Mrs. Martin picked up the phone on the nightstand beside my bed and consulted a paper menu in her hand. "Hello, Room Service? Can you please send up a bowl of vegetable soup, some crackers and some ginger ale? Thanks very much." She hung up the phone and laid her hand against my forehead. "You're probably just tired out from the trip," she said.

Cold air rushed into the room as Daddy opened the door. "How d'you like Vermont so far, Ronnie?" He tossed my suitcase on the bed.

I ignored him and stared down at the red leather Bible on the nightstand, clenching my teeth together to keep them from chattering. Mrs. Martin nodded toward the other room. "Zach, why don't you go unpack and make dinner reservations," she suggested. "I'll take care of Veronica." She sat down on the end of my bed and flipped through the TV guide. "Looks like they have some pretty good movies on cable tonight," she said. "We'll be back in an hour or so. The restaurant's right downstairs, but I think you'd better get in bed and stay warm." She turned back the bedspread and put one pillow on top of the other. "If you need us, you can pick up the phone and call the lobby."

So they're going out to dinner— I thought— *leaving me alone in this awful hotel room with a bowl of soup*. I stood stiffly beside the nightstand and ran my finger over the gold edges of the Bible. I wondered if the gold came off. It didn't.

Beside me, Mrs. Martin folded her arms and looked at me out of sharp black eyes. "Your father needs both of us right now, Veronica. Tomorrow is going to be really rough on him."

"He doesn't need me," I muttered.

"Of course he needs you," she replied. "You're his

oldest daughter." She leaned over and put her arms around me. "He told me how you took care of him last night. I admire that."

I didn't know what to say, so I just sat there and breathed in the woolly perfume of Mrs. Martin's navy blue coat sleeve. It felt good to be hugged, but after a moment, I shrugged her away. Then someone knocked at the door.

"Come in," Mrs. Martin called.

A waiter appeared, carrying a covered tray. Mrs. Martin moved the phone and the Bible off the nightstand. "You can put that here," she said. She reached into her coat pocket and took out a five-dollar bill. "Thank you."

The waiter had smooth, tanned skin that made his teeth shine whitely in the admiring smile he gave Mrs. Martin. "Thank *you*," he said and walked out.

Mrs. Martin uncovered the tray. I watched the steam curling up from the bowl of vegetable soup. Suddenly, I wanted to crawl in between the white sheets on the hotel bed and sleep forever. Mrs. Martin put her hand on my head again. It felt heavy and relaxing. I closed my eyes. For just an instant, her hand felt like Mother's.

"I'm going to go change for dinner," she murmured. "You might want to get into your pajamas and turn on the TV." She paused in the doorway and looked at me standing stiffly beside the nightstand. "Well . . . good night, Veronica," she said.

"It's Ronnie," I whispered as the door closed behind her. I got into bed with all my clothes on, even the turquoise jacket, and cupped my hands around the bowl of soup trying to get warm.

The next morning, I woke up to a light tap on the door. "Room Service!"

"Come in," I mumbled.

The same waiter from the night before walked in with a tray full of scrambled eggs, bacon, and fruit. "I'll put it here." He placed the tray on the small table by the door. "She said you'd be awake . . . I'm sorry!" His white teeth shone in a grin of apology, and then he was gone.

The other door swung open. Mrs. Martin appeared in beige wool pants and a matching jacket over a creamy silk blouse. "Oh, good, Ronnie, you're up," she said. "Have some breakfast and get dressed, okay? We're going over to the hospital soon."

In the daylight, Vermont was prettier than it had been the night before. Warmer, too. The houses were all painted blue, green, or red, with white gingerbread trim around the windows and doors. A thin layer of snow covered every roof, reminding me of the cream cheese frosting on the carrot cake Mother baked for my birthday every year.

Daddy drove the car up the road to a single brick building and sat there for a moment, just looking at it. Then Mrs. Martin touched his arm, and we got out of the car and walked up the icy stone path to the glass doors. I glanced at Daddy out of the corner of my eye. His eyes were red and squinty, as if he hadn't slept much. His thin lips looked pinched and unhappy under his mustache. I almost felt sorry for him until I remembered how he had lied to me.

"Mr. Davis' room," he said to the red-haired nurse at the desk.

"I'm going that way anyhow, hon," the nurse said, picking up a pitcher of ice water. "I'll take you there."

The nurse's bright head bobbed cheerfully down the hall. The thick rubber soles of her shoes thudded dully on the spotless tile floor. "Room twenty four." She pushed the door open.

I peered into the room. A bare mattress stood close to the door. Across the room, a thin shape sat up on the other bed. Daddy lurched forward, hands clenched at his sides. "Dad?" he whispered. Mrs. Martin and I stood in the doorway, watching Daddy bend over his father. I heard a coughing sort of sob.

"Where's Grandma Davis?" I whispered.

"Home, I guess," Mrs. Martin whispered back. "I thought she'd be here."

"Veronica?" The figure on the bed leaned over to peer at me.

"She wanted to see you," Daddy said. "Ronnie, come over and say hello to your grandfather."

I walked slowly toward the bed. The hospital room smelled like Tim's room when he used to wet his bed at night. I felt like throwing up.

The man in the bed looked nothing like the grandfather I remembered. Grandpa Davis had been a big, tall man. This man was tiny and so white he was almost purple. Even his scraggly mustache looked like it might crumble into dust if I touched it. Beneath the mustache, his mouth opened. "You look like your mother," he croaked. He reached out a white hand that was more bones than skin. A tube stuck out of his arm. I followed it, horrified, up to a plastic bag suspended on a pole. Clear liquid dripped down the tube and into his arm.

I screamed and ran out of the room.

Mrs. Martin walked swiftly down the hall after me. "Let's go down to the cafeteria," she suggested and put her arm around me. A couple of nurses sat at a table near a heater in the small cafeteria, huddling around cups of coffee. Mrs. Martin led me to a table next to them and brought me a Styrofoam cup of hot chocolate. "Hospitals are scary, aren't they?" Across from me, she stirred cream into her black coffee.

I wiped my eyes with the paper napkin she handed me. "He looks so different," I whispered.

"He has cancer. Your father says he smoked all the time." She sighed and rested her chin on one hand. "I'm glad I gave it up last year."

"*You* used to smoke?" I asked. Mrs. Martin looked as clean and neat as the hospital itself. I couldn't imagine her long, graceful fingers holding onto a dirty cigarette.

She nodded and gazed out the window. "Your poor, poor father," she murmured.

I scowled down at my hot chocolate. Mrs. Martin felt as sorry for Daddy as I'd felt for him the day before, when he'd told me back in Torrance that he needed me to take care of him. I thought of him up in that hospital room, and I hoped that Grandpa Davis was scaring Daddy as much as Daddy scared me.

"I heard Daddy tell Mother once that Grandpa Davis used to beat him up," I told Mrs. Martin. "That's why Daddy never comes to Vermont."

She put a finger to her red lips and glanced at the nurses. I looked away and out the window at a field covered with a smooth blanket of snow. I felt awkward having mentioned Mother to Mrs. Martin, and I was almost glad to see Daddy walking into the cafeteria. He looked nearly as pale as Grandpa Davis had looked. He gulped down the rest of Mrs. Martin's coffee, then said, "Let's go see my mother. Might as well get this all over with at once."

Daddy's parents lived in a small blue house surrounded by trees. Their branches stretched out against the gray sky as skinny as Grandpa Davis' fingers. We walked up to the front door. Daddy knocked, then blew on his knuckles.

"Zach!" A tall man with Katie's downward-tilted blue eyes and blond hair threw open the door. He caught Daddy up in a hug and shook hands with Mrs. Martin, then pulled me into the house. "This your little woman?"

"One of them," Daddy said. "This is Veronica. Ronnie, you remember your Uncle Bob."

I didn't remember him at all, but I twisted my lips into a polite smile and let Uncle Bob kiss my cheek. Daddy shut the door behind him, and we all shrugged off our coats in the warm room. "Mom here?" Daddy asked.

"Of course." Uncle Bob grinned. "She's a lot better this week. Almost seems liberated."

"She *is*," Daddy said. "Dad was a holy terror." The muscles in his face relaxed and he grinned back at Uncle Bob. "Still not married, huh?"

Uncle Bob screwed up his face in disgust. "Can't find a good woman," he said. "Maybe I should move out to California." He winked at Mrs. Martin and pulled my ponytail. "Curly hair like her mother's," he said to Daddy. "How is Maggie? Do you still talk, or are you one of those divorced couples who hate each other and call each other evil names on talk shows?"

Daddy shrugged and bent down to brush snow off his shoes. "Maggie's fine," he said.

A door opened somewhere down the hall. A little tan-colored dog with a wrinkled, smashed-in black face raced into the room. It yipped sharply and nipped at Uncle Bob's shoes.

"Dammit, Snippet, cut it out or I'll punt you across the living room!" Uncle Bob said.

Daddy bent down to scratch the dog's wrinkled head. "I can't believe this dog's still around."

"Yep." Uncle Bob rolled his eyes at me. "Snippet'll outlive all of us."

An old woman shuffled into the room— Grandma Davis, her back humped under a faded print dress. Snippet danced around her heels, threatening to trip her. "I was in the kitchen, fixing you all some lunch," my grandmother said by way of a greeting.

"Hi, Mom," Daddy said, giving her a quick hug. "This is Elsa Martin."

Mrs. Martin hugged Grandma Davis. "It's nice to meet you," she said. "I've heard a lot about you."

"None of it good, I'm sure," Grandma Davis replied in a thin, melancholy voice. She knelt down beside me and kissed me somewhere near my ear. I wrinkled my nose against the sour, dusty cotton of her dress. "Is this little Veronica?"

"I'm not little. I'm twelve," I said, embarrassed in front of Uncle Bob.

Grandma Davis raised one thin, pale eyebrow at Daddy. "She takes after you, Zachary." Snippet yipped and put his little paws on one of my hiking boots. "Come on, Snippet." Grandma Davis shuffled back down the hall. "Lunch is ready in the kitchen."

"Mom, we don't have time for lunch," Daddy said. "Elsa and I want to get back to the hospital. We have to leave tomorrow, you know."

Uncle Bob widened his eyes at Daddy. "You flew all the way across the country to stay for one day?"

Daddy shrugged again. "I have to be back in Los

Angeles on Friday for an appointment."

Uncle Bob looked at Mrs. Martin, who looked quickly away. Then he chuckled. He poked Daddy in the ribs and kissed Mrs. Martin on the cheek with a loud smack. "Ha! This appointment wouldn't happen to be at the courthouse, would it?"

Mrs. Martin looked at Daddy, then gave Uncle Bob a faint smile. "You guessed it," she said.

Daddy's face flushed pink. "We're going back to the hospital now," he told me. "I assume you'd rather stay here with your grandmother."

"I guess so," I muttered. I didn't want to go back to the hospital, but I didn't want to stay with Grandma Davis, either. Nothing about this trip to Vermont was turning out the way I thought it would. I was glad we'd be going back to California tomorrow.

"We'll be back around six," Daddy told me.

Mrs. Martin put a hand on my shoulder. "Why don't you go see what your grandma's made for lunch."

"I guess I'll tag along to the hospital with you two," Uncle Bob said. "Safety in numbers, and all that."

They left. I stood alone in the living room and looked around. I inspected a torn lace doily on the couch and walked over to a black and white photograph in a silver frame on top of the TV. A beautiful woman with curly dark hair leaned against a wooden fence, laughing up at a big man sitting astride it.

"That's your grandpa and me," Grandma Davis said behind me.

I jumped, startled. "Oh," I said, turning away from the picture. *Age is a mean thing—* I thought. Now my grandmother was old and ugly, and the corners of her mouth turned down in a permanent frown.

I followed her out to the kitchen and sat down in front of a plate of greasy fried chicken and peas. My stomach turned over. I wondered if I'd be able to eat at all. Mrs. Martin made delicious fried chicken, seasoned with thyme and basil and rolled in breadcrumbs. I picked up a drumstick and took a small bite. No seasoning.

That describes Grandma Davis as well as the chicken— I thought. She sat down across from me and began to eat. Her mouth barely moved as she chewed. I looked around for the salt, gave up, and dropped a piece of chicken under the table for Snippet. The peas mushed on my fork, but I managed to swallow a few bites.

"You like apple pie?" Grandma Davis asked me when she'd finished her chicken and peas.

"I . . . I think so," I said.

She shuffled over to open the oven door. Suddenly, the kitchen was full of a warm cinnamon and sugar smell. She cut a big piece of apple pie and put it on a plate. "Ice cream?"

"Yes, please!" I watched her spoon up a big scoop of vanilla.

"Here you go," she said, putting the pie down in front of me. "I wasn't sure what anyone would like to eat. I thought apple pie and ice cream would be safe. Even if it is winter." I chewed a mouthful of the pie and wondered how anyone who could make such awful fried chicken could make such a great pie. Grandma Davis sat down with her pie and ate silently. I wondered if she even tasted it. I looked above her at the picture of Jesus that hung on the wall. It showed just his brown-bearded head, floating peacefully in a purple cloud. On either side of the picture hung dusty crosses made out of matchsticks.

"Your father and your uncle made those in Sunday school when they were little boys." My grandmother pointed a crooked index finger at the crosses. "Does your father take you to church?"

"My mother took us for a while before they . . . um, split up," I explained through a mouthful of pie. I tried to scoop up all the ice cream before it melted into white puddles on my plate, but now Grandma Davis wanted to talk.

"I couldn't believe it when your father called to say that your mother took you all and left," she said in her quavering voice. "To move in with that woman . . . your father was devastated."

It took me a moment to figure out that "that woman" meant Ms. Whitney and not Mrs. Martin. "Ms. Whitney's okay," I said. "She's just . . . different."

"Exposing children to that lifestyle," Grandma Davis continued as if she hadn't heard me. "It's like spitting on the Bible."

I didn't know much about the Bible, but I was pretty sure it didn't say anything bad about living beside the beach and eating dinner with incense and candles in a roomful of couches. Didn't the three Wise Men bring the baby Jesus frankincense, which was sort of like incense?

"I like that lifestyle," I said as I scraped up the last of the piecrust with my fork. I stood up to put my plate in the sink. "You know, Daddy used to hit Mother," I said defensively.

From the table, Grandma Davis sighed so heavily that Snippet growled. "Zachary's always had a bad temper. He used to hit *me* when he was younger."

I stared at my grandmother. She bent down and put her plate on the ground beside Snippet. "He'll grow out of it," she said. "He has a lot of anger in him." She stood up and faced me, her little eyes surprisingly fierce. "And his behavior does not excuse your mother from turning her back on the Lord." She clattered her plate into the sink. "I'm gonna lie down for my nap now."

Grandma Davis shuffled down the hall. Snippet darted around her thick brown shoes. I wandered back into the living room and looked again at the picture in the silver frame. The young, laughing woman looked nothing like Grandma Davis, but something about her was familiar. I picked up the picture, turning it toward the gray light from the window. The round face, big eyes, and small, straight nose looked just like mine. I put the picture down on top of the TV and turned on a game show. *I will not look like my grandmother when I'm seventy—* I thought— *and I'll be nicer to my granddaughter when she comes to visit.*

When the game show was over, I walked around the house some more. I peeked into a dim room where Grandma Davis lay snoring. Her false teeth sat in a glass on the nightstand beside her. Snippet lay on the braided rug, flat, like he'd just been run over by a car. I found the bathroom and decided that I had to go. I sat on the toilet and glanced up at a shelf full of dusty perfume bottles and medicines that looked like they were at least a hundred years old. When I stood up from the toilet, I saw the water all blue and cloudy beneath me. I screamed.

Grandma Davis rushed in to find me hopping around the bathroom with my underwear and blue jeans twisted around my ankles. "Get it *off* me!" I screamed. "Get it *off*!"

"What're you talking about!" Grandma Davis demanded above Snippet's sharp barking.

"It's lye! I sat in lye!" I cried, straining to examine my bare behind. "It'll eat my skin off! Mother said so!"

Grandma Davis peered into the toilet. "That is nothing but Comet that I forgot to flush down the toilet," she said sternly, swiping at my behind with a wet washcloth. "There is no lye in Comet or on your skin. Your mother always did over-dramatize everything, even toilet cleanser."

I was sobbing now, half with humiliation and half with anger over what she'd said about Mother.

"Why's Ronnie crying?" Daddy opened the bathroom door and glared at Grandma Davis, who was helping me pull on my blue jeans.

"It's nothing, Zachary. She thought she'd sat in lye."

Daddy's eyes went from my face to Grandma Davis' toothless frown. He chuckled, and then he laughed his deep, loud laugh. I stopped crying and giggled a little, embarrassed at the thought of me dancing around the bathroom half-naked. It *was* pretty funny. I began to laugh, too.

"I came back to see if you want to go on a walk, just the two of us," Daddy said to me. "Elsa . . . Mrs. Martin's back at the hotel taking a nap."

"I guess so," I said.

"There's lye in Maggie's head," Grandma Davis muttered and flushed the toilet.

Daddy and I put on our coats and walked outside to the porch. The air was still cold, but it didn't tug at my skin the way it had the night before. "This is the house I grew up in," Daddy said. His breath puffed out into the air like a small dragon's smoke. Unlike the house he'd rented in Torrance, the houses on this road stood far apart, divided from each other by rows of tall trees with frost-covered branches. We began to walk. I stepped down into the gutter to hear the ice crunch under my boots. Birds chirped from somewhere above us. A little brown bird swooped down in front of us to examine a leaf.

"One time, I almost beat up your Uncle Bob because I thought he'd taken the gold necklace I gave your Grandma for her birthday," Daddy said. "We found it later, built into a jay's nest that fell out of a tree."

I thought of all the things I'd make a nest out of if I were a bird. Soft things— pieces of purple velvet, glittering green thread, Katie's blond hair, Mother's brown and gold. I tried to imagine what Mother was doing right now. Going on a walk with Daddy was all right, but across the country from this cold place, I knew Mother, Katie, and Tim were playing on the beach in the sun, the sand soft between their toes and the water cool and salty against their hands as they dug for sand crabs.

"That's my old school." Daddy's voice interrupted my thoughts. He pointed to a square brick building that looked a lot like the hospital Grandpa Davis was staying in.

"High school or grammar?" I asked for something to say.

"Grammar." We walked toward the school. Daddy brushed the snow off a low picnic table with his glove. I sat down beside him. "So, what d'you think of your grandmother?"

"She's a lot different from Grandma Hammond," I replied. Mother's mother owned a costume shop and a dance studio. She had fiery orange hair, and she was always busy working on some new, wonderful costume.

"You know, Ronnie, I loved your mother more than anything in the world," Daddy said suddenly. "It really was love at first sight, at least for me." His eyes grew dim, remembering. "She was sitting in the bleachers by herself, watching a minor league baseball game. All the men were staring at her, but she was so pretty that no one had the courage to go up to her. I thought she looked lonely . . . "

His words hovered around me, mingling with the steam from our breath. I shoved my hands in the pockets of my jacket and thought. There were so many things I wanted to ask Daddy, but I knew I had to find exactly the right words so that I wouldn't make him mad.

"I thought if you loved someone, you weren't supposed to yell at them or hit them," I said cautiously.

Daddy stared across the field at his old school. I tried to picture him Katie's age, walking up the brick path with a sack lunch, but I couldn't. Instead, I saw him as small as Tim, Grandpa Davis' bony bluish hand smacking him across the face. A chill ran up my back, and I shivered.

"I loved her, but she used to make me so angry." Daddy's voice broke, and his chin trembled. "I know I shouldn't have hit her, but she made me so angry." A tear slid down his cheek and got lost in his mustache. "I miss her, Ronnie. I miss her so much."

"Don't cry, Daddy," I begged. I put my arms around him and held him tightly. "Please don't cry."

"I'm sorry," he said into his hands. At last, he lifted his head. "Things have really piled up," he sighed. "And your mother . . . so confused . . . at first I couldn't believe it. I thought it was just to hurt me. But Ronnie," Daddy took a long, shuddering breath, and his eyes filled again, fading the yellow circles around his pupils into deep blue. "I want you to know how much help you've been. Without you, I don't think I could've made it through all this. You've really taken care of your old Dad."

He's not lying— I thought. I was the one who had been there when the phone call about his father came two nights before, and I was the one who helped with Katie and Tim and flew across the country in the seat beside him. *Mrs. Martin is right*— I thought— *Daddy needs me, too.*

I stood up and wiped snow off the back of my jeans.

"I'm freezing," I said. "Let's go back."

Daddy wiped his eyes with a crumpled tissue from his pocket. "I should've bought you a better coat," he said.

Before he could start to cry again, I said quickly, "It's all right." And it was.

We walked back to Grandma Davis' house hand in hand. Tiny flakes of snow began to drift down, melting as soon as they hit the pavement. "It might really snow tonight," Daddy said. At the door, he turned to me. "Should we have dinner here or go out?"

"Go out!" I said, remembering the fried chicken. "*Please!*"

Daddy winked at me, and we walked into the warm house laughing.

My grandmother said she'd rather eat with Grandpa Davis at the hospital than go out to dinner. Daddy, Mrs. Martin, and I dropped her off in front of the brick building and went off together. Daddy took us to an elegant restaurant with white tablecloths and candles on the tables. The waiter held my chair out for me. I ordered shrimp and tiny pasta called *orzo*, and Mrs. Martin poured me half a glass of red wine.

"It'd be a shame for Ronnie not to try this— it's so lovely," she said. "Besides, kids in Europe drink when they're her age."

Mrs. Martin and I began to talk about books, and Daddy ordered us dessert, which was swan in a chocolate lake. It wasn't really swan— just cream-filled puff pastry shaped to look like a swan, floating in a pool of warm chocolate. I wanted to take it home to look at. I thought Katie would like to see it too, but finally, I broke a piece of the tail part off and ate it. It was delicious.

"It's nice to be alone with you for a while, Ronnie," Mrs. Martin said. "Can you imagine bringing Tim to a restaurant like this?"

I shook my head and spooned up the dark chocolate. Tonight, I couldn't help wondering what it would be like to be an only child with Daddy and Mrs. Martin as parents.

I took off my jacket and sweater as soon as we stepped off the plane back in Los Angeles. The night air felt warm and damp against my cheeks as we walked to Daddy's car. "It's good to be home," Mrs. Martin sighed, stretching her legs out in the front seat.

I was surprised not to see the red Volkswagen bus in the driveway when we got home. "Where are Katie and Tim?" I asked. I half-hoped that they were going to stay with Mother a while longer.

"We're going to meet them tomorrow," Daddy said, hauling the suitcases up to the porch.

"Where?"

He turned the key in the lock and pushed the door open. "We're going to court tomorrow, Ronnie," he said. "You kids need to know once and for all where you're going to live, so we can all get on with our lives."

"Court? No one told me we were going to court!" Court sounded like a horrible place, almost like jail. "We're *all* going? Even Tim?"

Daddy nodded. "Mrs. Martin's coming, too." His voice was muffled as he hung up his coat in the hall closet.

Mrs. Martin opened the back door. Sweetie and King ran barking into the kitchen. "Hello, pretty dogs!" she said.

I stood in the front doorway so that Daddy would have to look at me on his way back out to the car. "But I'm not sure who I want to live with!" I said.

Daddy put his hands on my shoulders and looked into my eyes. "Mrs. Martin loves you very much," he said. "She told me on the plane that she'd love to have you for a daughter. And I . . . " He blinked, and his eyes filled with tears. "I'd hate to lose you, Ronnie. I think we'd make a wonderful family, don't you?"

"I guess so," I whispered.

We got to the courthouse at nine the next morning. Mother's red bus stood empty in the parking lot, close to the big, sand-colored building. "She probably got here early to try to bribe the judge," Daddy said as we walked across the grass.

"Everything will be fine, Zach." Mrs. Martin slipped a hand through his arm. She looked beautiful in a gray dress with a pattern of small white triangles and gray high heels to match. Daddy wore a navy blue suit and tie. I didn't known court was something to dress up for, so I had to change out of my blue jeans into a white dress with flowers all over it. I was glad Mrs. Martin had told me to bring a sweater. I could see only a ragged patch of blue sky beyond the thick gray clouds. Although Vermont was a thousand times colder, this morning in Los Angeles was definitely chilly.

We got into an elevator, and Daddy pushed the button for the fifth floor. I stepped out feeling sick and unsteady. I didn't look out at the view of the city from the tall, wide windows.

I saw Mother before she saw me. She stood near the windows with one arm around Tim's shoulders. Katie stood beside her, pointing to a black and white pigeon on the stone ledge. "Look, Mother, there's a pretty one!" she cried.

Mother turned to look at the pigeon, and then she saw me. She wore a brown sweater over a pair of black stretch pants and high heeled black shoes. Katie and Tim wore blue jeans and sweatshirts. I smoothed down my dress and pretended I liked being dressed up. "There weren't any leaves," I said, walking over to Katie. "Everything was dead."

"We went swimming and went to a fair," Katie said, lifting up her sweatshirt to show me a new T-shirt with a blue pig silk-screened on it. "You missed out."

I thought of the elegant dinner with Daddy and Mrs. Martin and didn't say anything.

"Ronnie . . . how are you?" Mother asked as Tim ran over to Daddy.

I stayed close to Mrs. Martin and waved to Mother behind Daddy's back. "Okay," I whispered.

Daddy found us a seat up in front of the small courtroom. I sat between him and Mrs. Martin. "Come sit with us, Tim." Mrs. Martin patted the empty seat beside her.

"No way!" He ran up the aisle to where Mother and Katie were sitting.

"Why are all these people here?" I looked around at the strange men and women sitting near us.

"They're all here for their own cases," Daddy said.

A short, fat man with a black goatee sat down beside Daddy. "How's it going, Zach?" he said. He reached up to brush white flakes off the shoulders of his black suit.

"Paul. It's going, I guess." Daddy shook the man's hand. "You've met Elsa, of course, but have you met Ronnie? She's my oldest." Daddy smiled at me, not a real smile, but a tense, fake smile. "Ronnie, this is my lawyer, Mr. Berkman."

Mr. Berkman leaned across Daddy and shook my hand. "It's very nice to meet you, Veronica," he said. His hand felt sweaty. As soon as he turned back to Daddy, I wiped my palm off on the seat cushion.

Mother sat with Katie and Tim a few rows behind us. I could hear them laughing and talking, but I didn't turn around even when Tim kept whispering, "Ronnie! Iss me! I your brother!"

Sitting with Daddy and Mrs. Martin, I felt like I'd taken sides, us against Mother. I didn't like it, but I didn't know what else to do. If I went and sat beside Mother, I might hurt Daddy's feelings. *Besides—* I told myself— *Mother already has two kids with her.*

"All rise," a man who looked like a policeman said. We stood up as the judge walked in. He was a tall, older man with white hair that stood out sharply against his black robe. He sat at a high desk at the front of the room and put on a pair of glasses, then shuffled through the papers on his desk.

"Wilson versus Sterns," he said. A young woman in denim shorts with her arm in a sling walked up to a long, low table in front of the judge and sat down, glaring at a bearded man with a tattooed dragon on his arm. I listened hard, but all I could figure out was that the man had broken the woman's arm because she drove his truck into his new girlfriend's car and almost killed her. It felt funny to be listening to other people's stories, like eavesdropping or television.

"Are all these other people going to listen to *us*?" I whispered to Mrs. Martin.

She nodded. Her hands were clenched tightly together in her lap. I wondered what she had to be nervous about. *I* was the one who was going to have to tell the judge who I wanted to live with.

Our case didn't come up until after lunch. The judge called an hour-long lunch break, promising Mr. Berkman that he'd get to us at one 'o' clock. Daddy, Mrs. Martin, and I walked down to the cafeteria. Mother was already there, helping Katie and Tim through the line for sandwiches and sodas.

Daddy bought Mrs. Martin and me lunch. We sat at a table far away from Mother. A blond woman in a lavender pantsuit sat down beside Mother and opened a briefcase. "That's some lawyer Maggie's got," Daddy whispered to Mrs. Martin. "I wonder where she dug her up."

Mrs. Martin drank black coffee and didn't eat her ham sandwich. "They're not going to put *me* on the stand, are they?" she asked Daddy. "I hate talking in front of people."

"What's the stand?" I asked her.

Daddy reached for her ham sandwich and began to eat it. "The stand is that box you saw people sitting in this morning, where they had to talk into a microphone and the man said, 'Do you promise to tell the truth, the whole truth, and all that stuff,'" he said. "It's *very* important to tell the truth in court, Ronnie," he added, looking soberly at me.

I glanced over at Mama's back as she bent over a stack of papers. My throat tightened, suddenly, and I couldn't swallow my bite of sandwich. *What is the truth—* I wondered. My ears were plugged up with a sound like the roar of the ocean in the big shell Ms. Whitney kept by the front door to use as a doorstop. I wanted to put my hands over my ears so I could think clearly, but Daddy was still looking at me. I swallowed my sandwich and reached for my soda.

At one o'clock, I stumbled behind Daddy and Mrs. Martin back to the courtroom. The judge announced "Davis versus Davis." Mr. Berkman and the woman in the lavender pantsuit walked up to the judge and spoke to him for a long time. I picked up the book Mrs. Martin had brought and flipped through the pages. It was a thick orange book called *The Thorn Birds*. I had just begun to read the first page when Mr. Berkman tapped me on the shoulder with one of his fat hands.

"The judge wants to speak to you alone," he said.

My ears were full of the rushing sound of water. I couldn't look at anyone— not Daddy, not Mrs. Martin, not Mother— as I followed the judge into a little room at the front of the courtroom. The nausea I'd felt from riding up the elevator crept into my throat and sat there sourly. I sat in a black chair across from the judge with my mouth closed tightly, terrified I'd throw up.

"You're Veronica," the judge said. I wasn't sure if it was a question or a statement, so I just nodded at him.

"Who do you want to live with?" The judge wiped his glasses on his robe and glanced out the window above his desk.

There it was. No small talk, no friendly smiles or questions about how I liked school. Just "Who do you want to live with?"

I stared at a coffee cup full of lollipops on a corner of the judge's desk. I'd thought all night about my answer, but when I gave it, it sounded wrong.

"I want to live with my father," I whispered, as if Mother might be on the other side of the door with her ear pressed against it, listening.

"I see," said the judge. His lined face relaxed slightly into a stern smile. "May I ask why?"

"I think . . . I think he needs me," I choked. Water roared against my ears. I couldn't hear my own words. "Can I please go back now?" I said past the roaring.

"Of course." The judge opened his door, and I

stumbled back down to my empty seat. Mrs. Martin put her arm around me. I struggled against the urge to put my fingers in my ears, to stop the sound of rushing water. I stared down at my hands, which were pleating the white flowered fabric of my dress into tiny accordions. I knew I'd never wear this dress again.

Katie talked to the judge next, and Tim followed, strutting behind the judge as if he were a cowboy or a policeman. I could never predict Tim. I wondered if, when the judge asked him who he wanted to live with, he'd say Mother or Daddy, and if the judge would take him seriously. Sometimes Tim liked to say things just to see people's reactions. Once, he told me he'd taken my diary to school and lost it, when actually, it had fallen between my bed and the wall.

I was sure Katie had told the judge that she wanted to live with Mother. If that were the case, then I might really be an only child, and Daddy would take Mrs. Martin and me out for dinner every weekend.

The judge came back in. The uniformed man standing near the door led Tim back to his seat. "I did it, Pop!" Tim said as he passed Daddy.

"The children may be excused from this part of the proceeding," the judge said. "Perhaps someone would like to take them down to the cafeteria."

"I'd be happy to." Mrs. Martin stood up and walked swiftly to the door. "Come on, kids," she said.

I waved to Mother once more as I walked up the aisle to Mrs. Martin, but she and her lawyer had their heads together over a folder of papers, so she didn't see me. "I'm glad we don't have to stay in there," I whispered to Mrs. Martin as we went downstairs to the cafeteria. "I hate court."

"That judge is nice," Katie said while Mrs. Martin went to get us something to drink. She reached into her jeans pocket and pulled out a yellow lollipop. "He gave me this."

"Who did you tell him you want to live with?" I asked.

Katie put her lollipop back in her pocket. "None of your beeswax."

Mrs. Martin came back to the table with cups full of hot chocolate and another cup of black coffee. "We'll have a little party until they call us back in," she said, taking a pack of Oreo cookies from her gray purse.

We sat in the cafeteria a long time, talking and laughing. Mrs. Martin quietly taught us a song called "K. . . .k . . . k . . . Katie," which Katie loved. I looked around at the dressed-up men and women who clutched their briefcases with grim faces. I knew I never wanted to be a lawyer.

Then Daddy's lawyer walked in. "The judge is ready to present his decision," he announced, smoothing down his goatee with one hand.

We filed back down the aisle in the courtroom and sat beside Mrs. Martin. People sat up in their seats and looked at us, as if they'd been following our case with interest. Daddy, Mother, and her lawyer sat at the long table in front. Mr. Berkman hurried over to sit beside Daddy. The judge shifted in his seat, glanced at a pile of papers and cleared his throat. My heart began to pound. Again, I fought the desire to put my hands over my ears.

"This has been a difficult decision," the judge said slowly, as if he were thinking hard about each word. "Obviously, both parents love these three children very much. Until now, the children have received the best care imaginable. But with the dissolution of a marriage, certain factors must come into play. I have considered the extremely different lifestyles each parent has to offer these children—one traditional and stable, the other . . . shall we say, *alternative*?"

A few people in the courtroom chuckled. I looked around, confused. Mrs. Martin's long fingers twisted a tissue until it shredded in her lap. I looked down at her hands and saw the flash of a diamond ring on one finger—a ring I'd never seen before. She saw me looking at it and turned her hand so that I could see the ring sparkling under the courtroom lights. "Beautiful, isn't it," she whispered.

"Love can only count for so much in these proceedings," the judge continued. "In the end, the court must make a decision with respect to both emotional and financial security, the primary focus being on what is best for the children. It is for this reason that the court has decided to award full physical custody to Zachary Davis. The court has awarded visitation rights to Margaret Davis, which are to be observed every other weekend, for a week at Christmas, and for a month during the summer."

Mother gasped, then dropped her head down onto her lawyer's shoulder. Even from where I sat, I could see her shoulders trembling. Daddy stood up and shook Mr. Berkman's hand hard, then almost ran to where we were sitting with Mrs. Martin. "We did it!" he said. He kissed Mrs. Martin on the lips. "We're a family now!"

He hugged each of us in turn— Tim, Katie, then me. I stiffened and couldn't hug him back. I stared down at the ground and tried not to hear Mother crying as we walked out of the courtroom. *It's over*— I repeated in my head, trying to hear my own thoughts— *we officially live with Daddy now.*

While we waited for the elevator, Mr. Berkman and Daddy began to discuss the L.A. Dodgers as if nothing at all had just happened in the courtroom. Mrs. Martin tried to take my hand as we stepped into the elevator, but I didn't have the energy to hold onto it. Her diamond ring caught the light from the windows and gleamed as she pushed the button for the first floor.

Just before the elevator door closed, Mother walked up with her lawyer. Her mascara had run and tears glistened on her cheeks, but when she saw me, she lifted her head and looked straight at me. She opened her mouth to speak, and finally, the roaring in my ears stopped. I heard her words, clear and strong, even though she whispered.

"We'll fight this," she said as the door shut between us.

Chapter 5

Christmas was a strange, sad holiday. Memories of the day in court crowded out the excitement I'd always felt before in December. But Katie and Tim still tied jingle bells on their sneakers and laughed at the Christmas cartoons on TV, even though Grandpa Davis had just died, Daddy and Mother had gotten a divorce, and Mrs. Martin was going to be our stepmother.

Daddy woke us up Christmas morning, ringing a string of sleigh bells outside our bedroom doors. "Come look what Santa brought!" he cried.

I got out of bed and walked slowly out to the plastic Christmas tree Mrs. Martin had bought. Katie and Tim were already ripping gleefully through piles of dolls and toy cars and clothes.

"What about the singing?" I asked Daddy, strapping on the narrow gold watch Mrs. Martin had given me. We always sang Christmas songs after we opened our presents, getting all tangled up in "The Twelve Days of Christmas" and in the happiness that was as thick and rich as the fudge Mother made and let us have for breakfast this one morning each year.

"That's your mother's thing," Daddy said. He sniffed at a bottle of cologne and made a face. "Can I exchange it?" he asked Mrs. Martin.

She took a piece of mistletoe from the tree and held it up over his head, kissing him under the shiny green leaves and white berries. "I love you," I heard her whisper.

"Me too," Daddy replied and bent down to help Tim unwrap a toy bulldozer.

After we'd examined all our presents a second time, and Mrs. Martin had made homemade waffles and something slimy called Eggs Benedict for breakfast, there were still two more hours before Mother could come to pick us up. Katie and Tim set up a new race track with glow-in-the-dark cars that could go backwards and forwards. They yelled over who got to control the red car, and Daddy swore trying to put together a ping pong table he'd bought us. Even through the noise, it felt like the whole house was waiting breathlessly for the sputter and chug of the red Volkswagen bus.

I was in the bathroom when the doorbell rang. I had wanted to meet Mother outside, so she wouldn't have to see us all gathered around the Christmas tree like some family in a commercial. I opened the bathroom door and found Katie pulling Mother into the hall. "Look at my new Barbie!" she cried.

Mother set her mouth in a hard line, barely glancing at the Barbie. "Are you kids ready to go?" she asked loudly. Sweetie and King looked up from the living room floor at Mother. King growled low in his throat.

Daddy and Mrs. Martin sat on the couch, sipping cups of eggnog. "Are you ready, Tim?" Daddy asked, not looking at Mother.

"Yep! My dozer come?"

Mrs. Martin shook her head slightly. "I think you'd better leave it here," she said. "It might get lost."

"You have lots of toys at your other house, Tim," Mother said from the hall. "Santa Claus comes to Carpinteria, too, believe it or not."

Daddy looked up at her sarcastic tone. Her eyes met his, angry and cold. "Go on, kids, we'll see you in a few days," he said quietly, then stood up and went into the kitchen.

I walked over and gave Mrs. Martin an awkward hug. "Um . . . thanks for the watch," I said. "It's really pretty."

"You're welcome." She kissed me on the cheek, smelling of cinnamon and rum.

"Bye!" Katie hollered, running out the door with her Barbie stuffed under her shirt so Mrs. Martin couldn't see it.

In the car, the lines in Mother's forehead smoothed out, and she hugged each of us tightly. "Merry Christmas!" she said. "Let's sing."

The sun was shining, so we rolled down the

windows and sang all the Christmas songs we knew. Gradually, happiness began to crowd the memory of that awful day in court out of my head. Mother taught us to sing "Silent Night" in German, and people in their cars turned to smile at us through open windows as we sang at a red light along the coastal highway.

"When Tim sings in English, it sounds like German," Katie observed, tying Seymour around her neck like a scarf. Mother and I laughed. Katie was right. Tim had a thick, slurred way of talking because his tongue was larger than most people's. His English did sound a little like German.

"A Christmas dog!" Tim said, pointing to a life-sized bronze sculpture of a large dog in front of a house in Carpinteria. The dog wore a Santa hat and a big brass bell around its neck.

"The owners of that house came into the newspaper office last week," Mother said. "The man told me he had the sculpture made when his favorite dog died, and now his wife dresses it up for every holiday."

She pulled into the driveway to Ms. Whitney's house. We got out and ran upstairs to where Ms. Whitney and her kids were lighting green and red candles all over the room. They'd waited until we arrived to open the presents piled around a real pine tree in a red pot.

"Sit over here, Ronnie." Max patted the spot beside him in front of the fireplace. Tim climbed onto Ms. Whitney's lap. Katie put on a Santa Claus hat and passed out presents. I took the shiny purple paper off of a box marked "To Ronnie, From Sage," and found a tiny silver hoop earring.

"It's for your belly button," Sage said, pointing to her own hoop earring below her cropped green and red sweatshirt.

"Maybe in a few years," Mother laughed, seeing my surprise. "I can just see Ronnie's father's face when she comes back with a pierced belly button."

I bit my lip and put down the earring. Tim kicked a ball of wrapping paper across the floor. "I stay here," he muttered. "Don't like Dad's house."

Katie sat on Pam's lap, watching her braid her Barbie's hair. Max put one skinny, freckled arm around my shoulders. I guess he knew that I wanted to stay here, too.

Mother stood up. "Let's go to the beach," she suggested. "We've never done that on Christmas Day before."

"I'll stay here and clean up," Ms. Whitney said. She looked almost pretty in the new blue and black-checked flannel shirt Mother had given her.

I walked over to Ms. Whitney and hugged her, holding my breath against the cigarette smell of her coarse hair. "Thank you for the book," I told her. She'd given me a copy of *Where the Red Fern Grows*.

"Sure," Ms. Whitney said. "It was my favorite book when I was your age."

Pam stuck a green bow on top of Sage's head. "We'll help you clean up the room, Ma." Max was already smoothing out wrapping paper to save for next year.

Mother took four candy canes from the tree, and she, Katie, Tim, and I walked down the street to the beach. We kicked off our shoes and left them in a pile on the sand.

"Thank you for the dress," I told Mother, holding the soft green fabric up out of the salt water as we waded down the beach.

"Thank *you* for the necklace," Mother said. She touched the gold double-heart at her throat.

"It's only gold painted," I said. "I wish it was solid gold."

"I'll wear it always," Mother assured me.

Even though we were talking, something still felt wrong between Mother and me. Right then seemed like a good time to tell her what I'd said to the judge, and why I'd said it, but the moment I got up the courage and opened my mouth, Katie screamed. We whirled around to find her sitting in the water, her new pink dress wet and her candy cane bobbing away on a wave. Tim was pointing and laughing. Katie pulled him down beside her, and a little wave came up, soaking them both. I remembered the snow in Vermont. I was glad I lived in California, where we could go to the beach on Christmas Day.

"Time to take a bath and have dinner," Mother said, pulling Tim and Katie up out of the water. "Ms. Whitney has a roast in the oven."

And then, even though it was Christmas, and we were with Mother, I felt miserable because I hadn't told her what I'd said to the judge. *If I'd said something different—* I thought— *we wouldn't have to go back to Daddy's house in six days.*

"I'm gonna hang out here for a few minutes," I told Mother.

"Are you all right, Ronnie?" she asked me, frowning.

I shrugged. "Yeah."

I thought she was going to insist that I come back with them, but all she said was, "Don't stay too long."

I watched her walk with Katie and Tim down the street. Then I sat on the sand and looked out over the cold blue ocean. Just below the water's surface, long tangles of seaweed drifted up to the shore, but before they could settle on the sand, they were yanked back out to sea by the powerful tide.

At the end of our week with Mother, I wished we never had to leave. We didn't sing on the way back to Daddy's house on New Year's Eve. Mother put the radio on low to a station that was still playing Christmas music, and we looked out the windows at the expensive houses along the ocean, all lit up with Christmas lights.

The lights nailed around Daddy's new house shone green and blue. They didn't look like Christmas at all.

"I wonder where my old lights are," Mother murmured as she pulled the bus into the driveway.

I knew where they were. One day after we'd gone to court, I'd been looking in the garage for our old hand-cranked ice-cream maker. I'd found a big box with "Maggie" written on it in Daddy's sharp handwriting. I opened it to find a lot of records and books, the ice-cream maker, a purple cotton dress, and the red, green, and white Christmas lights, neatly looped and tied. "I'll see if I can find them for you," I promised Mother.

The four of us stood on the porch, not wanting to go inside. Katie sniffled, and Tim shivered in his denim jacket.

"You kids go in now. It's cold," Mother said, hugging them quickly.

Mrs. Martin opened the door. Inside, I could hear more Christmas music. The spicy smell of gingerbread floated out. Mother looked at Mrs. Martin, and I could feel hurt and guilt and anger between them like a brick wall.

"Bye, Mother," I whispered, clutching her in a hug. "Are you . . . are you gonna be okay?"

"Of course." Her eyes flashed blue fire at Mrs. Martin. "Tonight when I get home, Ms. Whitney and I are going to a party, and tomorrow I have to work. I won't have time to think."

The timer in the kitchen began to beep, and Mrs. Martin turned and disappeared down the hall. Mother clung to me suddenly, her tears damp and hot against my cheek. "I love you, Ronnie," she said brokenly.

"I love you, too," I whispered, then followed Katie and Tim inside with my heart so full of pain that I was afraid it would rip a hole in my chest.

I thought I'd be miserable forever, but that same night, I made a friend. Her name was Bella, and she lived around the block. Her mother came over to babysit us because Daddy and Mrs. Martin were going out to celebrate their engagement and New Year's Eve.

"I don't need a babysitter," I protested to Mrs. Martin. "I'm old enough to stay by myself."

She stood at the mirror in her bra and half-slip, trying to hook a pearl necklace. "Help me, Katie-Cat, would you?" Katie jumped up from the bed and carefully clasped the necklace around Mrs. Martin's neck. "Mrs. DelGrosso is not for you, Ronnie," Mrs. Martin told me. She examined her eyebrows in the mirror, then ran a tiny brush across them. "She's for Katie and Tim." The door bell rang. Mrs. Martin hurriedly brushed blush on her cheeks, smiling hard so that her cheekbones stuck out.

"I'll get it!" Katie raced down the hall.

"Make sure that's really the babysitter, Ronnie," Mrs. Martin said. I left her outlining her lips with a red pencil and walked to the door.

A short, stout woman wearing a green smock over brown polyester pants followed Katie into the hall. Beside her was a pretty girl my height, with brown hair cut short and large green eyes.

"This is my daughter, Bella," Mrs. DelGrosso said in a peculiar, hoarse mutter. "I thought she'd be good company for you girls."

Bella pursed up her full lips, examining me. "What school do you go to?" she demanded. She had pale skin that was so clear it made me want to rush into Mrs. Martin's room to put concealer over the pimple on my chin. "*I* go to Saint Joseph's. It's the one next to your school. It's *private*," Bella told me.

Mrs. Martin walked into the hall in a navy blue silk dress, smelling of jasmine that clashed with Mrs. DelGrosso's musky perfume. I examined at the babysitter and realized that her stiff blond curls were actually a wig—underneath it, I glimpsed dark oily hair tangled in bobby pins.

"I'm sorry, Tina, we're running late," Mrs. Martin said. Daddy honked the horn from the driveway. "Help yourself to anything in the house. We'll be home at one."

"Fine, fine," Mrs. DelGrosso muttered. "Have a good time." She walked into the kitchen, poured herself a cup of coffee from the tall silver thermos and reached into the cookie jar shaped like a pink pig. "Oatmeal," she said approvingly. Crumbs sifted down to the floor Mrs. Martin had just mopped. Mrs. DelGrosso walked into the living room, where Tim was sitting with his nose almost touching the television.

"What're you watching?" she asked him.

"Brady Bunch," Tim said, not moving from the

screen.

Mrs. DelGrosso stood beside Tim and began to punch buttons, changing channels.

"Jerk!" Tim said, slamming his head into his hands.

Bella looked at Tim. I could tell she was trying to figure out what was unusual about him. She tossed her head so that her short hair swayed and turned to me. "I decided to come over 'cause I heard you guys were new and didn't know anyone."

That was only half-true. Katie already knew the whole neighborhood. She spent all of her time in between school and meals playing Barbies and riding bikes with Maria across the street. I still didn't have any good friends. Julia Goldberg was nice, but she went home for lunch. At school lunchtimes, I sat at a table close enough to a group of kids to look like I was a part of them and picked at the green paint on the bench, watching other girls in groups of two or three laughing and fluttering their eyelashes at boys.

I wanted a friend. Before Mother and Daddy had got a divorce, people called Trisha, Dolores, and me the Three Musketeers. But something about the haughty lift of Bella's chin and a mischevious spark in her cat-like eyes made me certain she wouldn't want to be friends with someone as quiet and serious as I'd become since the day the elevator door closed between Mother and me.

"D'you wanna play a game or something in my room?" I asked Bella shyly.

"No, *my* room!" Katie insisted. Katie's room was smaller than mine, but she had a pretty pink desk that matched her dresser. I had Mrs. Martin's old ebony dresser and nightstand, and I was terrified I'd scratch the polished black wood. Katie's window looked out towards the street. She could wave to Maria at night and even yell to her if both their windows were open. My window faced the house next to ours. All I could see was our old neighbor watering his spider plants and feeding his fish.

Bella stretched out her legs and put her feet in red sandals on Katie's yellow and white checked bedspread. "My name means 'beautiful girl' in Italian," she said. "My father's Italian, and that's what he and my mother thought of me when I was born." I couldn't imagine fat, greasy Mrs. DelGrosso giving birth to Bella. Bella looked like a slender, graceful fairy.

Her greatest joy, I found out immediately, was to torture her mother.

"Watch this," she said, getting up from the bed and tiptoeing out the door. "But be *quiet*."

Mrs. DelGrosso sat on the couch with her coffee cup. The flesh under her chin wobbled like a bullfrog's dew lap as she talked to the television. "You dumb chicky," she muttered. "Even I know the answer to that one. It takes brains to be on *Wheel of Fortune*, not beauty, miss."

Bella sneaked up behind her mother so quietly that Tim didn't even turn around. Katie and I watched from the kitchen. I had no idea what Bella was going to do. Her hand crept up above her mother's head, and then it blurred as she snatched off the blond wig.

"What's going on!" Mrs. DelGrosso leapt up from the couch, her head suddenly naked and frightening.

I remembered the time Mother was driving us up into the mountains for a picnic, and we passed a huge bird in the middle of the road. It had dark, dirty feathers and a terrible bald head that jerked sharply as it picked at a dead squirrel.

"Mother, what *is* that?" Katie had cried.

"A vulture," Mother replied.

Mrs. DelGrosso looked just like a vulture when Bella stole her wig.

Bella laughed so hard that she fell down on the carpet, waving the wig in the air. Katie giggled, and Tim looked up from the TV at Mrs. DelGrosso and then at me, unsure of whether it was okay to laugh. I shrank behind the door and hoped that Mrs. DelGrosso didn't seen me.

Bella threw the wig back to her mother and ran into Katie's room. "Top that," she told us proudly.

"Let's play a game," I suggested. "D'you like Monopoly?"

"Now *that's* boring," Bella said, tossing her head

again. "I know, let's play strip poker!"

"I don't know how," Katie said. "Is it with cards or dice?"

"Cards. Do you have any?"

We crept to the dining room, where Mrs. Martin had arranged all the games in a tall cabinet. I peeked into the living room. Mrs. DelGrosso had replaced her wig, and it vibrated as she breathed. Tim had his face smashed up against the TV screen, watching Vanna White's every move.

Bella dropped the deck of cards down her shirt. We tiptoed back to Katie's room and shut the door. I didn't know why we were being so quiet, but strip poker sounded strange and vaguely dangerous.

"The point is to try to get the highest score you can," Bella whispered. She shuffled the cards and dealt us each three. "For instance, Katie, you have an ace, a king, and a six. You can use your ace as a one or it can be the highest card in the deck. Of course, since you don't have a straight, you want to use it as your high card."

"No, I don't," Katie said. "It's a one. See, it has one diamond."

"Use it as your high card," Bella said. "Otherwise, you'll lose."

"I wanna lose," Katie replied, kicking off her white socks.

Bella shrugged. "Whatever. Okay, you have seventeen points then. Veronica," she scanned my cards. "You have eleven points, which means you're the loser, since I have a queen and two jacks."

"What do I have to do?" I asked nervously.

"You have to take one item of clothing off," Bella said.

I blinked at her. "Really? Does jewelry count?"

"Whatever."

I removed one of the gold hoop earrings Mother had given me and placed it on the bed beside me.

"You deal." Bella handed me the deck.

We played quickly, slapping the cards down and sweeping them back up as if Mrs. DelGrosso might come walking in at any moment. A car raced by outside. I heard kids screaming and laughing, probably on their way to a New Year's Eve party. I walked over in my T-shirt and underwear to shut the blinds. Bella sat in her underwear and a white lace bra and stuck her long legs out in front of her. "Some day, I'm gonna have tons of boyfriends," she said. "I'll have one for every day of the week."

"I'll have one for every day of the year," Katie said. She was completely naked except for her pink ruffled underwear.

I didn't say anything. None of the boys at school paid any attention to me except for Daniel, who sat next to me in English class and called me hippo girl.

"D'you like your school?" Bella asked me

"It's all right." I wished I could think of something more exciting to say.

"We have to wear the dumbest plaid skirts at my school," Bella said, "and all the boys have to wear ties." She leaned over to examine a photo of Daddy and Mrs. Martin in the pink ceramic picture frame on Katie's nightstand. "Your mom should be a model," Bella said. "Or an actress. I *adore* her accent."

"She's not our mom. She's gonna be our stepmother," I said.

I didn't feel like telling Bella anything about my mother just yet. Mother would be back at Carpinteria soon, getting ready for a party. I was glad she was going to have fun instead of sitting at home being sad. Sadness was a mean emotion— I could be doing something fun, like reading a good book or sitting here playing cards with Bella and Katie, and still, right beneath the happiness, I could feel sadness stabbing at me. I wondered if Mother felt that way, too.

"Daddy and Mrs. Martin are getting married in two months," Katie said. "You should come to the wedding."

"Ooh, I love weddings," Bella exclaimed. "My sister got married last year and when she did the money dance, her dress was just *covered* with twenty dollar bills."

"What's the money dance?" Katie asked.

"The bride dances with all the men and they have to pin money on her dress," Bella explained, whirling around the room in her underwear. "Some of them even put money down here," she said, pointing at her white lace bra.

We were silent a moment, thinking about weddings. Then Katie jumped up from the bed. "Let's go flash your mother!" she cried.

"Good idea!"

Katie and Bella ran out the door and down the hall to the living room. I pulled on my sweatpants and got there in time to see Katie swinging her hips and waving her arms in front of the TV.

Mrs. DelGrosso woke up with a snort. "Hey . . . hey . . . what's going on here? What's going on?"

"Strip!" Bella yelled, dancing around her mother. "Strip!"

"Strip!" Tim echoed, leaping up to do the moonwalk in his flannel pajamas. Bella and Katie jumped up on the overstuffed blue chairs Mrs. Martin had just bought. Tim bumped into the lamp, knocking it onto the carpet.

"Get in that room and put your clothes on!" Mrs. DelGrosso demanded with her chin trembling furiously. She glared at me. "You should know better, a big girl like you," she said, even though I was fully clothed. "I'm gonna tell your mother."

"You don't know her phone number!" Katie yelled, bumping her hip into Bella's.

"When she gets home, I'm gonna tell her, I promise you that," Mrs. DelGrosso said.

"Mrs. Martin is not their mother, stupid!" Bella tore off her bra and whipped it around her head like a lasso. Her breasts pointed straight at her mother. "Their parents are divorced. Don't you know *anything*? Strip! Strip!" She ran off down the hall. Katie and Tim followed her.

"No boys allowed," Katie said, slamming the door in Tim's face.

Before Tim could start to cry, I pulled him into my room. I got out colored paper and pens, and we made New Year's cards for Mother. I helped Tim write his name and draw a heart on his card. I could hear Bella and Katie giggling in the next room, but I didn't want to go in, in case Bella still had her bra off. Even in that brief moment in the living room, I could see that she had bigger breasts than I'd ever have.

Tim handed me a card full of people with long necks and twenty fingers and toes each. "Iss Mom, you, Katie, me," he explained, pointing.

"That's great, Tim." I said.

He yawned and smiled sweetly. "I watch TV now, okay, sister." He hugged me and disappeared into the hall.

I read the book Ms. Whitney had given me the rest of the night. I didn't even come out of my room when I heard Katie and Bella and people outside on the street yelling "Happy New Year!" I wondered what Mother was doing. My eyes stung with tears as I thought about how wonderful it would be to sit with her tonight in front of the fireplace in the house at Carpinteria.

I read until the headlights from Daddy's car swung across the walls of my room and the key turned in the back door. "We're home, kids! How was everyone?" Daddy said too loudly, so that I knew he and Mrs. Martin had drunk a bottle of wine.

Bella, Katie, and I filed into the living room where Mrs. DelGrosso had straightened the chairs and the lamp. "Fine, fine, everyone was fine," she said, not looking at us.

Tim hugged Mrs. Martin, crumpling her silk dress. "Strip!" he murmured, half-asleep.

"Now, where do you suppose he learned that word?" Mrs. Martin's black eyebrows arched with surprise.

Bella and Katie snickered behind their hands. Mrs. DelGrosso put on her coat and fumbled with the buttons. "Oh, you know, kids pick up all sorts of stuff from TV."

Daddy jangled his car keys in the palm of his hand. "I'll drive you home."

Mrs. DelGrosso shook her head. "No, no, it's just around the block. Bella and I'll walk." She backed out the door, Bella grinning behind her.

"Hey, Veronica, if you meet me at my house at

seven thirty on Monday, we can walk to school together," Bella said.

"Really?" I wasn't sure she was serious.

"See ya Monday!" Bella assured me. "Seven thirty!"

Monday morning, I walked around the block to Bella's house carrying the peanut butter sandwich Mrs. Martin had made me in a brown paper bag with my name in neat cursive on both sides. Red paint peeled off Bella's small house to reveal dirty yellow paint. The grass in her front yard came up to my knees, more dandelions and weeds than grass. I tapped softly on the front door and waited.

Mrs. DelGrosso waddled up, muttering to herself. She opened the door, and a strong smell of garlic and cat pee hit me in the face. "Oh, that girl, that girl," she grumbled. "One day she doesn't want any breakfast because she says she's too fat. Today she wants me to make her waffles with fresh strawberries and whipped cream."

"Mom, did you iron that skirt?" I heard Bella yell from the back of the house. Mrs. DelGrosso hurried off, leaving me to find my way to Bella's room. Her radio blared some song by Madonna. I had to yell to be heard over it.

"Hi, Bella!" I sat on her canopy-covered bed and looked at the pictures of Princess Diana taped all over the walls. "She's so pretty," I said.

"Everyone says I look just like her." Bella stepped out of the bathroom next to her bedroom in a purple, fake-satin robe. She handed me a jewelry box painted to look like a house. "Pick out earrings to go with my blue sweater."

By the time Bella had dressed and blown her hair dry, it was eight o'clock.

"I know a better way to get to school," she said, pulling me by the hand off the sidewalk and onto a dirt path. "It's kind of long, but it's more interesting." The path led to the railroad tracks behind a row of houses. We followed them all the way to our schools, each of us walking on one rail, balancing carefully. "If you fall off three times, the boy you like will never like you back," Bella said. I didn't tell her that there were no boys I liked in Torrance.

"Meetcha here at three," Bella said when we got to our schools.

By the time I slipped into homeroom, it was quarter after eight. Mrs. Ellis gave me a stern look when she handed back my spelling test. "Try to be on time please, Ronnie," she said.

Daniel kicked my metal desk leg. "You're late, hippo girl," he whispered.

"I had to put my little brother on the school bus," I lied.

I met Bella every morning after that. It was worth being late to school to be her friend. After school, we picked up Katie and Maria and walked home along the railroad tracks. Bella showed us how to lay pennies on the tracks for the trains to flatten, and we gave the paper-thin copper pieces to the younger girls, who sold them at their school for a dime.

Sometimes, not often, Bella would be ready when I arrived at her house in the morning, and she'd burst out the door. "Bring me a hot dog!" I heard a man's voice yell once as Bella grabbed my arm and propelled me down the driveway.

"Who's that?" I asked her.

Bella chewed viciously on a piece of gum. "No one. My father," she said, walking so fast that I had to run to keep up with her.

On those mornings that we got to school early, I sat on the cement wall with the other girls from my class, listening to them gossip. Bella walked to the baseball field between my school and hers and fed the seagulls pieces of the cold buttered toast Mrs. DelGrosso insisted she take with her. The birds flapped and screeched around her, examining her with shining black eyes that reminded me of Daniel's eyes when he teased me in homeroom. The girls sitting on the wall called Bella the Bird Lady, and some of them said it in a mean way. The boys in my class didn't call her anything, but they looked sideways at the plaid school skirt she wore pulled up very short and poked each other with their elbows.

I began to like school, especially the fifteen minutes after morning announcements when Mrs. Ellis took out a book and read to us. Some of the kids lay their heads down on their desks and fell asleep, but I followed every word of *Ellen Foster*— a book about an orphan girl living in the South. I understood how Ellen felt, being passed around from family to family. But Ellen's mother had died. Sometimes, when Mother didn't call for a few days, I remembered the time I though she might have died, and I lay awake terrified at night wondering what my life would be like without Mother to visit every other weekend.

One morning in a week when the gray January sky opened up and dumped out rain for days, Mrs. Ellis closed her book and passed out sheets of paper. "I'd like you all to write a poem about the rain," she said. "A good poem doesn't have to rhyme, but it should have a sort of rhythm, a flow like that of your own voice when you talk." She lay one square hand against her chest. "Or of your own heartbeat."

Daniel and some of the other boys snickered, but Mrs. Ellis put up her hand with a stern look that seldom came into her face and said, "Just listen."

It got very quiet in the classroom except for the rain pounding on the roof. The smell of wet asphalt and car exhaust seeped in through an open window. Beneath the rain, I heard the thump of my own heartbeat. I put two fingers on the pulse at my wrist. Suddenly, it was as if every kid's heart was beating at exactly the same time in the classroom— as if we had merged into one person.

"Now," Mrs. Ellis said, "Write."

I wrote.

A few days later, Mrs. Ellis brought my poem over to my desk during free-reading time. She knelt down beside me and looked into my face. "It's called plagiarism when you copy someone else's poem," she said very low.

I returned her serious look, confused. "I don't get it."

"You copied this poem, didn't you, Veronica," she said sadly.

"I did not!" I protested. Beside me, Daniel looked up, one eyebrow a curious black triangle.

Mrs. Ellis pursed up her full lips and frowned. "I'm sorry, Ronnie. I just don't see how you could've written this."

I turned red. I liked Mrs. Ellis so much, but now she was being horribly mean. "I *promise* I made it up," I said. I wished I could tear up my poem right there.

Mrs. Ellis looked down at the poem again, studying it. She stared hard into my eyes. Then she stood up abruptly and smiled. "All right then, Ronnie. I think you must have a talent for poetry."

I wanted to tell her about the songs Mother sang, how all of them rhymed and she'd sing the rhyming words extra loud so that Katie, Tim, and I heard how the song worked. But Mrs. Ellis had already walked back to her desk, the smile still on her lips.

Daniel reached over and tapped my shoulder. "Good recovery, hippo girl," he said. "So where'd you copy it from?"

That day, Mrs. Ellis announced that in March, everyone in the class was going to write an essay for the Torrance "Mother of the Year" contest. A little shiver of excitement ran down my neck. "Three hundred words or less about what makes your mother special," Mrs. Ellis said.

Eddie Cameron waved his arm frantically. "Can I be excused from this assignment, please? My mother isn't special."

The kids laughed, but Mrs. Ellis said soberly, "Everyone's mother is special in some way."

I thought of how Mrs. DelGrosso plodded around the house ironing Bella's blouses and giving her money to buy whatever she wanted at the 7-11 for lunch instead of replacing her own scuffed brown shoes. These things seemed special, not in a nice way, but in a way that set Mrs. DelGrosso apart from other mothers.

"I have two step-mothers besides my mom," Jane Gilmore said. "Which one should I write about?"

"Write about the mother you live with here in Torrance. This is a community contest, and the winning mother's picture will appear in the local newspaper," Mrs. Ellis explained.

I couldn't concentrate on the chapter of *Ellen Foster* she read that day. I chewed my thumbnail so far down that the tip of my thumb stung. I lived with Mrs. Martin. Mother lived a hundred miles away. I wondered if Carpinteria had a "Mother of the Year" contest. Maybe I could enter that one, too. I waited in the hall after school to ask Mrs. Ellis what I should do, but Bella pulled me away to the baseball field, where Roosevelt's boys' baseball team was practicing.

"Let's make clover necklaces." Bella lay down on the grass with her ankles crossed like a model. I sat down cross-legged beside her. We threaded clover stems into long chains, draping them around our heads. Some of the boys on the baseball team whistled at us while they were doing stretching exercises. Bella tossed her head and pretended not to see them.

"Which boy do you like best in your class?" she demanded.

I lay back on the grass and stared up at the sky which was blue for the first time in weeks. "I don't know. I don't know any of them real well." I started to tell Bella I'd seen her older brother, Travis, that morning while I waited for Mrs. DelGrosso to answer the door. He'd ducked past me, all curly brown hair and long, tanned legs, his backpack slung over one shoulder.

"My sister sure is a bitch," he'd said, pausing a moment to look down at me. "Why d'you hang out with her?" I'd turned bright red, and he'd jogged off down the street, laughing.

I didn't think Bella would like it if she knew I thought her brother was cute. "Does your dad live with you?" I asked to change the subject.

"Yeah, why?"

I chewed on a sour grass stem, wincing at the tartness on the front of my tongue. "I never see him."

"So?"

"Well, I just wondered where he is all the time."

When Bella didn't want to talk about something, she became silent and cold, the way I imagined Princess Diana used to be when reporters chased her. Bella stood up abruptly and began to walk home. I walked a little behind her, feeling like I should apologize, but not sure of what I'd done. She turned to glare at me when we reached her house, fists clenched at her sides. "If you tell anyone about my dad, I'll tell the whole city about your mom!"

"What *about* my mom?" I said, surprised. Bella had never even met Mother.

She stared at me hard, and her lips curled into a sneer. "*You* know."

I didn't know. "So what?" I said nervously.

"You don't have to meet me tomorrow morning if you don't want to," Bella said, looking calmly up into the sky.

"I want to meet you," I said quickly. "I'll be here tomorrow at seven-thirty."

"Whatever." She walked into the house, slamming the door behind her.

I walked home slowly, trying to imagine what Bella could tell anyone about my mother that would be bad. She couldn't possibly know that Mother had started to smoke cigarettes while she and Ms. Whitney drank bottles of beer out on the balcony after dinner. *Mother is nice and funny and smart*— I thought— *there's nothing bad anyone can say about her.*

Right then, a poem popped into my head. I sat under the willow tree in my father's front yard and scribbled the words down on the back of my math homework.

"About Mother," I wrote at the top, then underlined the title. I stretched my arms wide and gazed up into the branches of the tree. I knew this poem was even better than the one I'd written at school the day it rained. I couldn't wait to show it to Mrs. Ellis. She'd have to believe I'd written this one, because no one else in the world had such a wonderful mother.

Chapter 6

I sat in my bedroom the first Sunday night in March, staring blankly at a stack of lined paper on my desk. All day, the sky looked as if it had been trying to decide whether to rain or be sunny, just as I was trying to decide whether to write about Mrs. Martin or Mother for the Torrance "Mother of the Year" contest.

"It's a community contest," I heard Mrs. Ellis say in my head. "Write about the mother you live with here in Torrance." I chewed the black plastic cap of my pen and thought hard. Mother didn't like Torrance. She complained that her eyes and throat burned every time she drove down to pick us up. Katie and I told her about "Smog Days"— those days at both our schools when the smog hung thick and yellow in the air, and we were not allowed to play outside, but had to stay inside at recess and lunch playing Heads Up, 7-Up and Mum-Ball.

"I don't know why your father picked such a dirty city to move to," Mother said once in the driveway, loud enough for Daddy to hear from the side yard where he was fixing the lawnmower. "He used to be a real *nature* lover."

I glanced outside as light drops of rain began to hit my bedroom window. Finally, I took my pen out of my mouth and wrote my name on the first sheet of paper. I was certain that Mother would not want to be Torrance's Mother of the Year. I didn't know what to write about Mrs. Martin, though. After living with her for three months, I barely knew her. She spent most of her afternoons playing with Katie and Tim, or taking them with her to the grocery store and to the dry cleaners to pick up Daddy's starched shirts for work.

I knew she was clean. Every Friday afternoon was Chore Day, although she vacuumed, dusted, and watered her houseplants every other day of the week, too. But Katie was not allowed to go to Maria's and I was not allowed to hang out with Bella on Friday afternoons until we had cleaned our rooms completely. Last Friday, Mrs. Martin had run one finger over the black dresser in my bedroom and said, "Veronica, I could eat off this dresser, it's so clean."

"I could dust your dog statues for you," I'd suggested. Mrs. Martin had a whole collection of porcelain and glass dogs that she kept on top of the oak dresser in her bedroom.

"I think I'll keep that chore for now," Mrs. Martin had replied. "But," she'd handed me a soft white cloth, "you can dust the furniture in the living room if you'd like to."

I hunched over my desk and drew a big black circle in the middle of the first sheet of paper, then wrote "Mrs. M." inside it. I drew smaller circles around the big circle and wrote "Clean" in one of them.

Mrs. Martin was also a good cook, I reminded myself. I never groaned like the other kids, "It's pork chop night," or "Meatloaf . . . yuck!" Mrs. Martin coated her pork chops in oatmeal, herbs, and Parmesan cheese, and her meatloaf was delicious. On nights that we had macaroni and cheese, she let me stir the cheese into a white sauce until it got thick and creamy, and she showed me how to use the salad spinner so that the lettuce came out crisp and dry. She liked to send a plate of homemade oatmeal cookies with me in the mornings when I went to pick up Bella. Mrs. DelGrosso always peeled back the plastic wrap on the paper plate immediately and dunked two cookies in her cup of coffee. "Your mom's a good lady," she'd say as she tucked the rest of the cookies into Bella's backpack.

One Saturday night, Mrs. DelGrosso had walked over and handed Mrs. Martin a large metal pan of something called *spanikopita*. "Here, I made this for your family," she said. "Recipe straight from my mother in Greece."

Mrs. Martin hugged Mrs. DelGrosso and thanked her, but the next morning, she cut into a piece of the casserole and lifted a forkful to her eye. "I knew it. There's a hair in here." She wrinkled her nose and slid the entire casserole into the garbage can. "Don't tell her I did that," she said to me. "Tina means well."

"Good cook," I wrote in another circle on my paper. I felt suddenly lucky to have a neat, talented, soon-to-be stepmother.

In the middle of writing my first paragraph, the phone rang. I picked up the black phone Daddy had given me for Christmas. "Hello?" I said, still writing.

"Hi, honey," Mother's cheerful voice sang out.

"Hello?" Mrs. Martin said on the kitchen phone.

"It's for me!" I called.

"Oh. Sorry." Mrs. Martin hung up the phone, and I was alone with Mother.

"How are you?" she asked.

"Fine." I crumpled up the sheet of paper I'd written on and tossed it on the floor. "How're you?"

"All right. That cat Pam found had her kittens right on my bed last night. I can't wait for you to see them— they're so cute," Mother said. "Look, honey, I need to know if you and Katie are coming up this weekend for the horse show. It should be a lot of fun. The 4-H club I want you to join will be there, and afterwards, they're all going out for pizza."

I chewed on a hangnail, ripping off a tiny piece of skin with my teeth. "I sort of promised Bella that I'd go ice skating this weekend. I've never been before . . . "

I sensed Mother's disappointment before she'd said a word.

"I see," she said. "Is Katie there?"

I wanted to throw the phone across the room. It wasn't my fault that I wanted to hang out with Bella instead with of a bunch of kids I didn't even know.

"Katie!" I yelled down the hall.

My sister trotted into my room. Her blond ponytails bobbed up and down at the sides of her head like wings.

"What?"

"Mother's on the phone."

She reached for my phone, but I held it above my head. "Use the one in the kitchen," I said. "I have to study."

Katie stuck her middle finger up at me. She and Maria had just figured out what giving somebody the finger meant, so for the last week, they'd been going around giving everyone the finger. I gave it right back to her, and she disappeared into the hall.

"What're you studying?" Mother asked as we waited for Katie to pick up the other phone.

"Math," I lied.

"Maybe when you come up again we can work on it together the way we did when you . . . when you lived here."

Guilt hit me like a fist in my chest. It was all my fault that Mother wasn't around to help me with my math homework now. "I'll bring it when I come up this weekend," I promise.

Mother cleared her throat. "Did your father's girlfriend hang up the other phone?" she asked, more to Mrs. Martin than to me.

"Yeah."

She lowered her voice. "I've been talking to my lawyer about appealing the court's decision. It could take three months to a year before we're allowed to go back in front of a judge, but we *can* go back."

"I can wait," I said, then added quickly, "I have a friend now, so it'll be easier."

"I'm glad you have Bella," Mother said. "I worry about you, Ronnie."

She sounded like she might begin to cry. Just in time, Katie picked up the phone. "Mother, I want to wear my pink dress to the horse show this weekend! Can I?" she squeaked.

"Bye, Mother," I said. I hung up and began to work on the "Mother of the Year" essay. Rain pounded against the roof. I wrote for a long time without stopping, then copied the essay over neatly on lined paper and put it in my school folder.

The next morning, I walked around the block to Bella's house with the clean pan and a plate of Mrs. Martin's cookies. Mrs. DelGrosso waddled up to the door with a frayed pink towel wrapped around her head. I had a feeling she wasn't wearing her wig. "Oh, your mother," she said, the wrinkles in her broad face deepening with pleasure. "How'd you like that *spanikopita*, huh? That was real Greek *spanikopita*."

I hesitated, thinking of the mess at the bottom of the garbage can. "I don't really care for Greek food," I murmured and hurried into Bella's bedroom. I found her dancing naked in front of her mirror to a Blondie c.d.

"Don't you ever knock?" she screamed. She ran into the bathroom and slammed the door.

"You wouldn't have heard me anyhow!" I yelled back, red-faced at the sight of Bella's naked breasts. "The music's so loud!" I went over and turned down the volume on the stereo. "D'you want me to pick out some earrings for you?"

"No! God! Does this run in your family or something?"

"What're you talking about?" I sat down on her bed and looked at the newest picture of Princess Diana taped to Bella's wall. Diana wore a flowing white dress, and she was walking across a lawn with Prince Charles.

"Charles is kind of cute, don'tcha think?" I said in the direction of the bathroom.

"He's not your type," Bella yelled. "He's a *man*!"

I wondered if Bella would be angrier if I waited for her, or if I left for school without her. Finally, I wandered into the living room and sat down on a fuzzy, orange-flowered couch. The curtains were pulled closed, but I could still see a film of dust on the scratched end tables and lampshades. Beside me on one table stood a black and white photograph of a beautiful woman in a wedding dress. Dark curls flowed around her face, mingling with a white veil. A trail of lilies bloomed over her delicate hand.

Bella came out of her room wearing her plaid school skirt hiked up high and a white lace top that looked more like a bra than a blouse.

"Who's the picture of?" I asked her.

"My mother."

Some of my amazement that the beautiful bride had turned into ugly Mrs. DelGrosso faded as Bella moved closer to me. She was wearing make-up. I was instantly jealous of the blue powder on her eyelids and of her red lips— red like she'd been drinking cherry Kool-Aid but without the mustache.

"Let's go, silly," she said, tossing her head. She seemed to have forgotten about my walking in on her naked. We walked down the block. Bella chattered about some cute eighth grade boy and offered me a handful of M&Ms from a bag. "Hey!" she said, stopping suddenly. "The Bugs!"

We watched the three Volkswagen Bugs, each painted a different color— pink, blue, and yellow, even to the hub caps— as they chugged down the street.

"The most popular boys in high school," Bella sighed, hugging herself when the cars were out of sight. "Especially Bobby in the blue Bug. He lives on the next street, and someday, I'm gonna go over there and . . . "

She didn't finish. My school bell rang, and we took off running.

That month, Bella began spending more and more time over at my house. I liked a lot of time alone to read and think, but Bella spent most of her afternoons following Mrs. Martin around anyway, trying to copy her English accent. For weeks, she'd been carrying the cream-colored wedding invitation, addressed to "Mr. and Mrs. DelGrosso and Bella," in her backpack. She was more excited about the wedding than Katie and I were.

Mother dropped us off the Saturday night before the wedding, after taking us to see the musical *Annie* in Los Angeles. Neither Katie nor I had told her that Daddy and Mrs. Martin were getting married the next day. Our goodbye at the front door felt quiet and awkward, as if we were keeping a secret from Mother.

"I'll see you in ten days," Mother said. Tears filled her eyes as she hugged each of us in turn. "You kids be good."

"We will," Katie promised quickly, then ran in the house.

I stayed outside on the porch a while longer. "Does Carpinteria have a 'Mother of the Year' contest?" I asked Mother.

She shook her head. "I don't think so." She looked away from me and reached up to pull her hair off her neck. "Why? Are you . . . are you thinking about nominating me for one? Somehow, I don't think I'd win."

"I just wondered," I said.

Mother hugged me once more. And even though I hated to watch her get into her bus and pull out of the driveway, I stood on the front lawn and waved until she had disappeared down the street.

I walked slowly into the house and opened my bedroom door to find Bella waltzing around my room in a long, off the shoulder flowered dress.

Mrs. Martin looked across the room at me apologetically. "Bella didn't have anything to wear to the wedding tomorrow, so I took her shopping," she explained.

"We got you the same dress!" Bella reached into my closet to hand me the exact same floral dress in my size.

"You don't have to wear it if you don't want to," Mrs. Martin said, watching me run my hand over the stiff new fabric. "Bella just thought it would be nice if . . . "

"This way, everyone will think we're sisters," Bella said. "I'm over here so much that it's practically like we *are* sisters, isn't it?" Her green eyes pleaded for Mrs. Martin's answer.

Mrs. Martin twisted her long black hair up into a knot at the top of her head. "What do you think?" she asked us. "Should I wear it up or down?"

"Pretty!" Tim walked into my room in his flannel pajamas and the light blue bow tie he was supposed to wear the next day.

"With white flowers in your hair— maybe jasmine

since it looks like stars— it's *perfect*," Bella sighed.

Katie stood in the doorway and squinted up her eyes. "*Perfect*," she repeated, trying to knot her skinny blond ponytail up into a bun.

I couldn't help seeing how much happier everyone would be if Bella were to take my place in the family. *She* would never sit in her room reading for hours, refusing to play a family game of Monopoly or go bike riding with Katie. I thought of Mother driving alone on the dark and winding coastal road back to the beach and wished I could've gone home with her. The dull ache of every other Sunday night felt worse because it was only Saturday. Because Bella was there, I had to hang out and pretend to be happy and normal in a family that didn't feel like my own.

Bella stayed for dessert, which was a chocolate Bundt cake. We all sat in the living room, and Mrs. Martin put a CD of Beethoven's sonatas on low. She stretched out on the couch with her feet on Daddy's lap. He began to paint her toenails a careful, deep red. Bella and Katie leaned over the back of the couch, watching the toenail-painting with interest. I curled up in one of the blue chairs. Tim sat on the floor beside me, tickling the bottoms of my bare feet with a feather he'd found at Carpinteria Beach two weekends ago.

"We can't call you Mrs. Martin anymore," Katie said suddenly.

I looked up to find Daddy and Mrs. Martin smiling at each other— warm, intimate smiles that excluded everyone else. I wished I had someone to smile with like that.

"You'll have to call her Mother now," Bella said.

Katie's blond eyebrows furrowed at me. I knew what she was thinking. We already had a mother. It would be too confusing to call Mrs. Martin "Mother" or "Mom," and it would hurt Mother.

"How about Mother Elsa?" Daddy suggested.

Bella snorted delicately. "Mother Elsa makes her sound like a nun."

"Well, I'm hardly that, am I, Zach." Again, that smile, and Mrs. Martin reached up to kiss Daddy while Bella watched closely.

"What if we just call you Elsa?" I suggested. Mother had taught us not to call any adult by a first name unless asked, but it didn't look as though Mrs. Martin was going to ask us to call her anything.

"Elsa's fine," Mrs. Martin said. "It's my name."

Daddy finished painting her toenails, and she stepped carefully into the kitchen to wash the dessert dishes. Daddy carried Tim off to bed. Bella nudged me with her elbow. "I think you hurt her feelings," she whispered. "Why couldn't you just call her Mother? *I* would."

I bit my tongue hard so I wouldn't remind Bella that she'd never lost her mother in court and could see her any time she wanted instead of just two weekends a month. I doubted she'd care if she *did* lose her mother. She'd just adopt Elsa.

The next morning, the last Sunday in March, I woke up to a blue sky dotted with clouds as perfectly white and fluffy as the clouds in the pictures Katie drew and taped to her bedroom door.

"What a great day for a wedding!" Bella said, waving her spoon at me. She was already seating at the dining room table eating a bowl of oatmeal, with her hair rolled up in big pink curlers.

Mrs. Martin . . . Elsa stood at the stove in a white satin robe, stirring a pot of oatmeal. "Ronnie, you're the last one up this morning," she said. "Have a bowl of oatmeal, then take a shower. I hope Katie's left you some hot water." She set a bowl of oatmeal in front of me at the table. I reached for the bowl of brown sugar.

"Why're you over here so early?" I asked Bella.

"Couldn't sleep." Bella reached up to test her hair for dryness. "Weddings are sooo exciting!"

Katie stomped in and sat down at the table. Elsa handed her a bowl of oatmeal with a quiet "Good morning." My little sister was definitely not a morning person. Still, she was up and dressed in a short turquoise and black dress made out of some shimmering fabric with matching black lace shorts. I hurried into the bathroom to take a shower in water that quickly went from lukewarm to cold. Then I put on the floral dress.

I don't know why I expected it to look as nice on me as it did on Bella. One glance in the mirror assured me that where Bella's chest filled the top of the dress, on me it sagged gracelessly. Where Bella's shoulders rose up pale and smooth, I had to square my own narrow, freckled shoulders to keep the dress from falling down.

"That dress looks better on Bella," Katie said as she walked past my room.

I ran a brush through my hair, trying to smooth it down to look like Bella's own silky hair. I finally clipped it into a ponytail and turned unhappily away from my reflection. I looked like a little kid playing dress-up in adult clothes.

Bella stood in the living room, putting sprigs of jasmine into Elsa's black hair. Elsa glanced up as I came in. "You look nice," she murmured, bending down so that Bella could reach the top of her head. Elsa wore a plain, cream-colored dress that looked dull and faded beside Bella's dress. Our dresses.

My father was pacing up and down the hall in his dark blue suit. His graying sideburns glistened slightly with sweat. "Ronnie," he said when he saw me. "You look beautiful."

For a moment, I felt better.

"Go put your brother in the car, would you? He's practicing karate on the lawn, and he's gonna tear his pants." Daddy resumed his pacing.

I found Tim out on the lawn kicking his leg up into the air. I heard a faint rip of cloth.

"Great, Timmy. Turn around," I said. I examined his light blue pants for rips, but I couldn't find any. "Come sit in the car with me, and we'll sing." I walked carefully to the car, trying not to wobble on my half-inch heels. With my luck, I'd walk into the church and either trip and break my ankle, or my dress would fall down.

The wedding lasted only a few minutes. A few of Daddy's friends from the insurance company and some neighbors sat in the first four pews in the big church. Katie hurried to sit with Maria and her family. Bella and I sat together in our identical dresses. "Lucky!" she hissed in my ear. "No one ever gets to see their parents get married!"

I thought of Mother and her Las Vegas wedding in her purple bikini top, as I watched Daddy and Elsa repeat their vows. My father's voice rang out loud, echoing against the stained glass windows with their pictures of Jesus and the disciples that reminded me of Grandma Davis. Elsa stammered a little when she spoke, and she looked very stern. She kissed Daddy quickly on the lips as the minister pronounced them man and wife, then hurried over to hug us.

"Congratulations!" Bella cried, throwing her arms around Elsa.

"Congratulations!" Katie said, imitating Bella.

"Congratulations, Elsa," I said, feeling stupid.

Tim untied his bow tie. "Way to go, guys!"

The heavy door at the back of the church swung open. Mrs. DelGrosso appeared in a sudden ray of sunlight from outside.

"Oh, God! I told Travis *not* to drop her off!" Bella wailed. She ducked in back of Elsa as Mrs. DelGrosso waddled up the aisle clutching a gold-foil wrapped box with a huge white bow on top of it that looked like a bird about to take flight.

"I'm late, huh," she muttered. "Woke up this morning to find that one dressed and gone." Mrs. DelGrosso nodded at Bella. I saw that she was wearing a gold scarf in her wig that matched a gold sequined top over the brown polyester pants. "Travis forgot he was supposed to drive me here and went off to play basketball. Was it a nice ceremony?"

Elsa hugged Mrs. DelGrosso. "The reception is the best part, anyway, Tina."

The reception took place in the banquet room of a hotel overlooking a harbor. Bella and I walked over to inspect the small white wedding cake on a long table full of fruit, bread, and several kinds of sliced meat and cheese. Green bottles of champagne stuck out from three silver buckets of ice.

"Now, what would you girls like to drink?" Daddy's secretary, Mrs. Carson, walked up in a dress that looked like a turquoise pillowcase and a hat with a white peacock feather. I glanced at Daddy and Elsa, who stood a few feet away greeting guests. Champagne was obviously out of the question.

"A Coke, please," I said.

"Me, too." Bella walked over to another table to examine the pile of presents. I waited by the cake for Mrs. Carson to come back with our Cokes. I wanted to scoop up one of the white frosting scallops with one finger; I would've if I'd been Katie's age. *The only good thing about weddings is the cake* — I thought.

Mrs. DelGrosso walked up to Bella and leaned close to her, saying something I couldn't hear. I could see her chin trembling. Bella tossed her head and glided over to where Elsa stood. Elsa glanced down and put her arm around Bella, then continued talking to a woman who was holding a baby.

"Your mother doesn't know what a good man she left," Mrs. Carson said, returning with two glasses of soda. The feather in her hat nodded as she spoke. "Your father's been so good to me— lets me go home whenever I need to take care of my grandchildren, and he sends me the most beautiful bouquets for Secretary's Day."

I didn't tell Mrs. Carson that I used to go with Mother to the florist to pick out bouquets for her, and that after Mother left, Elsa had taken over the duty.

"I'd better go help with the champagne," Mrs. Carson said, handing me my Coke. The room was full now, and guests were raising their glasses in a toast.

"To the happy couple!" Daddy's boss from the insurance company, Mr. Spalding, raised his glass high over his head. Everyone clinked glasses, and I saw that Bella was holding a glass half-full of champagne. The guests drifted off into little groups again. Daddy and Elsa began to move among them, talking and laughing. I wandered out the glass doors and across the lawn to the cement path, where Katie and Tim were hanging over the iron railing looking at the boats.

"Weddings are boring," Katie said when she saw me. "Bella said they were supposed to be fun."

We watched the boats bobbing on the water and read the names painted on the sides. I thought if I ever owned a boat, I'd pick a better name than "Neptune's Daughter," or "Lazy Daze."

"What would you name your boat if you had one?" I asked Katie and Tim.

"Elsa," Katie replied firmly.

"Morris the Cat," Tim said.

I leaned against the cold rail and thought. If I had a boat, I'd sail it away from everyone I knew, and I'd name it after the first handsome pirate I met.

I heard a rumbling sound behind me and turned to see Bella pushing a black cart on a rolling metal stand. "I found it in front of a restaurant," she said. "We can push each other around in it."

"I wanna ride!" Tim said. Bella picked him up, and he scrambled into the cart. "Iss my car!" he said, smiling. When Tim smiled, his whole round face got into it, and he looked happier than anyone I'd ever seen. I didn't want to spoil his fun by suggesting that he might rip his new pants or get dirty. I stood near the glass doors in case Daddy or Elsa decided to come out and watched as Katie and Bella took turns rolling Tim around the harbor in the cart. A movement near the door caught my eye. I peered into the reception room. Mrs. DelGrosso stood near the door, drinking down a crystal glass of champagne like it was water. Mrs. Carson hurried over to pour her some more, then poured herself another glass. The two women clinked their glasses together. I could hear the bright tinkling sound even through the door. Then they put their heads together and laughed the way Bella and I had laughed last week when she'd spent the night, and we'd crept around the block and toilet-papered her own house. I was glad Mrs. DelGrosso had found a friend at the reception.

Across the room, I saw Daddy standing behind Elsa at the cake table. He held a big knife, and she had her hands over his on the knife.

"Hey, you guys, they're going to cut the cake!" I called across the lawn.

Katie and Bella raced down the sidewalk with Tim. The bus cart swayed on unsteady wheels. Suddenly, Bella rolled it over an uneven place in the sidewalk. Tim and the cart crashed to the lawn.

"Timmy!" I cried, yanking my dress up on my shoulders as I ran to him. "Are you all right?"

Tim sat on the grass looking dazed. He giggled a little, then looked up at me and burst into tears. A scratch above his left eyebrow began to turn red.

I put my arms around him. "It's okay," I said, rocking him gently. "They didn't mean to make you fall down."

"Good thing he fell on the grass. Otherwise, his head would've busted open," Bella observed.

"He ripped his pants," Katie said, pointing to a tear in the knee of one pants leg.

"What's going on here?" Elsa pushed past Katie and Bella and knelt down beside Tim. "What happened?"

"He fell down," I said.

Elsa's dark eyes narrowed. She looked at the bus cart tipped over beside us and then at me. She stood Tim up and examined the scratch above his eye. "I'm surprised at you, Veronica," she said in a voice colder than the gray mist that was beginning to settle over the harbor. "As the oldest, I thought you were a little more responsible than this." She stood up and carried Tim up to the reception room. At the glass door, she turned. "Bella, Katie, come inside and have some cake."

They ran inside, leaving me alone on the grass. I stood up and leaned against the iron rail. A waiter in a white coat walked by and picked up the bus cart. He looked at me curiously, then rolled the cart back to the restaurant. I decided I wasn't in the mood for cake anyway.

Elsa is officially my stepmother now— I thought. I knew a lot of fairy tales about evil stepmothers, and even though she was a lot better stepmother than most of the ones I'd read about, she wasn't Mother.

It's my own fault I'm living with her instead of Mother— I told myself. I should have told the judge I wanted to live with Mother. It was obvious now that Daddy didn't need me at all. He barely spoke to me in the evenings after work, and our snowy walk and the elegant dinner in Vermont seemed like a dream now. A bad dream.

Daddy came out to find me as the late afternoon sun grew pale behind the mist. I shivered in my thin dress, but he didn't offer me his jacket. He stood beside me and put one hand on the rail. "Tim's okay," he said, "but he could've been hurt worse."

"I know," I said, staring down at the damp grass. "I'm sorry."

Daddy had told me in Vermont that he'd loved my mother more than anything in the world. I supposed he felt that way about Elsa now. I didn't have the energy to try and explain what had really happened with Tim— anyhow, Daddy would only believe what Elsa told him. I poked at a pill bug with the toe of my high-heeled shoe. It curled up into a silver-gray ball. I wished I could curl up, too, but I had to follow Daddy back to the car where everyone was waiting for me. I sat smashed in the back seat between Mrs. DelGrosso and Tim. Elsa drove because Daddy had drunk a lot of champagne. Tim immediately went to sleep on my shoulder. I stared down at the bandage over the scratch above his eye and tried not to cry.

When we got home after dropping Bella and Mrs. DelGrosso off, Elsa reached into a box and pulled out the small top layer of the wedding cake. All the warmth rushed back into me at the thought of her noticing that I hadn't had a piece. I walked around the counter to hug her.

"Hand me the foil, Veronica," she said before I

reached her. "I'm going to wrap this up so your father and I can eat it next year on our anniversary. It's supposed to be good luck."

She wrapped up the layer and put it far back in the freezer. I walked into my room and shut the door. I hoped Daddy would let me have a bite of his piece of cake next March— I needed it for luck.

April arrived with a terrific thunderstorm that knocked out all the power lines that next Sunday. Mother didn't want to drive us home in the dark, and Daddy agreed with her for once, so we got to stay in Carpinteria an extra night.

"Good thing we're all used to eating by candlelight," Mother said as she served us stir-fried vegetables and rice on paper plates. The living room seemed empty with just the four of us. Pam and Sage were working, and Ms. Whitney was "out," Mother said. Sage had whispered to me earlier that her mother had been hanging out at a gay bar lately, dating a woman who drove a motorcycle.

"Dating a woman?" I'd repeated.

"Yeah, silly," Sage had laughed. "Didn't you know Ma's a lesbian?"

"Really?" I felt stupid for not knowing, but I'd never known any lesbians. I knew lesbians were women who liked other women, and that the worst thing the girls at school could call each other was "lesbo." "Why does your mom wear men's shirts and boots and no makeup if she likes women so much?" I asked Sage, confused.

She'd looked at me as if I were as young as Tim. "That's the kind of clothes other lesbians like, Ronnie."

"Oh," I'd said.

Ms. Whitney came home late that Sunday night. I woke up and peeked out of the bedroom door as she kicked off her brown boots. I felt a little disappointed— she didn't look any different than before I knew she liked women. *I wonder if Mother knows that Ms. Whitney is a lesbian*— I thought before I went back to sleep.

Mother dropped us off at our schools in Torrance

the next morning. It felt almost like old times, before she and Daddy got a divorce. She handed me the lunch she'd made me in a paper bag and kissed me goodbye. "Have a good day," she called after me in a shaky voice. I wanted to cry, too, knowing that the red bus wouldn't be in the school parking lot when I got out of class that day.

Mrs. Ellis had decided that we were going to act out Shakespeare's play, *A Midsummer Night's Dream*. She'd brought a big box of funny wigs and hats, and we were supposed to put them on while she assigned us each a part in the play. In the middle of trying to decide which kid would play Nick Bottom and walk around with a donkey mask on his head, she paused. "I want to make an announcement," she said. "I tried to wait until the end of the day, but it's too exciting."

Daniel leaned over to me. "She's pregnant. She did it with the principal, I bet."

Mrs. Ellis held up a lined paper that I recognized instantly. "I have here the essay that won the Torrance 'Mother of the Year' contest. It was written by your classmate, Veronica Davis."

Everyone clapped, and Daniel yelled, "Way to go, Hippo Writer!" My cheeks burned. Suddenly, I had to bite my lips hard to keep from crying. I couldn't believe I'd won the contest. And I couldn't believe that I'd written about Elsa instead of Mother.

"I'm going to read you Veronica's essay now," Mrs. Ellis said, smiling proudly at me.

I slumped down in my seat and tried not to listen. I wanted to rush to Mother, to get on a bus and go back to Carpinteria, so that I could throw my arms around her and keep her from finding out about the contest. I had to tell Mrs. Ellis that I couldn't accept the award. I'd written about the wrong mother.

Bella came to find me while I was waiting to talk to Mrs. Ellis in the hall after school. "Hey. Some girl told me you won a writing contest."

"Yeah."

"If I had your mother, I'd probably win, too," she

said with a glance at the group of boys walking past us.

"But she's not my mother," I whispered. "She's my stepmother."

Bella shrugged. "Same thing," she said. "Hey, aren't you supposed to pick up Katie today?"

She was right. Elsa had a hair appointment and couldn't pick Katie up after school. Reluctantly, I followed Bella down the hall and walked with her to Katie's school.

Katie rushed over when she saw us and started chattering about some fight she and Maria had gotten into. I didn't even hear her. All I could think about was how to keep both Elsa and Mother from finding out about the contest.

I didn't have to worry about Bella telling Elsa about the contest after school that day. There was a teen dance scheduled Friday night at the Torrance Recreation Center and Bella was full of plans.

"It's very important that you assert yourself socially," she told me, "because you're still so new in town." She shut my bedroom door and opened a compact full of pressed face powder to inspect her purple eyeshadow. I wanted to ask her if I could try on the eyeshadow, but Elsa didn't approve of girls wearing makeup.

"I'm not sure Elsa'll let me go to the dance," I said. "The other day, she had a fit cause Jimmy Van Meter called me up for a math assignment. He's a boy," I explained, shrugging at Bella's questioning eyebrows. "I'm not supposed to talk to boys, I guess."

"Let *me* ask Elsa." Bella smiled her slightly evil smile. She took my hand and pulled me into the kitchen, where Elsa was cleaning each leaf of a green and red coleus plant with a damp towel. Bella leaned over the counter and smiled so that the dimple in her right cheek deepened. "Elsa, would it be all right if Veronica went to the dance at the Rec Center this Friday? She's still kind of new, and I could introduce her to all my friends."

I almost laughed when Bella said that about her friends. As far as I could tell, I was her only friend.

Elsa pushed a plate of chocolate chip cookies

towards Bella and me. "I don't see any reason why Ronnie can't go to the dance, although she could've asked me herself."

I looked away, embarrassed. It was hard asking Elsa's permission for things. I was used to asking Daddy or Mother, but now, it seemed like I was only supposed to ask Elsa, and she said no a lot more than my parents used to.

"Will you need a dress?" Elsa wanted to know.

I shrugged. "I don't think so."

"She needs a black one," Bella said firmly.

Elsa frowned. "But it's April."

Bella nodded thoughtfully. "Yes, but black is always fashionable. Princess Diana once wore the most *gorgeous* black dress to an evening banquet."

I thought Elsa would tell Bella that the dance at the Rec Center was hardly an evening banquet, but she just smiled and nodded. "I'll take care of it," she said.

"Told you," Bella whispered in the hall. "You just have to tell parents what they want to hear."

Friday after school, Elsa took me to the mall and bought me a beautiful black dress with dots of gold and silver glitter all over it. "It's hard to believe that you're growing up already," she said, looking wistfully at the dress. "I used to love to dance, but your father hates crowds."

We walked out of the mall to find that fog had clouded over the sun. By the time Bella came over to help me dress, it was raining. "April showers bring May flowers," she sang, stripping off her yellow raincoat to reveal a short, tight black dress. "You'll have to put your hair up," she said, examining me critically. "You know it always gets fuzzy in rainy weather."

I sat obediently in my flannel robe as she pinned my hair into a French twist. I wasn't sure I wanted to go to the Rec Center. I didn't even know how to dance. I'd been so nervous that I practiced dancing in my room to Elsa's Beatles tapes all week.

Bella dropped the glittery black dress over my head and helped me zip it up the back. "I'll lend you my lipstick when we get there," she whispered, but when I turned around so she could inspect me, her eyes widened and she said, "Wow, Ronnie. You don't need lipstick."

I glanced in the mirror on the back of my door and didn't recognize myself. Somehow, the black dress made my eyes look bluer, and my cheeks were pink with excitement. Elsa had bought me a pair of low black pumps with rhinestones on them. My legs looked long and pretty in black nylons. *All of me looks pretty—* I thought happily.

Bella tossed her head. Her long, fake diamond earrings swung impatiently. "Let's go!" she said.

Elsa drove us to the Rec Center slowly, because the streets were slick with rain. Kids in dresses and suits leapt out of cars and raced up to the door, holding coats up over their heads to protect their clothes from the rain.

"Ronnie, you look stunning," Elsa said and kissed my cheek. "I'll pick you up at nine, girls. Have fun!"

Bella and I hurried up to the door, dodging raindrops. We each gave the woman behind the table a dollar. I hung my red raincoat carefully on the rack with everyone else's coats. Bella tapped her foot and sighed. "Come *on*, Ronnie! You're gonna make us late."

As we hurried down the hall toward the auditorium, several boys I'd never seen before whistled in admiration. Always before, when any boy whistled, I knew it was for Bella. But I remembered my reflection in the mirror at home, and I thought that just maybe, this time the whistles were for me, too.

The auditorium didn't look much different than it had the time I'd gone in with Elsa to pick up Katie and Maria from ballet class. A few pink and yellow balloons hovered limply in corners. The lights were so dim that I couldn't make out the faces of the kids standing across the room, but it was definitely just the Rec Center auditorium, and not the fancy ballroom I'd hoped it would be.

A man wearing a plaid beret stood on stage with a microphone and a pile of records. "*Get up and dance,*" he breathed into the microphone. He turned the music up so loud I could feel the beat of the drums in my stomach. Only a few kids were dancing— mostly girls in groups and Angela Scott and Bill Morris from my school, who'd been a couple since the second grade. Bella and I stood in a corner and looked at the group of boys near us out of the corners of our eyes. I recognized Eddie Cameron, who looked terrific in a white suit and green high-top sneakers, but he didn't even glance at me. The d.j. put on a different record, the Beatles' "Shake It Up, Baby." Finally, kids ran out on the dance floor.

"Elsa said that John Lennon smoked a ton of cigarettes before he recorded this song, so his voice would be all scratchy," I said nervously to Bella. My foot in its rhinestone shoe tapped the floor. Now I wished someone would ask me to dance, so I wouldn't have to stand awkwardly in the corner all night.

We stood there at least an hour. Boys kept walking up to us like they were going to ask us to dance. But Bella would peer at them from under her long lashes and whisper, "Too fat," or "Too short." Then she'd grab me like we were having this fascinating discussion and were much too busy for dancing. At last, Bella smoothed her black dress over her hips and frowned. "This is the most boring dance I've ever been to," she said. "Let's go outside."

The woman at the door stamped our hands with a green caterpillar so we could get back in. We stood outside under the roof, shivering in our thin dresses. "Maybe we should call Elsa and get her to take us home," I said, pointing to the pay phone. "We could rent a movie or something."

Bella shook her head, then lifted her chin and smiled. "Look." Daniel from my class was walking towards us with a tall blond boy.

"His name's Matt," Bella whispered. "He's the eighth grader I told you about, the one who plays soccer at the field on weekends."

The boys walked right up to us. Daniel said, "Well, if it isn't Hippo Girl." He was wearing jeans and a black turtleneck, and he looked fantastic.

"Hi," I said. Even the one syllable sounded stupid.

"Hi, Matt," Bella said in a low, sexy voice.

Matt jerked his head in greeting. His eyes wandered up and down Bella's body. I giggled, thinking he looked just like Tim whenever Elsa made a chocolate cake. Fat raindrops began to fall. I wished I'd grabbed my raincoat on my way outside.

"Wow! It's really raining," Daniel said. "Cool."

"Are you guys going to the dance?" Bella asked. She sounded like she could care less if they did or if they didn't.

"Are you kidding?" Matt scoffed. "Those dances are so lame."

Daniel grinned his wide, lopsided grin. "Hey, isn't there a pool here? We should go swimming."

There *was* a pool, around the back of the auditorium. Bella and I looked at each other. "Why not!" she said.

We scurried around the auditorium with the boys. Bella squealed as she stepped into a puddle. Mud seeped into her black velvet shoe, and I bent down to help her scrape it off with a leaf. The boys stopped in front of the high, chain-link fence surrounding the pool.

"They can't climb that," Matt said, jerking his head at us.

"I can," I said. I kicked off my heels and began to climb. Bella followed me, giggling. The boys raced each other to the top and leapt down to the cement. We tugged at the thick blue mat covering the pool. Bella stuck her hand under it to test the water.

"It's cold," she said. The rain made dark spots on her dress. I wrapped my arms around me, wishing I were in the warm auditorium instead of beside the dark, cold pool. No one said anything. I wondered if Bella and the boys were thinking what I was thinking. None of us had bathing suits. If we were really going to swim, we would have to swim in our underwear. I thought of the black lace underwear Elsa had bought me to go with my dress, and how I'd been too embarrassed to ask if she'd buy me a matching black bra for my practically nonexistent breasts.

Daniel and Matt raised their eyebrows at each other. Bella looked at her watch. "Veronica's mother is picking us up soon . . . " she said, so we all climbed back over the fence and stood in the wet grass. My hair had fallen out of its French twist and was hanging in damp strands across my face.

"Give you a piggy-back ride," Matt said to Bella, his voice ringing with challenge.

"Well, the grass is *awfully* wet," Bella said to me, hopping up on Matt's back.

"Giddy up, Hippo Girl," Daniel said, getting down on one knee. Without thinking, I climbed up onto his back and put my arms around his neck. He smelled like pine trees.

"Yee-ha!" the boys yelled, trotting us around the field behind the Rec Center. Matt tripped, or pretended to, and he and Bella fell on the grass together, laughing.

Daniel stopped trotting. For a moment, our heads stayed close together. His brown neck was warm and soft against my arms. I wondered if he could possibly like me, or if he was just showing off for Bella. "Hey, Hippo Girl," he said in a low voice, and for the first time, the joke of a name sounded sweet. "You look really nice tonight."

"Thanks," I whispered. "So do you."

Matt raced up with Bella, breaking the spell. "Oh, Ronnie!" Bella gasped with laughter. "It's almost nine!"

Elsa was already waiting in the parking lot, fifteen minutes early. When she saw us on the boys' backs coming from the direction of the field, she got out of the car.

"That's Veronica's mom," Bella said, pointing.

Matt gave a low whistle. "She's a babe!"

"Girls, get in the car." Even across the parking lot, I could tell that Elsa was furious.

Matt and Daniel dropped us abruptly to the ground and ran towards the auditorium. "See you in school, Hippo Girl!" Daniel called back.

Elsa looked coldly at my dripping hair and soaking wet dress. "Bella, you get in the front seat, since you're getting out first."

"But I thought I was spending the night," Bella said.

Elsa ignored her. Her eyes flashed at me in the

mirror, twin black coals of anger. "Veronica, what exactly were you doing with those boys?" she demanded.

"Playing in the rain!" I said. "What's wrong with that?"

"What's *wrong* with that?" Elsa's voice grew shrill as she drove away from the Rec Center, and even Bella shrank back in her seat. "You told me you were going to a dance, and instead, you spent the evening *playing* with some *boys*!" She turned to me at a red light. Her eyes burned into mine. "That makes you a liar and a slut."

The words struck me harder than her fist would've. I sat bewildered in the back seat.

"Only sluts do what you girls did tonight," Elsa said. "Bella, I am forced to tell your mother about this. And Veronica, you are grounded for two weeks."

"Grounded?" I cried. "But we were only walking around!" I'd never been grounded before. Mother believed in talking to me when I'd done something bad. I wondered if Elsa would take away my books for two weeks, since I didn't watch television or talk on the phone.

Elsa pulled up in front of Bella's house. Bella got out of the car and didn't say anything to me. She looked like her brother's orange cat, the time Travis had accidentally turned the sprinklers on it. "Thank you for driving me home," she said stiffly to Elsa. She turned to walk up the driveway.

"I'm sorry, Bella, but I have to tell your mother about this," Elsa said. She got out of the car, and they walked up the driveway together. Mrs. DelGrosso met them at the door. Even though it was still raining, I rolled down the window to hear better.

"Tina, I think you should know that Bella and Veronica didn't go to the dance," Elsa said. "I found them out behind the Center with two boys."

Mrs. DelGrosso chuckled, the sound almost like a growl. "Well, I was never big on those dances, either, if you know what I mean."

I could see Elsa's jaw tighten in the light from the porch lamp. "But they were playing around in the dark with *boys* like a couple of street-walkers. I've informed Veronica that this is completely inappropriate behavior, and I'm grounding her for two weeks."

"You can ground me, too," Bella said to her mother. For a moment, I felt happy, thinking she'd said it out of loyalty to me, her only friend. But then she moved closer to Elsa, and I heard her say, "I'm really sorry, Elsa. It was Ronnie's idea."

Mrs. DelGrosso looked long at Bella. Then she looked at Elsa. She reached up to straighten the purple scarf around her wig, and her tiny eyes narrowed. "I know my Bella is a good girl," she said clearly. "What you're saying seems pretty harsh to describe a bunch of kids having fun, and I'd . . . I'd appreciate you not saying mean things about my Bella."

Elsa stared at Mrs. DelGrosso. Mrs. DelGrosso gave one nervous chuckle but stared right back. Bella ran inside, slamming the door behind her.

"Well, Tina," Elsa said finally. "I didn't realize how lax you were in your discipline. I'll have to reconsider my choice of baby-sitters the next time I need one." She turned and walked to the car. "You will not play with Bella ever again," she told me when we got home. "I don't want her in this house."

Saturday afternoon, Daddy knocked on my door. "Hi, Ronnie," he said, sitting down on the edge of my bed. I looked up from my book and felt my shoulders tense. I waited for him to yell at me about last night. Instead, he picked up a blue stuffed rabbit Mother had made for me years ago and began playing with its floppy white ears, looking embarrassed. "The mail just came," he said. "Elsa says you won a writing contest."

I bit my lip and stared down at my book. *It's too late*— I thought— *Now Elsa knows about the "Mother of the Year" contest, and she'll tell Mother.*

"It means a lot to Elsa that you wrote about her," Daddy said.

I scowled. "It doesn't seem like it."

"Look Ronnie," Daddy said, "Elsa means well. She's just in a very difficult position, learning how to be your mother. Last night . . . "

He paused, and I wondered if he was going to tell me that I couldn't go to Mother's tonight with Katie and Tim. It was Spring Vacation next week, and we were supposed to spend five days with Mother, but maybe "grounded" meant I'd have to stay home. Daddy tied my rabbit's ears into a bow at the top of its head. He smiled, then gave the rabbit a little shake. "About last night . . . I think Elsa overreacted a little."

"She called me a slut," I said.

Daddy chewed on one knuckle and looked out my window at our old neighbor bent over his fish tank. "Look, Ronnie. I believe you were just hanging out with those boys and that there was no . . . uh, foul play. Elsa knows that. She's just trying to protect you. You know, she was raised in a pretty strict British household."

I shrugged. "She said I couldn't see Bella again."

Daddy stood up. "I think we both know she didn't mean that. Anyhow, I just wanted you to know that *I* think you're a good girl."

"Thanks," I said. I remembered Daniel's breath warm against my cheek when he'd said I looked pretty. I hadn't felt like a good girl just then. I'd wanted Daniel to kiss me.

"Where did you find this rabbit?" Daddy asked.

"In a box somewhere," I said vaguely. I took the rabbit from him and unknotted its ears. I hoped he wouldn't remember that the rabbit had been in the box labeled "Maggie" that sat in a dark corner of the garage. I'd smuggled the whole box into Mother's bus the last time she'd picked us up.

Daddy reached over and patted my shoulder. "By the way," he said on his way out the door, "Elsa and I have decided to go down to San Diego for the week. We're leaving tonight before your mother gets here, so Elsa'll have to dig up a baby-sitter somewhere." He winked at me and left.

As it turned out, Elsa couldn't find another baby-sitter on such short notice, so Mrs. DelGrosso and Bella walked over. Mrs. DelGrosso stood in the hallway not speaking to Elsa, and Bella stood there not speaking to me, so I was glad Daddy kissed us all quickly and whisked Elsa out the door. She didn't mention anything about the "Mother of the Year" contest before she left. I hoped she'd refuse to pose for the picture in the local newspaper, so that no one would ever have to know that I'd won.

Bella and I were eating pizza and not talking to each other when Mother knocked at the door. Katie ran to answer it. She led Mother into the kitchen.

"This is my mother," she told Mrs. DelGrosso.

"Nice to meet you," Mother said, laughing as Tim almost knocked her down from behind with a hug.

Mother put out her hand. Mrs. DelGrosso shook it for half a second, then wiped her hand on her polyester pants. "I guess you want the kids," she muttered. "Mrs. Davis looked so nice when they left. Can you believe he took her to San Diego for the whole week? She says they stay in the nicest hotels and eat in expensive restaurants when they go out. They make a lovely couple, don't they, Bella?"

Bella hadn't taken her eyes off Mother since she walked in. I could tell she was surprised by the way Mother looked. Mother wasn't fat, but she wasn't thin like Elsa. She was rather short and not the least bit elegant. She wore shorts and a faded green sweatshirt, and her nose was sunburnt. Tim and Katie clung to her hands. Mother smiled at me.

"Is this *the* Bella, Ronnie?"

"Yeah," I said. "Bella, this is my mom."

Bella stared at Mother through narrowed green eyes. That particular look of Bella's always made me feel like I'd done something so stupid that I'd never be able to hold my head up again. But Mother held hers up and met Bella's hostile eyes with an angry look I'd never seen her direct toward a kid. I only saw it for a moment. Then she turned and cuddled Tim to her side. "Ready to go, kids? I heard the Easter Bunny might be bringing baby bunnies next week."

"Wanna brown one, like Peter Rabbit," Tim said.

Mother glanced out the back door, where King and Sweetie stood on guard watching us all through the glass. "Who's taking care of the dogs?" she asked me.

"We'll come over to feed the dogs twice a day," Mrs. DelGrosso said to me. "Your dad should've left you all here. I could've stayed with you."

I didn't know what to say. Mrs. DelGrosso was being so rude. I knew I wasn't supposed to talk back to adults, but I didn't want to talk back to Mrs. DelGrosso anyway. I wanted to kick her.

"Time to go," Mother said, steering us all out the door.

Mrs. DelGrosso and Bella walked out with us. They watched us get into the red Volkswagen bus.

"I want the front seat first!" Katie wailed as Tim ducked ahead of her and sat down. Mother got them straightened out. She was getting in the car herself when Bella walked over.

"Wow," she said to Mother, her voice falsely sweet. "When Ronnie won the 'Mother of the Year' contest, I was sure Elsa was her *real* mother, cause she wrote such nice things about her. But of course, she wouldn't be allowed to write about *you*."

I froze in the back seat. My body went rigid, and I could barely breathe. Katie turned around to look at me. Tim drummed on the dashboard with his hands. "Wanna see bunnies!" he chanted.

"Well . . . I guess we'll see you later," Mother said to Bella and Mrs. DelGrosso. Neither of them said anything more to her. After a moment, she started the car. She drove down the street past them and turned the corner. "Your friend's a little different from what I'd expected, Ronnie," Mother said quietly, her eyes on the road. "You told me she was a nice girl."

"Not really," I said miserably. "She's not nice at all."

Chapter 7

"What's this about a 'Mother of the Year' contest?" Mother asked quietly.

We were on the freeway now, moving away from Torrance. I twisted a strand of my hair around and around one finger. "It's nothing," I mumbled behind Mother, glad I'd lost the battle for the front seat to Katie. "It was just some stupid writing assignment Mrs. Ellis had us do."

"Ronnie won!" Katie said. "Lots of people entered, even adults, but Ronnie won out of everyone. Bella told me."

"You wrote about your father's new wife?" Mother's voice was so low that I could barely hear her over the freeway traffic.

"I had to," I said tearfully. "Mrs. Ellis said we had to write about the mother we live with."

"But Elsa is not your mother," Mother said.

"I know."

I didn't blame her for being angry with me. I knew that no matter what Mrs. Ellis had said, I'd made a mistake writing about Elsa . . . Elsa who had called me a slut.

I wished I had been brave enough to explain to Mrs. Ellis that the only mother I had lived in Carpinteria, and I would write about her or not write an essay at all.

"I'm sorry," I said from the back seat. I tried to catch Mother's eye in the rear view mirror, but she was concentrating grimly on a green sports car weaving in and out of traffic in front of us.

The drive back to Carpinteria felt longer than usual. We stopped halfway at McDonalds for hot fudge sundaes and to switch seats, but I didn't remind Tim that it was my turn to sit in front. Instead, I leaned forward and helped him scrape the nuts off his sundae.

"Hate nuts!" he muttered. We were both surprised that Mother had not told the drive-thru man to leave the nuts off of one sundae. She always remembered, because Katie called Tim "Timothy-No-Nuts." I knew she must be really mad at me if she forgot about that.

Ms. Whitney and her kids weren't at the house when we got to Carpinteria. I helped Tim carry his backpack and a stack of coloring books through the empty garage bedroom and upstairs.

"Where's Ms. Whitney?" Katie asked. "She told me she'd teach me to strike a match on my teeth next time I was here."

"I don't know where she is, and I don't much care," Mother said shortly. She struggled to open a package of graham crackers in the kitchen, and finally stalked over to a desk in the corner of the living room and dug around the newspapers and pictures until she found a pair of scissors. She cut the package open and dumped the graham crackers on a plate. "Also, I thought it would be nice if she had her bedroom back, so tonight, let's have a slumber party in the living room," she announced.

Mother's two pillows— one for under her head, and the floppy blue one she put over her head to shut out light— already lay on the red velvet couch with her striped wool blanket. Tim and I spread sleeping bags across the floor, and Katie tossed all the pillows from the bedrooms at us. One pillow hit Tim right in the face. "Stop it, bitch!" he yelled.

Mother rushed in with a bag of marshmallows in one hand and stared at Tim. "What did you call your sister?" she demanded.

Katie poked me in the side with her elbow. "Did you hear what he said?" she giggled.

"Don't encourage him," Mother snapped. She glared at me. "Did you teach him that word?"

"No!" I said.

Mother's eyes narrowed at Katie, who swiftly turned her grin into a grimace of concern. "I heard Daddy call Elsa that word last week," she said. "Maybe Tim heard it, too."

Mother brushed her bangs back off her forehead and sighed. "Ronnie, go get four wire hangers out of your closet for marshmallows," she said. "Katie, you and Tim can put logs in the fireplace, but I'll light the match." She paused on her way back to the kitchen. She picked up Ms. Whitney's pillow in its red plaid pillowcase and stood looking down at it until Katie said, "Are you okay, Mommy?"

Mother nodded and walked off to put the pillow back in Ms. Whitney's bedroom.

We roasted almost the whole bag of marshmallows over the living room fire— burnt for Tim and me, Katie's and Mother's a patient golden-brown— and went to bed with our hands and mouths all sticky because Mother forgot to make us wash them.

I had never prayed before, but that night, listening to Mother sighing in her sleep, I tried to pray to someone. Maybe I prayed to Grandma Davis' God, or maybe I prayed to something else entirely. I listened to the low crash of waves breaking on the beach and to the sad, sad call of the foghorn, and I prayed that Mother would know how sorry I was for writing about Elsa for the "Mother of the Year" contest.

The next day, Mother was her usual cheerful self. She made a quick batch of pancakes and told us to get dressed, because we were going for a ride. I walked past Ms. Whitney's door on the way to the bathroom and peeked in. Her bed was still made, but I already knew that she hadn't come home last night because she would've tripped over all of us sleeping spread out between the couches on the living room floor.

We piled into the Volkswagen bus, and Mother drove away from the beach, toward the mountains. She had packed a picnic basket and piled a stack of blue jeans and jackets between Katie and me in the back seat. We drove for a long time, past ranches full of orange and avocado trees, and then past green fields bordered by hills that gave way to a purplish-green mountain range on all sides of us. Finally, the bus chugged down a mountain and we saw streets and houses again. At a red light, Mother turned to us, her face bright with excitement.

"I bought a house," she announced.

"Cool!" Katie cried. "Where?"

"In the town we're in now. It's called Santa Paula." We looked around at the tiny grocery store and at the barbershop with a red and white pole outside. We passed a railroad station that looked as if it should be crowded with women in long dresses and men with canes and curly, waxed mustaches. An old-fashioned black steam engine stood in back of the station. Santa Paula looked like a town out of the *Little House on the Prairie* books.

"Way to go, Mom!" Tim said.   Mother's blue eyes sparkled.

Relief rushed through me. *Mother couldn't be this happy if she were still mad about the contest*— I thought.

The light turned green. We passed past more groves of orange trees that sweetened the dry air and hid farmhouses behind their bright leaves.

"The newspaper promoted me to features editor last month," Mother told us. "And your grandma helped out quite a bit, too. I've never lived alone before," she added. "I married a boy right out of high school, and then I met your father."

I hated the way she said "your father," as if it were our fault that he was still part of her life, but I didn't say anything. Mother drove down a road lined with houses and fields of corn. She stopped in front of a small green house with a ragged lawn. A tire swing dangled from the oak tree in the front yard.

"This is it," Mother said, pointing to a real estate sign with another sign nailed diagonally over it that said "Sold" in big black letters.

"Can we see it?" Katie was already halfway out of the bus.

"Be careful," Mother cautioned, taking hold of Tim's hand. "This is Santa Paula's main street, and it's also a highway. Cars go really fast." She led us up to the front porch and fit a key into the lock, then swung open the door and grinned. "Ta-da! Welcome home!"

We ran through all the rooms, taking off our shoes to slide on the scratched hardwood floors in our socks.

Mother lifted up the dirty, heavy windowpanes, flooding the stuffy house with orange-scented air.

"Can we go outside?" I asked. My voice echoed in the empty hallway.

Mother led us through a blue and white tiled kitchen to the back door. "This is the first house I've ever bought, and I bought it for the backyard," she said.

The yard was enormous. We stepped into a vegetable garden bordered by a fence of crossed sticks. "The last owners left this for me," Mother said. "There's some lettuce and carrots, but we can plant corn and tomatoes— anything we want." Further on in the dirt yard, a big box stood on two wooden saw horses, covered with a sheet. Mother looked at the box and then at us, but we all three ran over to inspect a large, walk-in chicken coop. The coop was a tall, strong rectangle of chicken wire stapled to a wood frame. A long box sat at the far end of the coop, with holes just big enough for hens to climb in and lay eggs.

"Where're the chickens?" Katie wanted to know.

"We'll have to buy some," Mother said. "There's a feed store down the road." Tim gathered up a handful of white feathers from the ground and ran around making clucking noises. I looked past the coop and down to a dry creek bed full of stones. Mother's yard didn't end like normal yards do, with a fence or a wall. It just ran down into the creek bed and up into low mountains that were green and brown, covered with brush. *Chaparral*— I thought, remembering Sixth Grade Nature Camp with Dolores and Trisha back in Newbury Park last year.

Mother kept glancing at the sheet-covered box. I nudged Tim. "Go look under that sheet," I said.

Tim ran with his funny, bow-legged stride over to the box and peeked under the sheet. He jumped back, startled. "Bunnies?"

Katie and I rushed over and yanked off the sheet. Three baby rabbits— two light brown and one black and white— twitched their triangle noses at us from a wire hutch.

"The Easter Bunny came early," Mother said. "Now let's see . . . he told me the big brown rabbit is for Katie, the little one is Tim's, and Ronnie gets the black and white one." She slid the door open and handed Katie and me each a bunny. Mine was so small that he fit into one of my hands. I rubbed my cheek against his soft fur. He kicked at me with surprisingly strong hind legs. I sat down, setting him on the dirt with my hand on his back.

"I'm gonna call him Frisky," I said.

"Mine's name is Mopsy," Katie said. Her brown bunny was bigger than mine, and it blinked quietly in her arms. Mother held the smaller brown bunny so Tim could pet it. He stroked its back and smiled his most delighted smile.

"Name iss Morris," he said.

We sat in the backyard for a long time, playing with our bunnies. Mother brought out the picnic basket and a blanket, and we ate and watched the rabbits gnawing on carrot sticks. Tim tried to copy their fast chewing, but he bit his tongue.

"Poor bunny," he said, patting his own head.

"This is lots bigger than Daddy's yard," Katie observed with her mouth full of angel food cake. An orange and black butterfly sailed by her nose and disappeared into the waving green leaves of the cornfield next door.

I could walk across the backyard in Torrance in just seven steps— eight, and I'd run into the red brick wall that separated us from the neighbors behind us. At night, I'd go outside and try to look for stars, but some of the stores in Torrance never closed. The lights from the buildings were so bright that the sky always looked as though it were almost daytime on the horizon. If I sat out in the grass long enough, I could see just three stars in a straight, dim line, and if I put my hands over my ears, the hum of freeway traffic sounded almost like the ocean, but it wasn't the same as being out in the country.

"I love your new house," I said, snuggling up to Mother with Frisky in my arms.

"I knew you would," she replied. We all sat quietly a

while longer, then Katie and Tim took their rabbits inside the chicken coop to play. Mother lowered her voice and said, "I'm working on getting you kids back. The court system is very . . . slow, but my owning a house now should count for a lot."

She didn't say anything else about the "Mother of the Year" contest. I decided that my prayer had worked.

Ms. Whitney still wasn't home when we got back to Carpinteria. Katie looked disappointed. "Where *is* she?" she demanded.

"She has a new girlfriend," Mother said briefly, taking out a pack of ground turkey to thaw.

So Mother does know about Ms. Whitney being a lesbian— I said to myself.

"Oh," Katie said. "Can I call Maria?"

Katie doesn't get it— I thought— *I'll bet she doesn't even know what the word lesbian means.*

I'd almost forgotten about that day Sage had told me about her mother. Now that I remembered, I wanted to ask Mother what it was like to live with a lesbian. I wondered if Ms. Whitney had ever made a pass at Mother. Or maybe lesbians didn't make passes. Maybe they had a secret hand signal or something to let women know they were interested. *That must be why Mother's moving—* I thought— *Ms. Whitney must've given her a secret hand signal or something.*

Katie came back into the kitchen dismayed because Maria had another girl over to spend the night. Mother spent a long time explaining to her that some people were perfectly happy flitting around from friend to friend without making a commitment, while other, nicer people had just one or two close friends that they loved and stayed loyal to, and which type of person would Katie rather be friends with?

The months between Easter break and summer vacation passed quickly. I bought a blank notebook, and I began to write poetry in it. Sometimes, I would copy a poem for Mrs. Ellis. She would put it carefully into her roll book, saying, "Someday you'll be famous, and I'll be able to pull out these poems and tell everyone that I was your teacher."

I still walked the long way on the railroad tracks to school, but I was on time for homeroom every day now. I didn't see Bella, but I didn't miss her. Julia Goldberg invited me to her house twice to bake cookies and watch TV, and a group of girls who were putting together the seventh grade pages in the yearbook asked if I'd help them with the writing part.

Two weeks before school was over, Mrs. Ellis passed out yellow fliers in homeroom. "Cross Country Tryouts— June 10th," I read.

"Coach Lopez from the high school wants to coach an eighth grade team at our junior high to prepare them for the high school cross country team," Mrs. Ellis explained.

I studied the flier all the way home from school, remembering how I loved to run barefoot on the beach in Carpinteria. I taped the flier to the inside of my bedroom door.

"I think I'm gonna try out for the cross-country team at school," I told Daddy at dinner.

"Good," he said, leaning over to butter Tim's roll. "Elsa, pass me another pork chop."

On June 10th, I changed into shorts and a T-shirt in the bathroom after school and walked out to the baseball field, where our P.E. teacher, Ms. Lombard, was standing with a whistle. She had us line up together by the fence, then blew one shrill blast on her whistle for attention. I was glad to see that I wasn't the only girl trying out— there were nine girls and a lot of boys. Everyone was talking and laughing.

"You'll run around the perimeter of this field four times," Ms. Lombard explained. She pulled her baseball cap down further over her sunburnt face. "Coach Lopez had to go to a track meet today, but he wants me to find him six boys and six girls from our school. I'll choose the fastest." She pushed a button on her stopwatch. "When I say go, go!" she cried. "*Go!*"

I took off with the group of kids. My sneakers slapped against the wet, slippery grass. I forced my breathing into a synchronized rhythm with my pounding feet. I began to lose track of who was ahead of me and who was behind— after the first lap, kids ran spread out all over the edges of the field, and some of them walked, clutching their sides. My ponytail loosened and fell out of the rubber band so that my hair flew out behind me. I couldn't stop a smile from spreading across my face as I ran. Suddenly, I wanted to make the cross-country team more than anything in the world.

Ms. Lombard blew her whistle. "Okay, that's it!" She wrote busily on a clipboard. "I'll get together with Coach Lopez. We'll call you at home as soon as we've made up the team list."

I grabbed my backpack and kept jogging right off the field towards home. Halfway down the railroad tracks, I saw Bella and a tall, blond girl. Both of them wore the same plaid school skirts, pulled up as far as they could go without showing any underwear.

"Well, if it isn't Little Miss Lesbo Lover," Bella said loudly.

I ignored her and kept running down the tracks. A train whistle sounded in the distance. Over it, I could hear Bella yelling to the other girl. "That's the girl I told you about, the one whose mom is so *disgusting!*"

The next morning, as I slid into my seat in homeroom, someone behind me giggled, and a spitball hit me in the back of the head. Carefully, I felt in front of me to make sure I'd zipped my denim shorts up. Then I looked down at my desk. Someone had carved out the words "Lesbo Lover" in the wood. I looked over toward Daniel's desk. He was absent. I took out my grammar book and pretended not to have noticed my desk, but my mind spun in circles, trying to figure out how Bella had gotten into my classroom.

And how did she know which one was my desk— I wondered.

At lunch, I walked over to sit with the group of girls who were working on the yearbook pages. They all picked up their lunches and moved to another table.

"I think it's contagious," I heard one girl say to another, nodding in my direction.

I couldn't eat. I threw Elsa's turkey sandwich into the trash can and sat out on the field by myself under a tree. I wished I were brave enough to go for a run right there in front of all the kids.

I spotted Julia Goldberg walking across the street from her house. She knelt down by the backstop to tie her shoe, and I walked over to her. "Hi, Julia!" I said.

She blinked at me. At first, she stood up as if she were going to walk away. Then she paused. "Hi, Ronnie," she said, looking at the ground. "My mother says we're not allowed to be friends anymore."

"Why not?" I asked, bewildered.

"Because of your mom."

"What *about* my mom?" I cried.

Julia lowered her voice. "At first, I thought it was just a rumor," she said. "But then I told my mom, and she called that woman who worked with your mom on your old Girl Scout troop, and she said it was true."

"Said *what* was true?" I demanded, nearly in tears.

"That your mother's . . . well . . . gay," Julia said.

I clenched my fists. "You take that back!" I yelled. "She is not!"

Then Julia did walk away from me. "Get a clue, Veronica," she said over her shoulder.

I ran after her and grabbed her by one of her black curls. "I said *take it back!*"

"How can I, if it's true," she said.

I hit her. I'd never hit anyone in my life, but suddenly, my hand shot out, and I slapped her right across her red cheek. It turned even redder, and her eyes filled with tears. "They're right!" she yelled and pushed me down onto the gravel. "You *are* a lesbo lover!"

I stood up unsteadily. A crowd of kids surrounded us. They began to chant. "Lesbo lover! Lesbo lover!" I looked around wildly. Bella had done this, and no matter what I made up to tell about her, she'd make up something worse about me, a hundred times worse, because she was a hundred times meaner and smarter than I was.

I broke through the group of kids and ran home sobbing. Elsa's white car wasn't in the driveway. I sat on the back porch with King and Sweetie and sobbed into King's white and gold coat. Sweetie licked at my knee with her soft tongue. I looked down to find a thin line of blood trickling from my knee all the way down to my ankle. I went into the kitchen and washed off the blood and gravel from the school playground and stuck three Band-Aids over the cuts.

The kids called me "Lesbo Lover" all the rest of the school week, and they picked me last for kickball during P.E. every day. Someone drew a picture on my backpack of two girls kissing. No matter how hard I scrubbed at it with paper towels from the bathroom, the black ink wouldn't come off. *Now I'll have to ask Elsa for a new backpack for next year—* I thought, stuffing my old one far down into the trash can on the last day of school.

I didn't even want to think about returning to Torrance once we got into Mother's bus the first Friday evening of summer vacation.

"Let's celebrate!" she said when we got to her new house in Santa Paula. She opened the freezer and took out three different kinds of ice cream. She arranged the cartons on a long wooden table next to jars of hot fudge, caramel, and cherries. "We have a whole month together!"

It was hard not to remind her that up until last November, we'd had a whole life together.

We made our sundaes and went out on the back porch to eat them. Molly and Dolly, the two gray sister cats Mother had adopted from the Humane Society, rubbed against our ankles and purred. Katie took her bowl of ice cream over to the chicken coop to listen to the clucking of the new chickens. Stars began to appear one by one above the mountains, and I saw my three stars from Daddy's backyard in a bright line among the others. A low whir of sound, like a metallic humming, filled the air.

"What's that noise?" Katie asked, running back to us.

"Cicadas. They're a kind of insect," Mother said. "The frogs'll be out soon."

Right when she said that, a frog croaked from the garden, and then they all started up. The frogs and cicadas sounded like a fairy orchestra in the oak trees and bushes. For the first time in a week, I felt happy. "It's so weird to be in one place, then in two hours, to be in a totally different place," I said.

Mother didn't answer. I knew she didn't understand what I was talking about— she couldn't comprehend my fear that I might close my eyes and open them again to find myself sitting alone in Daddy's backyard on the prickly grass instead of with Mother on the wooden porch in Santa Paula. It was the first time I'd ever felt that Mother didn't understand me, and I felt sad beneath my happiness at getting to be with her for a month.

"Let's put on our pajamas and get out the coloring books," Mother said when the night got so black that we couldn't see the rabbits in their hutch.

Katie and I had a bedroom off at the back of the house with a window looking out toward the mountains. A bookshelf stood against one wall, full of toys and books. Beside that was a box of dress-up clothes— old clothes that Mother didn't wear anymore and discarded costumes from Grandma Hammond's shop. Our mattresses lay on the floor, made up with sheets and bedspreads. We had each arranged our stuffed animals around our beds. Katie flopped down on her low bed and draped her white blanket across her face.

"I *love* this room," she said, hugging Seymour to her chest.

We piled into Mother's king-sized bed with coloring books and crayons and grew quiet, concentrating on the pages in front of us. I thought about the way we colored, each with our own style. Tim still scribbled carelessly over the pictures, and Mother bought him ninety-nine cent coloring books because he could fill one a night. Katie was just past the scribbling stage. Every time she'd color out of the thick black lines, she'd look at us sideways. Then Mother would say, "Katie, that's a beautiful picture you've colored."

Mother, Katie, and I had adult coloring books with detailed black and white pictures on one side of the page and a history of fish or cowboys or hot air balloons on the other side. I tried to copy Mother's clean, neat coloring. First, she'd go over the black line with a crayon several times, and then she'd fill in the picture with a lighter color. Her strokes were always smooth and even. I could never get my pictures to look like hers.

All that month, we went to bed in stages— first Tim, pouting as Mother helped him into his pajamas. "*Not* sleepy," he'd protest, yawning so wide that Katie was worried he'd swallow his head. He said this a few times, loud enough for us to hear him from his bedroom, and then fell asleep instantly, sitting doubled over his pillow.

Katie went to bed next. She got to stay up half an hour later than Tim. We never knew how Mother figured this, since there wasn't a clock in her bedroom. Mother would simply say, "Bedtime," when Katie had finished her picture. Katie would pick up another crayon, pretending that it wasn't finished after all, or sometimes she'd ask Mother a question, hoping to earn herself another half hour of staying awake.

"Mother, why do bunnies have six or eight babies at a time, but humans usually have only one?" she asked once.

That particular question stumped Mother. She thought a while, then said, "I'm going to have to buy you a set of encyclopedias. Just because I'm a mother doesn't mean I know everything."

I was allowed to stay up as late as I wanted, because I was the oldest. I sat propped up on two pillows beside Mother and read the books she'd had when she was a girl. They had frayed cloth covers and names like *Bunny Brown and his Sister Sue*. They were illustrated with shiny pictures of chubby children with dimples and golden curls.

Mother read textbooks on Art History and

Literature, studying for classes she'd enrolled in next semester at the community college. "School keeps me busy at night," she told me, "so I don't think so much."

I knew what she meant about not wanting to think. In the middle of the night, if I thought too much about all that had happened to my family in the last year, I grew terrified and couldn't sleep for wondering what else might change or go wrong.

The first week we stayed with Mother, I missed the crash of the ocean in Carpinteria. Instead, I woke up to a yapping sound across the creek bed. One night, the sound came loud and close to the window. Katie sat up in bed and began to cry. Sharp voices echoed everywhere, bouncing off the hills. Katie pulled Seymour over her head and peeked out at me. "What *is* that, Ronnie?" she whispered.

Mother came in with Tim, who looked excited to be awake in the middle of the night. "Surprise!" he beamed. "Iss me!"

"D'you girls hear the coyotes?" Mother said. "They're having a midnight snack."

"What're coyotes?" Katie whimpered.

"They're sort of like wild dogs," Mother said. "They sleep during the day and wake up at night to have dinner and play."

I was glad Molly and Dolly were inside Mother's garage-office curled up on a piece of carpet. "Will the coyotes eat the rabbits?" I asked.

Mother sat down on Katie's mattress. Tim collapsed beside me and put one arm around my neck. "They're too scared to come into the yard," Mother said.

Katie sniffled. "They sound like they're laughing in a mean way."

"No, they just like to talk."

"Like my sisters," Tim said through a yawn. Mother and I laughed. We sat in the moonlit room listening to the coyotes down in the creek bed for a long time. I began to think they sounded almost pretty. After a while, their yapping faded away into the mountains, and Katie lay down and went back to sleep. Tim fell asleep, too, with his head heavy against my shoulder.

Mother came over and picked him up. "G'night, Ronnie," she whispered. She left the door cracked open so that a bright finger of light from the hall stretched across the room.

Every morning in Santa Paula, I woke up to the crowing of the rooster next door and to the sharp click of Mother's electric typewriter. The sky shone a soft gray through the bedroom curtains. Mother, the rooster, and I seemed to be the only ones awake in the whole world.

I never went back to sleep in those early summer mornings. If Mother was awake, then I wanted to be awake, too. I tiptoed out of the bedroom and shut the door. If Katie woke up, the magic of the morning would be over instantly.

The wood floors felt cold and smooth against my bare feet. I walked down the hall past the kitchen to Mother's office in the garage. The people who owned the house before her had cut windows into the garage walls and tacked strips of red carpet over the cement ground. Mother had her desk and typewriter against one wall, below a big bulletin board full of newspaper clippings. Some of the clippings said "By Maggie Hammond, Staff Writer" at the top.

"Good morning," I'd say. Then Mother would stop typing and hug me.

"Good morning, honey. Go make yourself some hot chocolate. And would you make me some coffee? There's instant beside the cocoa."

I felt important making Mother's morning coffee. Sometimes I added cinnamon to it, and sometimes chocolate chips. While I waited for the water to boil, I pulled back the curtains. Mother's kitchen window stood directly opposite our neighbors' kitchen window. In the dim, early mornings, I saw our neighbors— an old Latino man and woman with white hair— moving around their kitchen, making coffee and getting ready for the day. One morning, the woman pulled back her curtains just as I was pulling ours back. She waved at me, and I waved back, the early morning like a secret between us.

"Wait just a minute," Mother would say when I came back to the garage with the steaming mugs. She would finish typing a sentence, and then she'd sip her coffee and nod. "That's delicious, Ronnie. Let's go out and check the garden."

I loved our morning walks around the yard more than any other part of the day. The little, cold pebbles stung my bare feet as we walked. We stepped carefully over the crossed sticks and bent down to inspect the rows of tiny, lacy carrot tops and yellow wax beans dangling from low bushes.

"Somebody's been at the lettuce," Mother would say, or "Those stupid snails got a whole row of carrots," but she refused to spray poison on the plants. Instead, she counted the number of snails and slugs that had drowned overnight in her tin pie pans full of beer. "They died happy," she'd assure me, dumping the pans on top of the compost pile. "What d'you think about trying to grow pumpkins for Halloween?"

I remembered Halloween last year, and how I didn't dress up, but watched a dumb movie with Elsa's ex-step-daughter, Donna. I didn't know if we'd be with Mother this year at Halloween, but I closed my mind to any thought of Torrance. "I think we should plant pumpkins," I said firmly.

After we inspected the garden, we filled the rabbits' water bottle and poured grayish-green pellets into their food dishes. The rabbits twitched their noses at us and swiped at the silver ball on the end of the water bottle with quick pink tongues.   Molly and Dolly walked purring between our legs, nearly tripping us on our way to the chicken coop.

Mother unlatched the door to the coop and went in to scatter grain over the ground. The hens poked their heads out of their nesting box, clucking nervously.

"G'morning, girls," Mother greeted them. "Ready for breakfast?" The hens refused to come out until she walked out of the coop and latched the door behind her. As we walked away, they rushed over to the grain in a blur of white feathers and red feathers from the one small chicken called a Rhode Island Red.

By the time Mother and I had fed the cats twin bowls of Friskies, the sun had risen over the mountains. If there were clouds, they were tinted a pale pink that turned swiftly to orange in the deepening blue sky.

"The Native Americans used all those plants on the hills for food and medicine," Mother told me one morning, pointing up at the green and brown chaparral. "There's a bush called chemise, which is good for aches and pains, and all sorts of sages grow up there. They're good for everything. And all those oak trees for acorn bread."

I thought about running away from Daddy's house to live in the mountains across from Mother. I'd eat plants and acorns, and I'd learn to move silently, like a deer. No one, not even Mother, would know I was there, but I would be close to her. Then I remembered the coyotes.

Up on the wooden fence between our neighbors' yard and ours, the rooster crowed almost in my ear. He strutted red and yellow across the fence boards, crowing at our hens. "He's asking them for a date," Mother said.

I giggled, and the old man I'd seen in the kitchen across from ours poked his head up over the fence. "Morning, Maggie. That one of your girls?"

"This is my oldest daughter, Veronica," Mother said. "Ronnie, this is Uncle George."

Uncle George looked as if he were at least eighty years old. He was a big, dark-skinned man with a white mustache that drooped down both sides of his mouth. He wore a wide straw hat pulled down low over his face. When Mother introduced us, he chuckled under his mustache and the lines around his eyes crinkled cheerfully. "Gotta go find those dang gophers," he said, waving his shovel above his head. "Don't mind sharing a little corn with 'em, but they're greedy little boogers."

"Why do you call him *Uncle* George?" I whispered to Mother as the man disappeared into the cornstalks. "You aren't related to him."

"Everyone in Santa Paula calls him that," Mother explained. "Uncle George and Aunt Danielita have lived in that house for sixty years. They know everyone and everyone knows them."

Afternoons in Santa Paula, the air hung hot and heavy like the inside of a canvas tent. It was not fun to play outside then. I lay on my bed and read. Katie hung around Mother's office, bored. Mother tried to persuade her to take a nap when she tucked Tim in, but Katie refused.

"All right, then," Mother would sigh. I knew she'd rather play with us than work, but she had to make payments on the new house. "Go take some money out of the coconut and walk down to the little store," she'd say. "*Carefully.*"

Mother had found the coconut at a garage sale. It was the actual hull of a coconut, but the darker brown "nut" was plastic, with a scalloped top. She kept spare change in the nut part. Every afternoon, Katie came to get me so I could help her count out dimes and nickels. "Forty cents each," I'd say, giving Katie her share.

We'd walk down to the store, clutching our money in sweaty palms. We stepped cautiously to the right of the white line running down the road, half-believing Mother when she said that if we set one foot to the left of it, we'd be smashed flat instantly like the dead, reeking possums we passed.

The store was four houses and a school away from Mother's house. The grammar school was small, like everything else in Santa Paula. The swings and slides glared at us from the shimmering blacktop of the schoolyard. I stared down at the white line as we walked by, not wanting to look at the school. *If we lived with Mother—* I thought— *Katie would go to this school, and then maybe it would feel friendly.* For now, it was grim and strange behind the black metal fence.

A fat, red-faced man owned the little store, or at least he was the only person Katie and I ever saw there. He sat on a high stool watching TV shows about cowboys. A fan whirred full-blast at his back. We never saw him get up from his stool, but once, when I bent down to inspect the lower candy rack, I saw him aim his thumb and forefinger at the TV and make a shooting motion.

It took Katie and me a long time to select our candy. I liked anything chocolate— Hershey bars, little packages of Oreos, and Tootsie Rolls. Katie liked Everlasting Gobstoppers and candy necklaces. But we both almost always settled on the colored sugar that came in three joined packets with a candy stick for dipping.

"Eighty cents even," the fat man said every time, guns cracking in the background. "Havva nice day, girls."

On the way back home, we each made a little tear in one of our packets and dipped our sticks in. Katie ate red first and I ate blue, because purple was the best flavor and had to be saved for last. We winced at the tart sweetness and compared colored tongues.

After the first week of staying with Mother, we knew all the people who lived between her house and the store. Our favorite neighbors were Uncle George and Aunt Danielita. Aunt Danielita sat in a cushioned chair on her shady front porch every afternoon and snapped beans, sliced apples, or husked corn. One day, a week after we came to stay with Mother, she called to us from her front porch.

"Hello, girls. Wanna come over and help me with these peas?"

Katie looked confused. "Who is that man?" she whispered.

"It's a woman," I whispered back as we walked up the porch steps.

Aunt Danielita wore men's overalls, several sizes too big, over a red and white checkered blouse. Her white hair stuck out under a man's felt hat, looking like she'd hacked it off with the knife Mother used to cut tomatoes.

"How d'you shell peas?" I asked, setting my packet of colored sugar carefully down in a pot of red geraniums.

Aunt Danielita got up and turned over two white

buckets. "Sit," she told Katie and me. She held up a shiny green pea pod. "Gouge one end of the pod with your fingernail and rip off the string," she demonstrated swiftly, "then pop the peas into a bowl."

Katie and I grabbed handfuls of pea pods and began shelling. It was tricky to pull off the string, especially since I'd bitten my nails down, but finally, I got the hang of it.

"Does your Mother like corn on the cob?" Aunt Danielita asked.

Katie nodded enthusiastically. "She loves it!"

"I'll send some over with you when you go. Take some peas, too." She dipped her wrinkled brown hand into the bowl of peas and swirled it around. "I love fresh peas, don't you?"

Katie wrinkled her nose. "Yuck."

"We don't really like them," I said politely.

"*Pues*, then you haven't had peas fresh from the vine. Here!"

I chewed the pea she offered me. It was sweet and tender, not at all like the mushy dark peas they served in the junior high school cafeteria in Torrance.

"They're good," I said, hoping Aunt Juanita hadn't seen Katie spit hers into her hand and drop it on the grass behind her.

"You can eat the pods, too," Aunt Juanita said. "Just make sure you get the strings off both sides."

Mother stuck her head over the fence. "There you are, girls. I thought you were roadkill. Hello, Aunt Juanita, how are you?"

Aunt Juanita got up and brushed the pea pods off her overalls. "*Bíen*, Maggie. Your girls have been a lot of help. I promised them some corn." She disappeared into the kitchen and returned with a paper bag full of corn.

"We can't eat this much," Mother protested. "Besides, Uncle George told me this is the first of your harvest."

"*Madre de Díos*, if there's one thing George and I have, it's corn," she chuckled. "My grandson's coming to visit in a day or so," she said to Katie, who still looked a little afraid of Aunt Juanita. "He's about your age. I'll send him over to play."

"Cool!" Katie grinned. I knew she needed someone her own age to play with, someone who didn't read all the time like I did. But all the same, I couldn't help feeling a little insulted.

Aunt Juanita's grandson came over the next day, carrying a grocery bag of yellow squash. Katie and I were trying to hang a tire swing in the backyard oak tree when he pushed through the corn stalks and walked through the gate.

"Hey!" he said shrilly, "which one of you's Katie?"

"Me," Katie said. She let go of the tire so that I almost fell out of the tree along with the rope. I dropped down to the hard ground, the bottoms of my feet stinging.

"Are you Aunt Juanita's grandson?" I asked.

"Yep. I'm Angel." *He looks like an angel—* I thought. He was small, with smooth brown skin and hair so black it had purple lights in it. He wore baggy blue shorts and a T-shirt with a picture of a skateboard on it. Even though I knew he was two or three years younger than me, my face got hot, and I wondered if my ponytail was crooked. He kicked at the tire lying on the ground with one sandaled foot.

"You guys trying to hang that?"

Katie nodded. Her blond hair curled in damp spirals around her face. "It's pretty heavy."

"No problem." Angel hoisted himself up into the tree. "Throw me the rope," he commanded. He pulled the tire up and tied the rope several times around the branch of the oak tree. "Try it!" he told Katie. She climbed into the tire. The swing held, and Angel jumped down and pushed her. Then she pushed him, giggling. Neither of them even spoke to me.

I wandered over and took my rabbit, Frisky, out of his hutch.

"Cool rabbit!" Angel ran over to pet Frisky.

"I saw a man in the library make a chicken play

dead yesterday," Katie said. "He flipped it over and snapped in front of its eyes until it went into a trance."

Angel narrowed his eyes at Frisky. "I bet I could make that ol' rabbit play dead."

I held Frisky tightly to me, one hand around his front paws. "Frisky and I are going inside," I said coldly.

"Oooh, she's mad," Angel said. He and Katie laughed and ran off toward the chicken coop.

One of Katie's and my favorite things to do that summer was to sit in the big coop and wait for the hens to lay eggs. There was something fascinating about the egg-laying process; after all, eggs being laid were a little like babies being born. We'd go out to the coop right after breakfast and sit patiently in the dirt. The hens eyed us nervously from their boxes and clucked to each other. If Katie and I sat still long enough, they'd begin the long, drawn-out clucking that we were sure signaled the coming of the egg. Outside, the dew dried on the cucumber vines. The sun rose smoking in the sky as we waited. Sweat trickled down our backs and beaded Katie's upper lip.

"Maybe the egg's stuck," she'd say finally. "I'll check." The hens squawked wildly as she lifted their behinds to look for eggs. After a while, I'd get bored and go read, but Katie sat in the coop for hours, talking to the hens and making up songs for them.

I watched Angel and Katie walk into the coop. Then I took Frisky inside with me and kept him in my room until Angel went home.

That night, we stretched out on Mother's bed with our coloring books. Katie asked, "Mother, what time was I born? Angel was born at nine in the morning on the ninth day of the ninth month."

Mother shook her head. "Honey, I can't remember that far back."

"Did I cry a lot?" Katie wanted to know.

Mother bent over to color a turtle turquoise. "No, you were my good baby. You slept most of the time after you were born. But your sister . . . " Mother glared playfully at me. "Your sister would not sleep more than an hour at a

time until she was two years old. And she cried constantly."
Katie giggled at this information.

"That's funny— it's the other way around now," I
said meanly. "She cries all the time."

Katie jabbed her elbow into my side, and my pink
crayon skidded across the page. "I'm not a crybaby, *you*
are!" she said.

"It's good to cry, " Mother said. "It's not healthy to
hold all those tears inside you." She smiled at me. "I
remember when you were little, Ronnie, you thought Katie
was *your* baby. You'd carry her around and dress her up,
and you wouldn't let anyone else touch her."

Mother's eyes grew soft, remembering, and I knew I
should feel close and loving towards Katie now that I'd
heard about the way I used to take care of her. But all I
wanted to do was smack her. I was still angry over the way
she and Angel had ignored me, like I was some big nerd
who didn't know how to have fun. The tire swing had been
my idea in the first place.

"I have your baby books around here somewhere,"
Mother said. "Should I try to find them?"

"Yeah!" Tim said. He'd been asleep over his coloring
book, but now he sat up, wide awake.

Mother dug through her dresser drawers for a
while, then handed us three books. Mine was tall and
white, with a picture of a stork carrying a baby on the front.
I opened it. On the first page, it said "To Maggie and
Zachary for recording the joyous first years of Veronica's
life." I flipped through the pages covered in Mother's loose,
round handwriting and found a plastic bag full of soft
brown hair.

"Your first haircut," Mother said over my shoulder.
"And there's the baby bracelet you wore in the hospital."

I examined the bracelet. My name and birthday
were typed neatly inside the plastic strip. I looked over at
Katie's yellow book with the duck on the front. She was
trying to feel her own curl of blond hair through the plastic
bag.

Tim's blue book didn't have a bag of hair. I was

about to ask where it was, but then I remembered. The first time Tim got a haircut, Mother took him to the barber's, hoping he could do something to hide the flat spot at the back of Tim's head. The barber had accidentally nicked Tim's ear with the scissors. Daddy yelled at Mother that night until she cried.

I leaned against Mother and thought about how this felt like family to me, all of us hanging out on her bed reading and coloring. When we went back to Torrence, we were a completely different sort of family with Daddy and Elsa. I liked *this* family— Mother and Katie and Tim and me— but now we could only be a family every other weekend and a month in the summer.

"I hate living with Elsa and Daddy," I told Mother after Tim and Katie had gone to bed. "It's like Daddy isn't even our father anymore. He leaves all the decisions to Elsa, and she's so critical. She had a fit once because she let me make brownies out of a box, and when I poured them into the pan, I hadn't stirred them enough and there was all this brownie powder at the bottom of the bowl. She said it'd be a long time before she let me cook again." I looked down at a picture of Bunny Brown making his trick dog jump through a hoop while Sister Sue clapped and laughed. "When can we move here with you?"

Mother put down her book. "I don't know," she said slowly. "The court is pretty much against it."

"But it's not fair!" I said. "We never even see Daddy!"

"I know, honey. But the court system isn't always fair." She ran her hand through her brown hair and looked away from me. "*Life* isn't always fair," she murmured.

I hated her simple answers, but I didn't say anything. I knew the real reason we weren't living with her was because I'd told the judge I wanted to live with Daddy. The memory of that day in court had been aching inside me for months. Tears rushed to my eyes as I remembered how Mother's shoulders had slumped when she heard the judge's decision. And suddenly, I was sobbing into the pillow.

Mother hugged me, and she began to cry, too. "Ronnie, it'll work out somehow. We're still a family."

"But not for real," I sobbed. "I'm so sorry about the . . . about the stupid 'Mother of the Year' contest, and, oh, Mother . . . " I looked up at her and it felt good to cry, good to confess. "When the judge asked me who I wanted to live with, I said I wanted to live with Daddy."

Mother nodded, then leaned over for a tissue and wiped my eyes. She looked into my face, and her own face was very serious. "Ronnie, that's not the reason I didn't get custody of you kids," she said. "Whatever you had said to that judge wouldn't have made a difference."

"It wouldn't have?" I sniffled.

"Honey, in almost *every* custody battle, the mother gets custody of the children. . . " she said quietly.

"So why didn't *you* get custody of us?" I demanded.

Mother fell silent, staring down at the open art book in her hands. Outside, the frogs and cicadas hummed. A single coyote yapped somewhere in the distance.

Finally, she looked at me. Her gaze was steady and strong, reminding me of the way she had looked that day in court before the elevator door had closed between us.

"I didn't get custody of you because I'm a lesbian," she said.

Chapter 8

Mother's quiet words seemed to silence the fairy orchestra of frogs and cicadas under her open bedroom window. For a moment, the whole world seemed to hold its breath, and then the long howl of a coyote tore across the night.

"You're a . . . a lesbian?" I repeated finally.

Mother clenched her hands together in her lap. The backs of her hands were scratched from replacing some of the worn-out chicken wire that covered the backyard coop. "I know I should've told you sooner," she said, "but I . . . I thought you had enough to handle already."

My mind raced backward to the first day she'd taken us to Ms. Whitney's house. She'd known where the spare key was— just reached for it up behind the porch light. Then my mind ran forward, tumbling over images of Mother in her underwear and T-shirt and Ms. Whitney with her freckled arms around her; Elsa telling Katie that Mother was "sick"; the disgust Grandma Davis had shown in Vermont; and Bella, who knew about my mother before I did and told my whole class.

I leapt up from Mother's bed and ran to the doorway, fighting back tears. "Bella . . . told all the kids. . . " I choked. "They called me names . . . I got into a *fight* because of you!" Suddenly, I was furious— so furious that I had to clutch at the doorway for support. "I can't believe you didn't tell me!" I cried. "Everyone, even *Mrs. DelGrosso*, knew before me!"

Mother sat up rigid on the bed with the sheet pulled up to her neck. "Ronnie, we need to talk about this," she said.

"No way!" I yelled. "I think it's disgusting!" I ran to my room and fell on the mattress, sobbing. For once, Mother didn't follow me.

Katie turned over on her bed and opened her eyes. "What's *your* problem?"

"You!" I muttered. But my problem wasn't Katie. It was Mother. My mother was a lesbian. I didn't want to believe it, but why would Mother lie about something as horrible as that?

I tossed and turned all night, falling asleep only to have nightmares. I dreamt that women crowded around my bed hugging and kissing, yelling "Lesbo Lover!" at me. All the women howled with laughter, and then one of them turned to me. It was Ms. Whitney, one hand around a beer which she held out to me with a cracked grin that split her face in two.

I woke up feeling like I hadn't slept at all. A bright shaft of sunlight shone through the curtains, lighting up Katie's empty bed. I tiptoed out to the kitchen to make myself some hot chocolate. Tim had the TV on in the living room. Through the window, I could see Mother and Katie walking through the garden. I studied Mother as she leaned over the corn stalks. I'd never thought about lesbians until Sage told me about Ms. Whitney. I'd seen gay men on TV— thin, handsome men like that swimmer from the Olympics who told everyone that he was HIV positive. I remembered that once, a woman tennis player who looked like a man was featured on the cover of Daddy's sports magazine. He called her "another one of those damned lesbians," and then he dropped the magazine into the trash.

It was easy to believe that the handsome swimmer and the tennis player— and even Ms. Whitney— were gay. But not my mother.

I stirred a packet of hot chocolate mix into my mug of hot water and walked into the living room. I sat down on the carpet next to Tim. "Want a drink?" I held out the mug to him.

"Like it cold," he said with his eyes fixed on the TV. I didn't recognize the cartoon— something about a big blue dog and a Martian. Whatever it was, it looked stupid.

I wandered into Mother's room and looked around. I wanted to find something to reassure me that she wasn't gay, that she was the same Mother she'd always been. She hadn't made her bed yet— the white striped blanket lay in a heap on the floor, and Molly and Dolly were curled up and purring in the folds. Pictures of Katie, Tim, and me hung on every wall except for one, which was covered by a big animal fur— a bear or a cow, I guess. The fur bothered me. Mother would never have had something like that hanging on her wall in her blue satin and lace bedroom in Newbury Park. *Maybe all lesbians have animal skins hanging on their walls—* I thought.

I grabbed my baby book off her nightstand and went into my room to read it. I really had been a bad baby, I discovered. Mother wrote that I used to cry all the time unless I was near her. I wondered if I'd known, even as a baby, that I'd get taken away from her.

Mother came to the door and stuck her head in. "Ronnie, I'm making waffles. How many do you want?"

Her eyes looked red and tired, as if she hadn't slept well either.

"I'm not hungry," I muttered, staring down at my baby book.

She walked across the room and began to open the curtains. Then she stopped, glanced at me, and walked out the door. I could tell that she didn't know what to say. Neither did I, so I just lay there pretending to read my baby book all morning. But inside, I kept remembering the way the kids at school had made fun of me, how they wouldn't go near me the whole last week of school, as if being a lesbian was contagious. Is *it contagious*— I wondered.

Katie and Angel burst into the bedroom. "Ronnie, we got one!" Katie cried, holding out a brown egg. "Look! It's still warm!"

Angel's being there must've brought Katie good luck in the chicken coop. I touched the egg. It was smooth and warm against my fingers.

"That just came out of a chicken's butt," I scoffed, turning away. "How gross." I hoped Angel realized that I was much older than he was, and that I didn't care what he and Katie did.

"It's like a baby. " Katie stroked the egg fondly.

Mother appeared in the doorway again.

"Look!" Katie cried, holding out the egg.

Mother examined it all over, as if it were the first time she'd ever seen an egg. "I'll hard boil it for you," she offered. "You and Angel can split it for lunch."

"No thank you!"

Neither Katie nor I liked fresh eggs. The yolk was too yellow and new tasting. The only time we'd eat eggs from the hens that summer was if Mother disguised them in chocolate chip cookies.

"I have to boil eggs to put on top of the potato salad anyhow," Mother said. "Uncle George and Aunt Juanita invited us for lunch," she added to me.

"Oh," I said, looking down at my baby book. "I'll stay here."

"That's fine," Mother said and walked off down the

hall with Angel and Katie.

But I got bored just sitting in my room all day. When I heard everyone getting ready to go next door, I put on a tie-dyed sundress and walked into the kitchen. "I guess I'll go," I mumbled.

"Good," Mother said.

We walked next door. Mother carried potato salad in a blue glass bowl, and I brought a plate of peanut butter cookies I'd made the day before.

"Please come in," Aunt Juanita said formally, as if she and Mother hadn't just yesterday had a long conversation over the fence about how to trap gophers. "Sientaté, Maggie," she said, pointing to a chair in the cool, dark living room. Tim immediately stretched and dumped his bucket of toy cars on the brown shag rug. Katie and Angel raced outside to play in the cornfield.

Aunt Juanita nodded at me. "You can put those cookies in the kitchen, Veronica. It's all I can do not to eat them all right now, they smell so good."

I loved the way she said my name in her Spanish accent. "Veh-roh-nee-ca," I whispered in the kitchen. Daniel Castillo from my school in Torrance didn't have a Spanish accent when he called me "Hippo Girl." I wondered what he was doing this summer, and if he still remembered the night he'd given me a piggyback ride in the rain.

It was strange to stand in the kitchen across from Mother's house. Pink and white ducks marched across Aunt Juanita's curtains and across a magenta border on the walls. I looked out the window to our kitchen and saw the pictures Tim had colored and taped to Mother's refrigerator. Katie's avocado plant sat on the windowsill. I could almost picture myself half-asleep, pulling open the curtains and yawning into the early morning before making Mother's coffee.

I set the plate of cookies on the table and walked back down the hall to the living room. Mother was talking to Aunt Juanita in a low voice. I paused. I didn't want to play with Katie and Angel, but I didn't really want to be in the same room with Mother either.

"I don't know what to do, Juanita," she was saying tearfully. "My job and my new friends only make me feel worse. I've even thought about adopting some kids. I miss being a mother so much."

I froze in the hallway, my knees suddenly weak. There was no way I could go back in the living room now. I stumbled out to the backyard and sat on the warm porch boards. Tears slipped down my cheeks.

Uncle George walked up to me with an armful of corn. "Wanna help me shuck this?" he asked.

"Okay," I mumbled, wiping my eyes on my sleeve.

"Grip the husk and try to grab all of it, so when you yank it," he tugged the green husk down to reveal perfect rows of yellow and white kernels, "you get all the strings, too."

The strings were corn silk that clung to my fingers and stuck in my hair. I tried to husk as fast as Uncle George, but he did three ears to my one.

Uncle George cleared his throat and spat into the bushes beside him. "I don't know you girls well, but I'd say something's on your mind," he said.

I glanced at him, surprised, but his straw hat was bent over the corn. "Maybe you don't want to talk about it, but maybe it's better if you do." He raised his head and winked at me.

I looked sideways at his kind brown eyes above his white mustache. "We got taken away from our mother. I guess you know that," I said softly.

"I suspected," Uncle George said. "Wasn't your fault or your mother's, was it?"

Yesterday, I would've confessed that it was all my fault. *I* was the one who had said I wanted to live with Daddy. But Mother had said last night that the court wouldn't let us live with her because she was a lesbian. So maybe it was *her* fault.

"It's not fair," I told Uncle George without explaining.

He squinted up at the sun. "Nope, it's not. But

aren't you happy you get to see your mother on weekends, when you don't have to worry about school or homework?"

I flicked a furry green worm off the ear I was husking. "Every *other* weekend. Anyhow, I bet we won't see her at all now. She wants to adopt some kids."

"Humph," Uncle George said. "Your mother's just sad and lonely because she misses you all. You and your brother and sister are all she ever talks about to Juanita and me."

I shrugged. "Whatever," I said, feeling as knowing and mean as Bella.

Just then, Katie crawled out from under the wooden porch. Her red cheeks were shiny with tears.

"What's wrong?" Uncle George asked. "Bump your head?"

"Found you!" Angel ran around the side of the house and tackled my little sister. They wrestled on the ground like puppies, and when Katie stood up again, she was giggling.

Uncle George patted my knee. "Thanks for your help, Veronica. I'll go put the corn on the barbecue." He picked up the clean, glistening ears of corn. "Everything will work out fine," he told me. I nodded, even though I knew now that this was a lie adults told children to make them think that the world was a safe and happy place.

Still, I wished more than anything that I could believe Uncle George.

I barely spoke to Mother the whole last week we stayed with her. But I watched her a lot, when she was busy cooking or making paper maché masks with Tim and Katie at the dining room table. Now that I knew she was a lesbian, I thought she should look different or act different. But she didn't even drink beer now that Ms. Whitney wasn't around. She carried around a bottle of water all day, and in the evenings, she made hot chocolate for all of us. Several times I saw her looking at me with worried eyes over the top of her mug.

In those last evenings in Santa Paula, I went to bed

at the same time Katie did, not wanting to be alone with Mother. But one evening as we closed our coloring books, Mother put her hand on mine. "Ronnie, stay in here for a few minutes, please," she said.

I sat on the edge of the bed and listened to her telling Katie good night. My shoulders stiffened as she walked back into her bedroom.

"We need to talk," she said. Her voice was stern, and I knew that even if I hated her guts for not telling me about being a lesbian sooner, I was still going to have to sit still and listen to her.

But Mother wanted *me* to talk.

"I want you to ask me questions— all the questions you can think of— and I'll do my best to answer them as honestly as I can." She propped herself up on the pillows and smiled weakly at me. "It'll be kind of like a game show."

"It's not a game— it's my *life*," I muttered.

"You're right," she said. "But did you know that there's a tribe somewhere— I forget where— and their whole philosophy has to do with life being like a game. I think they play a game . . . maybe soccer . . . once a year, and the captain of the losing team gets to cut off the head of the captain of the winning team, just to keep things in perspective."

"So?" I said. I glared at Mother, wondering what any of this had to do with me.

"Of course, that's going overboard, but don't you like the idea of seeing life as a game? It's amazing what people'll do to amuse themselves." Her voice shook, and she bit her lip the way I did when I was nervous.

"Life's a pretty rotten game," I said.

"Sometimes it is," Mother sighed. "So ask me something, Ronnie."

"Okay," I snapped. "*Fine*. Why'd you marry Daddy if you knew you were a lesbian?"

"I didn't exactly *know* I was," Mother replied slowly. "When I was growing up, girls were just expected to get married. That's what I did."

"So then when did you figure out you were . . . uh . . . gay?" I didn't like the word lesbian. It sounded harsh, like an insult— like something Bella would say to hurt me.

Mother settled herself against the pillows. "Some women know right away. Ms. Whitney knew when she was your age. But I didn't know until she came along."

"So you had sex with her," I said flatly.

"Briefly." Mother looked out the dark window. "I would've been happy to stay with her forever, but she found someone she liked better."

I looked down at my knees below my pajama shorts. I could still see the gravel embedded in the left one from the day Julia Goldberg had pushed me. "Do you date other women when we're not around?" I asked.

"No," Mother said. "But I do belong to a group of lesbian mothers who have lost their kids to the court system. We have meetings, and sometimes those can be almost fun . . . well, fun and depressing."

"Are they like Tupperware parties?" I asked.

Mother smiled sadly. "It's funny now to think that somewhere there's a group of women taking Tupperware as seriously as what we talk about in our meetings."

"What d'you talk about?"

"We talk about how to get our kids back."

I rolled over on my stomach and lay across the bed. I hung my arms down over the side and took a deep breath. "Does this mean I'll be gay, too, when I grow up?"

"Not necessarily," Mother said. "Scientists have found that homosexuality is genetic, which means that it's predetermined before a person's born . . . not just a choice someone makes, but I don't know exactly how that works . . . " Her voice trailed off, and I looked up at her. The whites of her eyes looked pink and strained— exhausted. "It's been a hard year, Ronnie," she said. "I've been told I'm mentally unstable and sick. I've lost my kids to a monster because of what goes on in my bedroom, which shouldn't be anyone else's business but my own."

Mother had never talked this way to me before. I

felt uncomfortable, but at the same time, I felt strangely exhilarated, as if I could almost feel myself growing older and more experienced by the minute.

"You didn't have to lose us," I pointed out. "You didn't have to move in with Ms. Whitney. We could've moved in with one of your . . . other friends." I blushed. I'd almost said "one of your normal friends," but I'd caught myself.

Mother winced as if my words had hurt her. She stood up and walked over to shut the window. The coyotes sounded so close tonight, almost as if they were yapping right outside the bedroom. "I was naive," she said finally. "I didn't know what to do or how to do it. It was terrifying to contemplate living alone with three little kids, trying to feed and clothe you all, find you decent daycare while I worked and scrounged up enough money for things like health insurance."

"Daddy did it," I said.

Mother shot me an angry look. "Your father had a built-in baby-sitter, cook, and housekeeper. *I* took care of you kids all day. He just provided the money." Her voice rose higher. "And Elsa doesn't work either, does she?"

Tim appeared in the doorway, rubbing his eyes. "Iss too much noise," he said.

Mother went in to put him back to bed. I lay across her bed trying to imagine what it must have been like for her almost a year ago to pack us all in the Volkswagen bus and drive away from Daddy. She said it had been terrifying for her. I'd been terrified, too.

Mother came back in and sat down on the bed next to me. I let her put one hand on my head. "Ronnie, you have to understand . . . Ms. Whitney offered me a place to stay, rent-free," she said quietly. "She had kids who could look after you when I had to work. And she herself was a good person, kinder than any man, and most women, I know. I had no idea the court would react so strongly. I mean, we're supposed to be this *evolved* society . . ."

"Are you still in love with Ms. Whitney?" I asked. My cheeks flamed with embarrassment.

"I don't know. Probably a little."

We sat in silence, listening to a lone coyote wailing in the distance. Finally, I turned to Mother. "Do you *want* Katie and me to be gay when we grow up?" I asked her. "I mean, because of the way Daddy hit you?"

Mother shook her head. "Absolutely not. There's so much hatred, so much prejudice. Homosexuals get murdered all the time . . . " She put a fist against her mouth. "I'm sorry, Ronnie. I'm exaggerating. I want you to be whatever you want to be," she said. "But I want life to be easy for my children. I don't want you to have to struggle and fight."

I thought of the fight I'd had with Julia Goldberg the week before school got out. "It's too late," I said. "I'm already fighting."

Mother sat with her hands tightly folded and didn't look at me. "I know," she said.

I went to bed then, but I stayed awake long into the night, knowing that this time next week, I would be lying awake in Torrance listening to diesel trucks on the freeway instead of to coyotes in the hills, and Mother would be in this house alone.

The next morning, I woke up and looked over at Katie's bed. She was gone, but I could hear her crying down the hall. I found her in Mother's room with her head buried in Mother's lap and her shoulders heaving with sobs.

"What happened?" I demanded, grouchy from sleeping so late.

Mother looked at me over Katie's tangled blond head. "The coyotes got the chickens last night."

"How!" I looked out the window. The empty coop, small in the distance, looked intact. "Maybe the chickens are in their nesting boxes," I suggested.

"Katie and I walked out this morning and found a big hole dug under the coop," Mother explained quietly.

"Tell Ronnie what else we found." Katie's voice was muffled against Mother's lap.

Mother shook her head. "Oh, honey, I'm sure she

doesn't want to hear all the gory details."

"We found their heads and feet!" Katie sobbed, pounding her fists on the bed. "I *loved* them! They were my *friends*!"

"We'll get some more chickens, honey. We'll buy some baby chicks, so you can watch them grow," Mother said.

Katie shoved her roughly away. "Why? They'll just die again!" She glared at Mother, challenging her. I looked at Mother, too, waiting to hear what she'd say.

Mother pulled her hair off her neck and tied it into a loose ponytail. "Girls, little animals die. That's the chance you take when you love them. But we can build an even stronger coop closer to the house, so the coyotes won't get them anymore."

"I want to see how they got in," I said.

I walked out to the coop with my stomach churning. *Not just animals die—* I thought. Anyone could die, anytime. One moment they were alive, and the next minute they were gone. Even Mother could get murdered, simply for liking women instead of men.

There was a big, scraped-up hole in the dirt under the coop, and the chicken wire had been bent up. White feathers floated across the ground. I looked for chicken parts, but Mother must've cleaned them up already. I unlatched the door and walked into the empty coop, then knelt down beside the nesting box to feel for eggs. Something hard and sharp tapped at my hand. I snatched my hand out of the box and bent to see the red hen glaring out at me.

"She hid in the corner of the box!" I said, running into the kitchen. I dragged Katie and Mother out to see the hen, who was scratching for grain among the white feathers. Katie turned away.

"I'm not gonna love anything ever again!" she said with her arms crossed tightly against her chest.

I knew how she felt. Loving was dangerous. I loved Mother more than anything in the world, and I'd lost most of her already. *Am I going to lose the rest of her, now that she's gay—* I wondered.

The last morning we spent in Santa Paula, I woke up in the half-light of dawn and tiptoed into Mother's office.

"Hi," I said glumly, sitting on a folding chair.

"Good morning," Mother said, as if this were no different from any other morning. "I'll be done in a minute. Why don't you go make some hot chocolate. Oh, and honey, will you make me some coffee?"

I brought the mugs in and set her coffee down a safe distance away from the typewriter. "We have to go back to Torrance today," I said.

Mother continued typing, concentrating. *She's probably thinking about the kids she'll adopt as soon as we're back in Torrance—* I thought miserably. My being so angry at her probably made her want to adopt some kids even more. Maybe she'd find herself a new daughter who was more evolved than me.

I wanted to sit very still that day. I thought that if I didn't move, time would go slower. But Katie wanted me to play dolls because Angel had gone home two days before, and Mother took us out for ice cream at the neighborhood park. The Santa Paula band was giving a concert under a round wooden pavilion, and all the locals had set up lawn chairs and blankets on the grass. Little kids marched around the pavilion to a marching song, and when the band started playing "Tomorrow" from *Annie*, they marched to that, too.

"Let's stay a few minutes!" Mother said, sitting down at a green picnic table. I sat beside her. Katie and Tim ran to join the marchers. We licked at our ice cream cones and watched all the people. The day was hot, but I was comfortable in shorts and a tank top. The music was quiet enough to listen to and talk over at the same time.

My mother crunched the last of her ice cream cone and motioned to a group of women standing a little way in front of us. "Those women are part of a lesbian bicycling club I'm thinking of joining," she whispered to me.

I stared. The four women looked normal, just standing there with their bicycles. They all wore bright yellow T-shirts and black biking shorts, and they were a lot prettier than some of the other women at the park who were wearing thin, shapeless house dresses. They seemed to be having fun. A short, round, Asian woman with glasses kept leaning over to the others and whispering something that would make them all burst out laughing.

"They're gay?" I whispered. Chocolate ice cream trickled down my hand. I licked it off and kept staring.

"This county has a large lesbian population," Mother said. "Some of the women are more out— more open about it— than others, and they have regular meetings where women go just to talk."

"Do you go?" I asked.

Mother shook her head. "I work for the newspaper, where everyone knows everything about everybody, so I have to be careful. Sometimes people lose their jobs because they're gay."

"They lose their jobs?" I repeated, shocked. "I don't see why *anybody* would want to be gay."

"Exactly," Mother said. "But why would anyone want to be black, or Latino, or a woman? We're all victims of prejudice," she said bitterly. "Unless you're a white man with money, no one's safe. And to use one of Katie's favorite words, it *sucks*."

Something else occurred to me, but I finished my ice cream and wiped my hands and mouth on a napkin before turning to Mother. "Do you hate men? I mean, because of what Daddy did to you?"

Mother tapped her bare foot in time to "You're a Grand Old Flag." Then she stood up on the bench to look for Katie and Tim. They were up near the front of the pavilion with the other little kids having a contest to see who could march with their knees up the highest.

"I like men," Mother said, sitting down again. "There are lots of men like your father out there, but I've met some wonderful men at the newspaper office— the editor, for example."

So why not date him— I thought. I looked again at the group of women standing near us with their bikes and tried to decide whether or not I was attracted to them. Mother had said that Ms. Whitney knew she was gay when she was my age. I'd never thought much about sex, but I tried to picture myself kissing the short, Asian woman who was making everyone laugh. Then I pictured myself kissing Daniel.

Daniel won.

Mother nodded at a darkly tanned, wrinkled woman sitting in a lawn chair with a cowboy hat pulled down low over her closely-shaved head. "That's Cynthia Wright," she said. "She's a poet. She puts out an anthology of local poetry each year. I think you should send her a couple of your poems."

I looked at the woman. Her cigarette extended like a pointed index finger from her stern frown. I knew I would never be brave enough to show her my poetry. "Is she a lesbian?" I whispered.

"Some of us are easier to spot than others," Mother replied.

When we got home, we had just enough time for an early dinner of beans and hot dogs before it was four o'clock and time to leave for Torrance. I hurried outside to say goodbye to the rabbits, the cats, and the one red chicken.

I'll be back in ten days— I thought— *That's less than two weeks.*

Mother looked at me strangely when I went back inside. "Where's your sister?" she asked.

"I don't know," I said. "She isn't out back."

"She isn't in the house, either. I've looked in every room."

I helped Mother search the house again. We looked under the beds and in the closets, but Katie was gone.

"I know she wouldn't go to the store by herself," Mother said, clasping her hands together.

"I'll run down and check," I said. I jogged past the houses and glanced over at the grammar school. I knew

Katie wouldn't go there. The fat man looked up from the TV as I walked in.

"Is my sister here?" I panted.

He shook his head. "Haven't seen her, darlin'." I looked all around the store, just to make sure, then ran back home. The long wail of a siren cut through the hot summer air, and my heart jumped. An ambulance with frantic, flashing red lights raced past Mother's house and up the road, disappearing into the mountains.

My knees shook so that I could hardly walk. I met Mother about to walk out the door. Tim's feet were sticking out from under the couch.

"He thought Katie might be under there, and now he's looking for spare change," Mother said. "I called your father and told him we're running late. I'm going over to see if she's next door."

I coaxed Tim out from under the couch. "I find six pennies!" he said, jingling them in his hand. I took him next door with me. The front door was open. We walked in and found Mother and Aunt Juanita searching every room. I went out back and stood on the stone steps. I looked out above the waving tops of the cornfield, wondering if Katie had stolen my idea about living in the hills. Off in a far corner of the field, a bunch of stalks rustled suddenly, and then I knew where Katie was. I called to Mother.

"She's in the cornfield," I whispered, pointing.

I left Tim standing with Aunt Juanita and hurried through the rows of corn after Mother. We found Katie crouched into a tight little ball, crying in the middle of the tall green stalks.

Mother knelt down beside Katie and gathered her up in her arms. "Honey, what's wrong?" she asked, tipping up Katie's chin to look at her.

Katie's face looked red and splotchy, and there was a thick streak of dirt on her cheek. "I'm not going back to Daddy's!" she sobbed.

Mother nodded as if she'd expected this and took Katie's hands. "Honey, you'll be back in ten days," she said in a voice that wasn't quite steady. "And next time the peaches on the tree will be ripe, and we can make cobbler and even ice cream. Ronnie brought me my old ice cream maker, the kind you turn the handle on . . . "

"There won't be room for me in ten days," Katie wailed, kicking at a dirt clod.

"What d'you mean?" Mother said, puzzled.

Katie clamped her lips together and looked away. Mother glanced at me. I shrugged. I had no idea what was going on in Katie's head.

"Come on. Tell me what's wrong, honey," Mother pleaded. When Katie still wouldn't answer, she said, "You know, Katie, you're going to get me in a lot of trouble if you don't go back to your father's. The police can come and put me in jail."

Katie lay still in Mother's arms for a moment, then leapt up. "I heard Ronnie say you were going to adopt some kids to take our place!" she cried, bursting into tears again.

Mother looked at me, her eyes slowly comprehending. "Ronnie. Why didn't you tell me you'd heard me?"

I shrugged, wanting to kick a few dirt clods myself.

"I shouldn't have said that about adopting. I have bad days, when I miss all of you so much I can barely stand it . . . " Mother sniffed and blinked hard. "But I'd never find three kids as wonderful as you." She stood up and cuddled Katie to her. "We have to focus on the good stuff," she said. "We're a family, girls. No one can separate us in our hearts. We get to see each other every other weekend, and next summer, we'll have another whole month."

I couldn't stop the tears from running down my face. I hugged Mother and Katie in Uncle George's cornfield and sobbed. It was almost unbearable to think that in two hours I'd be sitting alone in my room at Daddy's house.

"Remember." Mother swallowed hard, then continued. "It's the *quality*, not the quantity of our time together that counts."

We walked back to the house. Tim was telling Aunt Juanita and Uncle George that he had a black stallion at

Daddy's house. They were nodding and asking him questions. "What's your horse eat?" Uncle George asked Tim.

"Pizza," Tim replied.

"We've gotta get going," Mother told them. "Thanks for watching Tim."

Aunt Juanita and Uncle George followed us out to the bus. I let Katie have the front seat and helped Tim arrange his coloring books and his pillow in the back seat. Mother started the bus. Aunt Juanita waved her pink dishcloth. "Adios, niños!" she cried. Her brown eyes glistened in their folds of wrinkles. "See you next time!"

Uncle George walked over the window and leaned down to speak to Katie. "I'll shoot those darned coyotes the next time they go after your chickens," he said.

Katie gave him a small, brave smile, and we pulled out on the road back to Daddy's.

When we got to Daddy's house, he was waiting for us, pacing up and down the front lawn with a shoebox in his hands. "I thought maybe you weren't going to show up," he said to Mother. His thick fingers drummed angrily against the shoebox.

"It's not like I wanted to," she said, her eyes flashing.

Now I thought I understood a little better why Daddy was so mean to Mother. She had left him for a woman. That had to be the ultimate insult for a man as loud and tough as Daddy.

Mother leaned down to kiss me goodbye. "Remember. We're a family," she whispered in my ear.

Daddy stood beside me and watched Mother's red bus pull away. As it turned the corner, he shook his head and began to walk toward the house. I walked behind him with my heart aching inside of me. I didn't know how I was going to survive the ten days until I saw Mother again. I didn't even have Bella or Julia to play with. The rest of the summer stretched out long and dull before me.

Then, at the door, Daddy turned and handed me the shoebox in his hands. "Some coach from the high school called and asked you to come to a meeting tomorrow afternoon," he told me. "He said that you made the cross country team."

Chapter 9

The next afternoon, I walked over to the high school track and sat on the blacktop with the other girls from my school who had made the cross-country team. They were all warming up, stretching out their leg muscles and comparing tans. Most of them kept glancing under their eyelashes at the group of boys sitting near us. I didn't look at the boys, but I was glad they were there. I liked the way they goofed around, pushing each other and laughing. I wished I had the nerve to go sit with them, but I didn't want anyone to notice me and remember the last week of school, when they all called me Lesbo Lover because of Mother.

Everyone seemed to have forgotten all about it. Cathy Kirby said, "Veronica's got a great tan," and Marissa Lee said, "We're planning a cross-country pool party at my house— can you come?"

Across the field, I saw Isabel, who had been in my Home Economics class last year. Her long, skinny legs carried her, giraffe-like, over the grass toward us. Isabel had been in my cooking group in Home Ec. She'd hated cooking so much that I had to show her how to crack an egg. I didn't know her well, and I was surprised when she loped over and collapsed next to me. "Hi, Ronnie," she said breathlessly.

"Hi," I said.

"So you're a runner, too. Wait'll you meet Coach Lopez. He's a fireball."

"Oh," I said. I was afraid to say anything else. Isabel had not been part of the group who had called me Lesbo Lover, but I didn't trust anyone anymore.

Coach Lopez was a short, balding man with muscular bowed legs. He was also the high school Spanish teacher. "My older sister took a class from him," Isabel whispered to me. "He flunks kids in his Spanish classes if they can't roll their "R's."

"Holá." Coach Lopez planted his feet in front of us on the blacktop. "So you all want to run?"

We nodded as a group. Isabel poked me in the side with her elbow and giggled. Coach Lopez began to call roll from a list in his hand.

"Barker, Angela?"

"Here!"

"Davis, Ronnie?"

My heart pounded as I called out "Here!"

"Castillo, Daniel?" the coach barked.

"Here!" Daniel from my homeroom class came running across the field wearing a white baseball cap with a picture of a sun on it and worn, dirty running shoes. "Sorry I'm late, Coach! I was playing basketball with my brother, and I didn't have a watch."

I thought Coach Lopez might yell at Daniel, but instead his stern lips twitched into a smile. "How's your older brother? Still running?"

"Yeah." Daniel sat down with the other boys on the blacktop. "In the Air Force."

Coach Lopez turned back to the group. "Running cross-country on my team demands speed, dedication, and most important, *practice*," he said. He let his narrowed black eyes rest on each of us for a moment. "If you're lacking any one of those three things, now would be a good time to leave." He looked pointedly at Isabel, who was still giggling behind her hand. Some of the boys cleared their throats loudly and looked over at the girls.

"Actually, gentlemen, the women on my team have historically proved to be far more dedicated athletes than the men," Coach Lopez said. "Sadly, our boys' team doesn't take its practices as seriously as it should. Last year, all they could handle was a half-mile run to the local park to play basketball."

Daniel laughed with the other boys, and then he looked right at me and grinned. I looked down quickly and pretended to adjust the laces on one of the blue and white running shoes Daddy had given me yesterday.

"Looks like you have a boyfriend," Isabel whispered, poking me in the side again.

Coach Lopez told everyone to stretch a while longer. Then he wanted to see us run. "Six laps around the track!" he said. He stood at the edge of the track and called out commands to us. "Head down, Marissa— you're running like an ostrich. Isabel, use your long legs to *stride*! Concentrate on breathing, Daniel, not on the girls! Veronica!" Coach Lopez stopped me after the first lap. I stood in front of him, panting.

"Veronica, you have speed, that is obvious," he said, with just a trace of a Spanish accent. "But you run bent over, and you're losing a lot of power that way. Pretend there's a yardstick taped to your back. If you can't pretend, I'll tape one there."

"I can pretend," I said and took off again. I tried to keep my back straight as I matched my breathing to my strides. "Breathe . . . one, two. Breathe . . . one, two." The rhythm pounded through my head, blocking out all my memories of the wonderful month I'd just spent in Santa Paula. I didn't want to stop running after the sixth lap. I wanted to run past my sadness, past the awful aching feeling of missing Mother, and at the same time being mad at her, until there was only exhaustion.

"Much better, Veronica," Coach Lopez said as I jogged up to him.

"You can call me Ronnie," I said. "It's easier."

"Veronica is a lovely name," Coach Lopez said. Beside me, Isabel nodded. "Practice next Wednesday, four o'clock," Coach Lopez barked. "Come prepared to run three miles— that's the length of a typical cross-country course. Daniel, stay here a minute, will you?"

"Sure, Coach." Daniel walked over to me. "If you hang out a minute, I'll walk you home, Veronica," he said.

"I was going to ask if you wanted to come over and watch TV," Isabel whispered in my ear. "I didn't realize you had a date. Maybe next week?"

I nodded. I felt my cheeks flush with excitement

and surprise as I waited for Coach Lopez to finish talking to Daniel. My hair was plastered in damp strings to my neck. I tried to smooth it back into a ponytail.

"Can you run six miles at a time without hurting your legs?" Coach Lopez asked Daniel.

Daniel nodded. "I can run ten if I stretch a lot before and after."

"Your stride is good, and I think you can make Varsity by your sophomore year," Coach Lopez said. "Even so, I want to speak to your doctor."

I watched a white seagull glide down to the football field. It began to peck in the grass for food. I remembered that Mother said you could always tell when it was going to rain because the seagulls came inland. I watched the seagull and tried to hear everything Coach Lopez was saying without looking like I was listening. I wondered what was wrong with Daniel's legs. He did run kind of stiffly with his feet turned out, but he was fast.

Daniel walked up to me and put his hand on my arm for an instant. "Thanks for waiting, Veronica. Let's go."

We walked across the field together, toward the high school. The seagull looked curiously at us out of bright black eyes. I was curious, too.

"I didn't know you ran," I said shyly. We walked down the outside hall of the high school. It was a nice-looking school— big, with lots of grass and trees.

"I've been running since I was little," Daniel said. "I used to pretend I was one of those guys from the Olympics, and I'd try to jump saw horses in the backyard like they were hurdles."

"Is that how you hurt yourself?" I asked.

"What d'you mean?" Daniel's voice tightened, and his brown eyes narrowed under his thick black eyebrows.

"I'm sorry . . . I was right there when the coach was talking to you," I explained, embarrassed. I looked away from him and in through the open door of one of the school buildings. I recognized printing machines that looked like the ones in Mother's newspaper office.   I heard kids laughing and talking inside and thought about how much fun it would be to write for a high school newspaper and hang out at school over the summer with friends.

"Sorry." Daniel touched my arm again lightly. "I get sort of self-conscious about the way I run. The kids at school used to laugh at me."

I know what that's like— I thought. Daniel had not been one of the kids who called me Lesbo Lover. I remembered now that he'd missed the whole last week of school.

"Where were you right before school got out?" I asked him.

"My grandmother has a restaurant in San Diego. She was having a thirty-five year anniversary celebration, so my family drove down to help."

"Was it fun?" I asked.

He nodded. "Yeah. My Nana's a great cook— she made these killer enchiladas and chilis rellenos and homemade beans, and she drank my dad under the table."

"Really?" Daniel's grandma didn't sound like either of my grandmothers. I couldn't help smiling, imagining Grandma Davis drinking beer out of a bottle with her little dog, Snippet, yipping at her heels.

"My mom's worried about how much longer she'll be able to run the restaurant," Daniel said. "Nana's feet swell up something awful from standing and cooking all day, but she just laughs and soaks them in the bathtub all night."

"Against the assault of laughter, nothing can stand," I said as we crossed the street in front of rows of waiting cars on both sides.

"I like that," Daniel said. "Did you make that up?"

"No, Mark Twain did," I giggled.

Daniel laughed. "Hey, I'll race you to the end of the block. There's a liquor store at the end, so whoever loses has to by the winner a popsicle."

Before I had time to argue, he yelled "Go!" and we took off down the street. I ran down in the gutter against the traffic. Daniel ran on the sidewalk, dodging people. He was a little ahead of me when he ran right into an elderly couple walking out of a pawnshop. I reached the liquor store before he was finished apologizing to them.

"All right, what flavor," Daniel grumbled, loping up to me with his funny stride.

"Grape," I said.

We ate our popsicles and walked home slowly, talking the whole way. Talking to Daniel was not like talking to Bella or Isabel. There was more teasing involved, and I felt very warm in spite of the popsicle.

"You know, I would have bought you a popsicle even if you'd lost," Daniel said, as we walked around the corner to my street.

I didn't know what to say to that. I looked up the street and saw Katie riding her bike with Maria. They were trying to jump curbs.

"I had polio when I was a kid," Daniel said. "That's why Coach Lopez was worried."

"Oh." I licked my hand where the popsicle had dripped. Once, I'd read a book about a girl who got polio and learned to walk again because she wanted to ride her horse so badly. "Did you have to learn to walk again?" I asked Daniel.

He shook his head. "I had to wear a brace on my leg all through grammar school, though," he said. "All the kids thought I was weird."

"It's good to be weird," I said. "Who wants to be normal?"

"*You're* not weird," Daniel said.

If Daniel knew about Mother being gay — I thought — *he'd think I was weirder than weird.* I was sure he wouldn't even be standing with me now, half a block from my house, if he knew.

Tim came running out of the house. He stood on the sidewalk and stared down the street at me. A slow smile of recognition spread across his round face. "Sister!" he cried, racing down the sidewalk. He threw his arms around me, almost knocking me over. "Dinner time!"

"Um . . . this is my brother, Tim," I said to Daniel.

Tim stuck out his hand and Daniel shook it. "Nice to meet you," he said to Tim.

"Cool!" Tim said.

When I was Katie's age, I used to think that Tim looked like everyone else. But his tongue, protruding slightly from his full lips, and his eyes with their slanted lids, made kids stop and stare at him. I wondered what Daniel would say about Tim, and if he'd laugh at him.

But Daniel only grinned at Tim. "My aunt works with adults like you, finding them jobs and stuff."

"Cool," Tim said again. He pulled on my arm, his blue eyes impatient. "Sister, *dinnertime*."

I looked at Daniel. "Well, I guess I'd better go."

He nodded. "Hey, thanks for letting me walk you home, Veronica. It was fun. Bye, Tim." He turned and began to jog down the street with his feet slightly splayed. "See you next week at practice!" he called back. "I'll walk you home again!"

I followed Tim inside, shivering with happiness. The walk home *had* been kind of like a date, just as Isabel said, and Daniel hadn't called me Hippo Girl once.

The second weekend in August was hot. Friday evening at Mother's house in Santa Paula, we ate dinner outside because it was cooler in the backyard than in the house. After we'd eaten, Mother turned on the sprinklers in the front yard so we could run through them. Then she brought out a carrot cake with thirteen candles on it for my birthday, which had been two weeks before.

"I'm only a few weeks late," she said. She tried to smile cheerfully, but her eyes were sad. "I guess we'll have to get used to celebrating our holidays at strange times. Make a wish before the wax drips all over, Ronnie."

I blew out the candles without making a wish. Before Mother had told me that she was a lesbian, I'd wished on the first star every night that I could come back and live with her. Now I didn't know what to wish.

Mother cut us all big pieces of cake, and we hung around in the yard trying to stay cool. I was pushing Katie on the tire swing hanging from the oak tree in the front yard when a little blue convertible pulled up. Rock music blared from the stereo.

A tall, tanned woman got out and brushed back her short, graying black hair, then pushed her glasses back firmly on her nose. "Hey, Maggie!" she called, waving.

"Hi." Mother walked down to the driveway and gave the woman a hug. "This is Annie," she told us. "Annie, these are my kids."

Tim immediately hugged Annie around her long legs. Katie jumped off the swing and stuck out her hand. "Charmed," she said, in an imitation of some old Fred Astaire musical she'd been watching on TV earlier.

I looked up at Annie. She had a wide, friendly smile, and her hand was warm and firm when I put mine into it.

"You're Ronnie, I'll bet. The oldest." When Annie said this, I knew she understood what it was like to have to be the responsible one. The one who had to help take care of Katie and Tim and pretend to be brave and happy so that Mother would not feel so horrible when she dropped us off at Daddy's house.

Annie sat down on the grass and ate two pieces of carrot cake. Then she spun Tim and Katie around on the tire swing as many times as they asked her to. Mother laughed a lot that evening. She went in to use the bathroom, and when she came out, she was wearing pink lipstick.

I didn't protest when she said, "Annie's going to stay with you tomorrow morning because I have to go interview the mayor." I found myself looking forward to the next morning, and when I peeked through the curtains later and saw Annie kiss my mother on the cheek before driving off in her convertible, I didn't raise my eyebrows at Mother when she came in, but smiled cautiously.

"Is she a baby-sitter?" I asked.

"No, she's my friend. I met her at the bicycling club I told you about."

"Oh." I thought about that day at the park— how Mother had pointed out members of the lesbian bicycling club who were standing with their bikes and laughing in their matching yellow jerseys. "I like her, I guess."

Mother ran her hand absently over my ponytail. "I'm glad she meets with your approval."

I thought that Annie would baby-sit us at Mother's house Saturday morning— we'd get out the Monopoly board and make cookies— but the moment Mother drove down the road in her navy blue suit and high heels, Annie turned to us and said "Let's go!"

"Where're we going?" Katie asked, bouncing up and down in the back seat of the blue convertible.

Annie buckled Tim in beside Katie. "Oldest gets the front seat first," she said.

I climbed into the car beside her and put the visor down. Annie reached over and flipped it back up. "The cool way to ride in a convertible is with the visors up and the windows down," she said. "And your sunglasses on."

"I don't have any sunglasses," I said.

"Then we'll have to get you some."

Annie pulled out of the driveway and turned on the stereo. Music rushed through the little car. I waved at Aunt Juanita, who was sitting on her porch reading the newspaper that Mother wrote for. "I thought we'd go get some breakfast in Oxnard!" Annie yelled over the music. "Is Speedy's okay?"

"Can I have a hamburger?" Katie yelled back.

"That's what I'm having!" Annie said.

"Fries!" Tim kicked off his shoes and crossed his legs on the back seat.

"Tim, one leg down, please," Annie said firmly. "Your mom told me lots of disabled kids like to sit cross-legged," she said in response to my surprised look. "It's really inappropriate in public, don't you think?"

I hadn't really thought about it. Tim was just Tim to me. I hadn't even noticed his disability much until Daniel met him on the sidewalk after cross-country practice.

Annie swung into Speedy's drive-thru and turned the music down one notch.

"Welcome to Speedy's— may I help you?" The flat, mechanical voice came out of a plastic purple hamburger.

"Well, yes you may," Annie said. "I'd like a double cheeseburger, large fries, and a large Coke."

"Can you repeat that please, ma'am. I can hardly hear you."

"I said I'd like a double cheeseburger, large fries, and a large Coke!" Annie yelled into the hamburger.

"And a hamburger, fries, and a chocolate milkshake!" Katie yelled.

"Fries!" Tim echoed.

"Ronnie, what would you like?"

I reached over and turned the music on the stereo down. "I'd like a cheeseburger, small fries, and a chocolate shake, please," I told the hamburger. I wanted to tell Annie that I'd written a poem about hell being an eternity of ordering fast food at a drive-thru, but I didn't trust her not to laugh.

Somehow, the hamburger read our order back correctly. Annie drove to the pick-up window. A boy with pimples covering most of his red face took Annie's money and handed her three bulging bags. Annie examined the bags to make sure all our food was in them. "You do a good job," she said, handing the boy back a dollar. "Ronnie, dole out the food!"

I passed Katie and Tim their burgers and fries and offered to unwrap Annie's cheeseburger for her.

"I hate eating in the car," she said. "Let's go to the park." She drove through a maze of streets and pulled up at a park with a playground and picnic tables. Katie and Tim stuffed fries in their mouth and ran to play on the swings and the slide. I sucked on my milkshake and watched Annie as she ate her fries. She licked the salty grease off her fingers the way I did, although Elsa always nagged me to use my napkin.

"Are you . . .are you dating my mother?" I said at last, as I studied the initials carved into the table. "M.J. + R.D." enclosed in a lopsided heart.

"I guess you could call it that," Annie replied.

"We've been seeing each other pretty much every day for two weeks."

I thought about that. Mother hadn't even told me about Annie. But I hadn't told her about Daniel, either. He was too important, and I wanted to see what was going to happen between us before I told Mother about him. Maybe that's what she was doing with Annie— waiting to see what would happen.

"You must bike a whole lot," I said, looking at Annie's long, muscular legs in denim shorts.

She laughed a deep, amused laugh. "I'm a weekend cyclist— not hard-core like some of these other nuts who ride fifty miles a day. Do you ride?"

I shook my head. "I run."

"Another fine sport!" she exclaimed. She finished her cheeseburger in three large bites, then stood up. "Come on, kids, let's go to the mall!" she called to Katie and Tim, and we all climbed back into the blue convertible.

Three men in white sailor suits pulled up beside Annie's car, which was practically shaking from the force of her booming stereo at a red light. Katie and I looked over at them. They looked back at us, grinning and elbowing each other.

Annie nodded at the driver. "How's it going?"

The driver had a crew cut and wire-rimmed glasses. He gunned his engine in a challenge to Annie. She gunned hers back. "Ready?" she asked us.

"Go!" Tim cried. Annie took off at the green light. The sailors took off beside us. They pulled ahead, then we did. Katie giggled shrilly. I glanced at the speedometer. We were only going forty miles an hour, but it seemed much faster. The wind blew my hair out of its ponytail and tangled it into curls. I screamed with laughter, and the wind carried the sound away instantly. The sailors pulled off into the turn-lane near the Navy Base. The driver blew us a kiss.

"That was for you, Ronnie," Annie said, and I glowed inside.

Katie shrieked. "Annie, Tim threw his socks out of

the car!"

Annie pulled over to the side of the road and turned to look at Tim's bare pink toes and the red sneakers he held in both hands. "Why'd you do that, Tim?" she demanded.

Tim scowled. "Has holes. I hate 'em." Katie and I pointed and laughed at the white socks curled up in the middle of the road behind us.

"He likes to throw things out the window," I explained to Annie. "But his socks really did have holes. My mother said she'd get him some new ones this weekend."

"Let's do that right now," Annie said. She headed for the mall. We walked into a big department store, and she said, "Why don't you girls pick out a new outfit? Your mom and I are taking you out tonight."

Katie rushed to the racks of girls' clothes and grabbed an armful of dresses. "Can I try these on?"

Annie nodded. "Ronnie, you help her, and I'll help Tim, okay? Don't forget to pick out something pretty for yourself."

I frowned as Annie walked off with Tim. *Why's she buying clothes for three kids she'd only met yesterday—* I wondered. Katie wasn't worried, though. She'd already found her way to the dressing room.

Annie met us back at the register with Tim and three packages of white socks, a boy's striped T-shirt, and a pink stuffed mole. Tim grabbed the pink mole and bounced it up and down. The mole made a squeaking noise, and Tim laughed. "Rowse!" he said. "Name iss Rowse!"

Katie had picked out a blue jumper, a white blouse and white tights. "Perfect," Annie said. "What'd you find, Ronnie?"

I held out the yellow sundress I'd found. Annie shook her head when she saw the red fifty-percent-off sticker. "Veronica, I make plenty of money, and I love to go shopping. I know your mom doesn't have much money right now, and I'm doing this as a favor to her. So go pick out something you really want. Consider it a late birthday present."

I came back to the register holding a pair of blue

jeans with daisies on the pockets that matched the daisies on a blue scoop neck T-shirt. "Are these okay?"

Annie took off the hangers and put my new clothes up on the counter for the cashier to ring up. "These are much better."

That same night, she came over with a box of makeup. "Who wants her face painted?" she asked.

"But it's not even Halloween yet!" Katie cried.

"Well, it's never too early to practice." Annie dumped tubes of makeup all over the table.

"We should get out the dress-up clothes," Mother said. I followed her into my room and helped her slide the box of old clothes and wigs into the living room. Katie and I buttoned Tim into a floral mini-dress of Mother's that hung to his ankles. I dropped a curly brown wig on top of his head.

"He looks like a munchkin from *The Wizard of Oz*!" Katie giggled. Annie had turned her into a black cat with whiskers and white stripes down her forehead. Katie fished around in the old clothes until she found a black cape and put it on over her new blue jumper.

"Okay, Ronnie, your turn. Do you want to be beautiful or scary?" Annie asked me.

"Scary," I said.

"Then I've got the perfect nose for you." Annie produced a long green plastic nose with a wart on the tip of it. "First, I'll put on foundation." She dipped a sponge into a container of green makeup and patted it all over my face. I studied her face as she leaned close to me. She had wrinkles around her eyes, and her own nose was kind of big. I decided that she was not pretty, but she was interesting-looking, which was better. Her blue-gray eyes were full of laughter as she handed me a mirror.

I stared at my new face. She'd stuck the nose on with cement and blended the make-up carefully so that my whole face and neck were mottled green and brown. I looked terrifying.

"Thanks, Annie!" I cried.

"Where should we go now that we're all beautiful?"

Annie asked Mother after she'd put lipstick and eye shadow on Tim.

"The beach?" I suggested. I slipped on a long black dress that used to hang in Grandma Hammond's costume shop.

"Disneyland?" Katie said hopefully.

"Oz!" Tim cried.

Mother got her purse. "Let's go the Pancake House. It's near the beach."

We ended up in a booth beside two sailors who were wolfing down chicken-fried steak. They chuckled as we walked in, and Katie began to speak to them in a fake British accent.

"How splendid to meet you," she said, holding out her hand for them to shake. "This is my family— my sister, the Witch. My brother, the Munchkin. My mother, and my Annie."

"Charmed, I'm sure," I said, imitating her accent.

Tim bounced the pink mole on the table so that it chirped. "This my Rowse," he told the sailors.

The sailors laughed and talked with us as we waited for our pancakes. I said, "Charmed, I'm sure," several more times, and Mother and Annie rolled their eyes in mock disgust at me. Then the sailors stopped laughing. They looked over at Mother and Annie, then looked away. I saw that Annie had her hand over Mother's hand and was looking at her with soft eyes, not paying attention to any of us.

"Sing pirate songs!" Tim begged the sailors, but they got up and paid their check and didn't say goodbye to us.

Annie took her hand off Mother's to help Tim pour more syrup on his pancakes. Mother glanced at me over the rim of her coffee cup, then looked away. The steam from my cup of hot chocolate loosened the cement, and my witch's nose tumbled off into my pancakes. Everyone else laughed, and the evening should've been fun and happy again, but it wasn't.

Daddy and Elsa seemed colder and stricter than ever after that weekend. Daddy was standing outside watering the lawn when we pulled up in Mother's bus at seven thirty on Sunday night. He stared at Annie in the front seat, then said, "Kids, dinner's been ready for half an hour. Maggie, I really wish you'd try to have them here on time. Elsa and I would appreciate it."

Mother's eyes flashed blue steel. "And *I* would appreciate it if you did your half of the driving," she said. "When are you going to start meeting me halfway like you said you would?"

"You left me," Daddy snorted, and he herded us into the house.

Elsa had made corned beef. She put the platter on the table as we walked in, so we didn't even have time to wave to Mother and Annie from the window.

I loved corned beef— loved the cabbage and red potatoes Elsa fixed with it. I had just put a large piece of each into my mouth when she said, "The very idea of two people of the same sex sleeping together makes me ill."

Daddy nodded. "It's disgusting," he said through a mouthful of food. "Don't you think so, Ronnie?"

I looked down at my plate. "I don't know. I haven't really thought about it," I said.

Daddy pounded his fist down beside my plate. My corned beef and potatoes bounced. "Well, maybe you should *start* thinking about it!" he said. "And look at me when I'm talking to you!"

I looked up at him, and my heart began to pound. Tim and Elsa kept on eating. Katie squeezed my knee under the table. After a moment, Daddy began talking with Elsa in a normal voice about a strange noise her car was making. But I couldn't swallow another bite. "Can I be excused?" I whispered with the sound of Daddy's fist still ringing in my ears.

"Fine," Daddy said and waved me away from the table with one hand.

I couldn't concentrate on my book or on the new poem I was working on after dinner. I lay on the carpet in my room and thought about how much fun I'd had over the weekend. Annie was nice and funny, and I wasn't even sure I cared what she and Mother did in bed.

"It's very unnatural," I heard Elsa telling Katie in the kitchen. "Two women can be friends, but they're not supposed to sleep together."

I slammed my pillow over my head to shut out her precise, brittle voice. I was glad it was Katie's night to help with the dishes. She wouldn't even understand what Elsa was talking about.

Talking with Elsa was dangerous. She had a way of saying things in her firm British accent that convinced me they were true, even if I thought they were wrong. Now, every time Daniel walked me home from cross-country practice, I wondered if I *was* a slut, just as Elsa had said. *What if she's right about Mother—* I thought— *what if Mother and Annie sleeping together* is *disgusting*.

An ache like the worst stomachache I'd ever had crawled up into my rib cage and sat there heavily. I needed to talk to someone. I thought about calling Isabel from my cross-country team, but I didn't know her well enough to start spilling my guts.

The phone on my nightstand rang, startling me. Before I could pick it up, I heard Daddy get it in the kitchen. "Veronica? Just a minute."

He stuck his head in the door, smiling at me as if his fist had never smacked the dinner table beside my plate. "Phone's for you, Ronnie. I didn't tell Elsa it was a boy." He winked and disappeared down the hall. I picked up the phone.

"Hey, Veronica, you're back. Can you go running with me tomorrow?" Daniel's voice sang out cheerfully.

"How'd you get my phone number," I said, twisting the black phone cord around my wrist.

"I have my ways," he laughed. "Anyway, can you go running? Early, like, eight A.M.?"

"Fine," I said. The cord pinched my wrist. For a moment I couldn't loosen it. I imagined my hand turning blue and falling off.

"You all right?" he asked me. "You sound kind of weird."

"I'm fine, " I assured him. "I . . . I just need to talk to you about something tomorrow. I'll meet you at the high school track at eight."

I hung up the phone and collapsed on my bed. For the rest of the night, I rehearsed over and over in my head the words I would say the next morning when I told Daniel about my mother.

Chapter 10

I set my alarm for six thirty Monday morning, hoping to slip out of the house without seeing anyone. I walked into the kitchen to find Daddy already sitting at the dining room table, eating a bowl of bran cereal and reading the sports section of the *L.A. Times*.

"Morning," he said when he saw me. "Going running? Better take a windbreaker. It's cold out."

I had on a pair of black sweatpants I'd cut off into shorts and a blue T-shirt that I thought made my eyes look bluer. I hoped Daddy wouldn't see that I'd put on the gold hoop earrings Mother had given me. Then he'd know for sure that I was going running with a boy.

I made two pieces of toast and spread butter in a thin layer over each. Elsa kept trying to get me to use jelly instead of butter— she said it was less fattening— but strawberry jelly in the morning made me want to throw up.

"Well, I guess I'll go run," I said, wrapping the toast in a napkin.

Daddy looked up from his cereal. "If you wait a few minutes, I'll go with you."

I froze. "Um . . . that's okay. I mean, don't you have to go to work?"

"I can get there late. We always used to run together, remember?"

I did remember. Before Mother left, I used to go with Daddy to the high school track in Newbury Park Saturday mornings. I'd jog four laps, and then sit on the bleachers to watch Daddy run five more miles. Sometimes I'd climb one of the goal posts on the football field and balance high up, clutching the metal cylinder beneath me as the post swayed in the breeze.

After our run, we'd drive home sweaty and hot, and Daddy would say, "Ronnie, I know it's not right to have favorites, but you're my oldest child, and that's something special."

Now, standing in the kitchen with my toast getting soggy in the napkin, I thought of all the times Daddy had said that to me. Then I remembered the crash of his fist beside my plate at the dinner table the night before. I could still hear the sound in my mind, and even though he was sitting there quietly eating cereal in his work pants and a white T-shirt, I was afraid of him.

"I'd rather go running alone," I said and hurried out the door before he could say anything else.

The high school was half a mile away. I walked slowly down the street, shivering in my T-shirt. Daddy was right— it was cold out. I ate my toast, then jogged down the railroad tracks to the high school. I was almost to the metal bleachers when I saw someone sitting there— Daniel, in red shorts and a black windbreaker. Under his baseball cap, his black hair looked like chicken feathers all messed up from jogging in the mist. I liked it.

"You're early," he said as I sat down beside him.

"So are you," I said. "By about an hour." We looked at each other and laughed.

Daniel reached into the pocket of his windbreaker and took out a paperback book. "I brought you something," he said. "I know you like to read."

"Science fiction," I said doubtfully, looking at the orange cat in a space helmet on the cover.

"It's about giant cats," Daniel said. "I read it. It's good."

It wasn't exactly Mark Twain, but I felt my cheeks flush with pleasure. "Thanks," I said awkwardly.

Daniel swung around on the bench so that he was facing me. "You said you had something to tell me."

Now that Daniel was right there in front of me, confiding in him about Mother didn't seem like such a good idea. *What if he doesn't want to be my friend anymore—* I thought. But I had to talk to someone.

"I'm not sure what you'll say, but I want you to know," I said slowly. "It's important to me."

"So what is it, already?" Daniel's brown eyes looked into mine.

I stared down at my blue and white running shoes. "It's about my mom," I stammered. "She's a . . . um . . . well, she's gay."

"So what?" Daniel said. Then he grinned. "Jeez, Veronica, I thought you were going to tell me you couldn't go out with me or something."

So what— I thought, shocked— *My mother being gay is 'so what?'* Out loud, I said, "I'm not 'going out' with you."

"Oh, no?" The seriousness in Daniel's eyes faded into teasing. "What are you doing right now?"

"Running." I got up and jogged off down the track. Daniel followed me.

"Honestly, Veronica," he said, "it's no big deal about your mom. Anyhow, I already knew."

I stopped jogging and stared at him. "You *knew*?"

"Yeah. That weird girl you used to hang out with . . . Bella . . . she told my friend Matt." Daniel put his hand on my arm, and I stopped jogging. "He said the kids at school teased you pretty bad."

I nodded, feeling tears rush to my eyes. "Yeah. They did."

Daniel pulled me over to the blacktop in the middle of the football field and sat down. He began to stretch. I stared down at the round brown muscle of his calf. "You gotta understand, Veronica, kids are mean," he said. "They pick on anything that's different, 'cause everyone's so scared to be different."

"You're not scared," I murmured.

Daniel snorted. "Yeah, I am. Every time I walk into a store, people look at me like I'm gonna rip something off.

And why?" He stuck out one arm and slapped it with his other hand. "Because I'm Mexican."

I remembered what Mother had said about how no one would choose to be gay or black or Latino in this world. Something about her words had confused me, though. Of course Daniel couldn't choose the color of his skin, but couldn't Mother choose who she dated?

"A lot of people say it's unnatural . . . to be gay, I mean," I told Daniel. "A lot of people say it's disgusting."

"A lot of people are pretty stupid," Daniel replied. "You have to come to make your own decisions about stuff like that." He looked up at me over his left shoulder as he stretched the long muscle in his back. "Sounds like you haven't quite made your decision yet."

I'd been hoping that Daniel would help me make my decision, but he was only confusing me more. "So . . . what d'you do when people stare at you in the store?" I asked to change the subject.

"What did you do when the kids started picking on you at school?" Daniel countered.

I sat down and leaned over my right leg, feeling my hamstring muscle pull tight as I grabbed the top of my shoe. "I tried to beat up Julia Goldberg," I said. "But that's when I didn't know my mother was gay. I was . . . well, I was trying to defend her."

"Why?"

Daniel's questions were beginning to make me mad. He acted like he knew so much more than me. "Why? Because she's my mom, and they were saying mean things about her!" I yelled.

"So why should you stop defending her when people say mean things about her now, just 'cause she likes women?" he asked me.

I shrugged unhappily and shivered in the early morning mist. "I don't know."

"Boys are so weird," Isabel said the next week after cross-country practice. We were sitting on the floor of her parents' living room, eating cream cheese and celery and trying to design a T-shirt for our eighth grade cross country team. "All those guys on the team can be so friendly to me at practice, but when I see them at the tennis courts on weekends, they totally ignore me."

I was sketching what I hoped looked like a dolphin on a piece of paper. I drew jogging shoes on its fins. "Why can't we be the Torrance Tigers or the Bears?" I complained. "What can you do with a dolphin!"

Isabel tilted her head and examined my picture, then spoke with her pencil between her teeth. "Maybe the guys are afraid they'll have to ask me out if they speak to me on weekends. You know, Ronnie, I'm so tall that sometimes I wonder if I'll ever get a date."

"Of course you will," I said absently, sketching a baseball cap on the dolphin. "You're beautiful."

I bit my lip and looked up at Isabel, half-scared that she'd call me Lesbo Lover and kick me out of her house.

Instead, she leaned over and hugged me. "Thanks," she said. "You're really nice to say that."

"I mean it," I said. Sure, Isabel was tall and skinny and silver braces gleamed on her teeth, and she also had a wide, friendly smile and long, thick brown hair that framed her cheerful face.

She reached for another piece of celery and cream cheese and got up to change the channel on the TV. "This talk show's stupid. Let's watch April Arias."

April Arias had long, curly hair the color of a candy apple and a passion for leopard prints. Today, she was wearing a leopard-print beret and a long leopard coat over a red mini-dress.

"We're interviewing adults whose parents have disowned them because they're gay," April said into the microphone in a low, scratchy voice that she obviously thought sounded sexy.

"Who's gay? The parents or their kids?" Isabel wanted to know.

"Um . . . I think the kids are gay, and the parents disowned them, but the kids are actually adults now. . . I guess." I pretended to be concentrating on my dolphin picture, but I listened carefully to April as she interviewed two men and a woman. All of them talked about how sad it was not to see their parents anymore.

"It's funny," one of the men was saying. "Even if I'd just murdered someone, my mom and dad would still come visit me in prison. But here I am, happy, healthy, with a wonderful partner . . . " The camera panned in on a blond man smiling shyly in the audience.

"He's a babe," Isabel said, stretching out on the couch. If she remembered what Bella had told everyone about my mother last June, she wasn't letting on.

"Has Daniel asked you to be his girlfriend?" she asked me during a commercial.

"No," I said. "We've only gone running together once. But he gave me a book."

"A book," Isabel said blankly.

"Yeah. About giant cats."

Isabel laughed so hard she fell off the couch. I laughed, too, and by the time we'd recovered, April Arias had said goodbye into the microphone. "Tomorrow, we'll interview the parents who've disowned their kids," she said.

"Would you ever do that?" Isabel said, crunching the last piece of celery.

"What?" I started gathering up paper and pencils to cover my nervousness.

"Not see your kid anymore just because she's gay."

"I . . . don't know."

"I'd see mine," Isabel said firmly. "I don't think there's anything wrong with it."

The second Friday in September, Annie was sitting in the passenger's seat of Mother's red bus when I walked outside. I wanted to remind Mother that it was my turn to sit in the front seat, but Annie looked too tall to squeeze into the back seat. I got into the back. Katie and Tim immediately started tossing Tim's pink stuffed mole back and forth like a squeaking football. Mother started the bus and glanced at Annie. I saw her nod in the direction of the living room window. Elsa stood looking out between the curtains.

Annie laughed and patted Mother's knee, then turned around to talk to us. "Do you kids know how to sing any rounds?"

"We know Freré Jacques and Edelweiss," Katie offered.

I watched Torrance disappear behind us on the freeway in a cloud of gray smog. Daniel had called the night before to see if I could go running Saturday morning, and I'd told him reluctantly that I had to go to my mother's house. I liked him so much that it was almost worth staying with my father and Elsa for the weekend so I could see him.

"Edelweiss isn't a round," I told Katie.

"But it sounds pretty when you sing it in two parts, like they do in *The Sound of Music*," Mother said.

Annie beamed. "One of my favorite movies. Let's sing."

Her voice lingered sweet and pure at the end of each round, with Tim chanting nonsense syllables, just so he could sing with her. We sang every round we knew, songs from every musical, and even some Beatles' songs. When we stopped at McDonalds for sundaes, we sang our order for ice cream sundaes into the drive-thru speaker.

"Caramel . . . " Annie said, drawing out the note in a deep voice.

"Strawberry . . . " Katie said, copying her in a higher voice.

"Hot fudge . . . " Tim and I sang the top note together.

"And a cup of black coffee," Mother said into the speaker. "Please."

I thought Annie would go home when we got to Mother's house in Santa Paula, but instead, she went into the kitchen to heat up milk for five cups of hot chocolate. From my room, I heard the sound of a hot air popper making popcorn. I didn't remember Mother having a hot air popper. She always made popcorn in a pot over the stove. I walked into her room and sat on the bed beside her as she took off her shoes.

"Is Annie staying overnight?" I asked her.

Mother looked soberly at me. "I've asked her if she wants to move in with me."

"Oh." I looked around the bedroom. It looked as though Annie had already moved in. There was a blue glass lamp I'd never seen before and a framed picture of a nude woman lying in some Greek-looking gazebo with a man— or maybe it was a woman— looking down at her.

"Maxfield Parrish painted that," Mother said, following my eyes. "He's Annie's favorite artist."

"How long have you known Annie?" I asked. "Didn't you just meet her a month ago?"

"I've known her about a year, I guess. We met at a party while I was still with Ms. Whitney."

"Oh." I knew Mother didn't have to ask my permission to let Annie move in— it was her house— but I still felt angry. "Where's she gonna sleep?" I demanded.

Mother began to fold the clean clothes in the pile that lay on her bed. "I've already thought about that. I can't have Katie and Tim going home and telling your father that Annie and I sleep together. . ." She paused, and I could tell that she was trying to decide how much information she could give me. "If he asks you, tell him I can't afford the mortgage on this place all by myself, and that Annie's just a roommate. She'll just have to sleep on the couch while you kids are here, at least for now."

In spite of my anger, I still felt a little sorry for Annie. Every other weekend, she'd have to sleep on the lumpy orange couch, all the way at the front of the house, with the headlights from passing cars lighting up the living room every few minutes. "That's pretty stupid," I scoffed. "If she sleeps in your room while we're gone, she might as well sleep there when we're here."

"Is everything okay, Ronnie?" Mother pulled me close to her. She smelled different than usual, like vanilla perfume. "I need to know what you're feeling."

"I'm fine," I said, looking down at my bare feet. "It's just that . . . well, I thought we were going back to court, and *I* was going to come live with you."

Mother held both my hands in hers firmly. "I want you to live with me more than anything, Ronnie. I've been doing some research, and it sounds like you need to appeal to the court and tell them you want to come live with me. The older you are, the more they'll take your opinion into consideration . . . but you're still pretty young," she finished sadly.

"I just turned thirteen," I reminded her.

"That's true," she said. "My lawyer said you'll have a lot better chance of moving in with me when you're sixteen, old enough to drive up here any time you want."

"But that's in three years!" I cried.

Mother rubbed her eyes with her index fingers. "I know. Could you wait that long if you had to?"

I thought of Daniel and Isabel and how they made life almost bearable in Torrance. And there was the cross-country team. "I could wait," I said. "If I had to."

Mother ran her hand over my ponytail absently. "Why don't we go see what everyone else is up to."

"Wait," I said. There was something I had to ask her, something that had been bugging me ever since that afternoon I'd watched April Arias on Isabel's TV. "Do you still talk to Grandma Hammond?"

"Why wouldn't I?" Mother said. "Last weekend, I met her at a hotel halfway between here and King City, and we watched this horrible Doris Day festival on TV and ate junk food all night. We had a wonderful time. She's coming down the end of this month to visit," Mother added as we walked into the living room. "Can you be here the fourth weekend, or do you have plans?"

"I can be here," I assured her, relieved to hear that Grandma Hammond hadn't disowned Mother for being gay.

Annie and Katie sat on the living room couch with twin pink mugs of hot chocolate. Tim lay stretched out on the floor beside a bowl of popcorn.

"We waited for you before we started the movie," Annie said, nodding at two more mugs of hot chocolate on the coffee table.

I cupped my hands around my blue mug with the unicorn on it. *Annie even knows which mug is mine, and she's barely moved in with Mother*— I thought.

I wasn't at all sure I liked that.

The next night, Annie and Mother took us to the drive-in to see a movie. Tim sat on Annie's lap, holding his stuffed mole, Rowse. Katie and I sat smashed together in the back, watching the movie between the front seats. It was a story about a mermaid who came up on land and fell in love with a man, so she turned herself into a human. Our favorite part was when she took a bath in the bathtub. She poured salt into the bathwater, and her legs turned into a sparkling green mermaid tail.

When the movie was over, Tim stood up to climb into the back seat. "Oh . . . gross!" Annie exclaimed, pointing at a large wet spot on one leg of her jeans.

"What *is* that?" Katie screeched.

Annie looked at Mother. "Your son peed on me."

Katie and I thought that was hilarious. We giggled all the way home. Annie and Mother tried not to laugh, but every once in a while, they'd chuckle behind their hands.

"You know, you're too big to be wetting your pants, Tim," Annie said when we got in the house.

"He does it all the time in Torrance," Katie said. "The other day, Elsa found him smearing poop and baby powder all over his walls."

"Is that true, Ronnie?" Mother asked with a frown.

"Yeah. Elsa said he was doing it for attention."

"Can you help him start a bath, girls?" Mother followed Annie into her bedroom. "I'll be out in a minute." I heard her voice — sounding worried — through the wall.

I filled the bathtub with warm water and went to get Tim, who was sitting on a towel in front of the TV. "Bathtime," I announced.

"No way!" Tim crossed his arms against his chest.

"But you love baths!" I said.

"Nope."

I tugged on his arm. "Come on, Timmy, you smell."

"*No!*" Tim hollered.

Mother and Annie walked out of the bedroom. "What's wrong with him?" Annie asked. She was still wearing the jeans Tim had peed on.

"He won't take a bath," I explained.

"Tim, you have to get clean," Mother said.

Tim shrieked again and stuck out his chin, pouting. "Not gonna!"

Katie emerged from our room in a long purple robe and a rainbow-colored wig from the box of dress-up clothes. "He's afraid he'll grow a tail, my dears," she said in her best fake British accent.

"What?" Annie shook her head, confused.

"Like in the movie!" I cried. "Tim's afraid if he gets in the bathtub, he'll grow a mermaid's tail!"

Mother covered her smile with one hand and took Tim's hand with the other. "I'll stay in there with you," she promised. She sat on the toilet seat and sang to Tim while he cautiously washed his legs with a washcloth. Then the phone rang in Mother's office.

"Maggie, it's for you!" Annie called.

"I'll be right back," Mother said to Tim.

Across the living room, Katie and I looked at each other. For once, we had the same idea. I watched for Annie from the doorway of the bathroom, while Katie ran to get the salt shaker from the kitchen.

"Tim," she whispered, holding the shaker up. "*Salt* in the bathwater."

Tim's shriek sent Mother and Annie flying into the bathroom. "What in the world is going on here?" Mother demanded.

Katie and I choked back laughter. Tim fell sobbing out of the bathtub and huddled shivering and naked on the floor.

Annie spotted the salt shaker, half-hidden in Katie's clasped hands. She held out her hand, and Katie obediently gave the shaker to her. "It'll be your fault if Tim never takes a bath again," she said sternly, but her blue-gray eyes crinkled with amusement.

"You girls go get your pajamas on. It's late," Mother sighed, drying Tim off.

It was then that I realized Annie really had moved in. I put on my pajama top and shorts and stood in the doorway of Mother's room. "Can I come in and talk?"

Mother sat propped up on pillows on one side of the bed. "Come on in, honey," she said through a yawn.

Annie appeared in the doorway with two cups of tea. "Oh, I'm sorry, Ronnie, I didn't know you were still up." She glanced at Mother who shifted uncomfortably on the pillows and looked away from me.

"It's okay, I'm going to bed," I said. I walked over to the nightstand to pick up the book I'd been reading two weekends ago. "There's not room for three of us." I muttered, shutting the door hard behind me.

That Sunday, we had a picnic dinner in the backyard. The sun shone warm, and the mountains behind the house gleamed green and gold. I made a little fence out of chicken wire and bamboo sticks so that the rabbits could run around on the grass. Frisky sat on his hind legs and sniffed the autumn air. Six chickens clucked in the hen house. They were too old to be babies and too young to lay eggs yet. "Teenagers," Annie called them. They had funny new feathers that stuck out awkwardly from their necks and tails. Katie wouldn't go near them. She stood in the kitchen, helping Mother dish up spaghetti.

I helped Annie put the tablecloth on the picnic table, which was a piece of plywood propped up on two sawhorses. Annie set a red geranium blossom in a vanilla bottle in the middle of the table and reached down to pet Molly and Dolly, who purred and rolled around on the grass, showing off their white stomachs. "Guess you've got to go back to your dad's soon," she said to me.

I felt my shoulders tense. *What a stupid thing for her to say—* I thought— *Of course we have to go back, but not for another two hours.* It was too soon to feel empty and lonely inside. Right now, I just wanted to eat dinner and enjoy the time I had left with Mother.

Mother brought out a big yellow platter of spaghetti and meatballs. Katie followed with the salad, and Tim carried a basket of garlic bread on his head. Next door, Uncle George's rooster crowed.

"He wants to come over for dinner," Annie said. Tim pretended to throw the rooster a piece of garlic bread, then stuffed the whole thing into his mouth. I served myself some spaghetti, and a meatball slid off the spoon and onto my white pants.

Mother stood up. "Ronnie, I told you not to put on your clothes from your father's house until *after* dinner!" She dipped her paper napkin into her water glass and held it out to me. "Put this on it. Do you think it'll stain?" she asked Annie, looking at the warm red circle on my pants. "Elsa has a fit if they stain their clothes."

"Wash them in cold water right now," Annie suggested, leaning over me to examine the stain.

I jumped up from the table, knocking my water glass over. "They're *my* pants!" I cried. "Just leave me alone!" I ran into the house and slammed the door to my bedroom shut, then threw myself down on my mattress.

At home when I cried, Daddy and Elsa ignored me. I'd even missed dinner a couple of times because I was too embarrassed to come out after one of my crying spells. No one ever came to get me. I didn't think Mother would come in now, but in a moment, there was a light tap at the door.

"Honey, what's wrong?" Mother sat at the foot of the mattress and leaned over to stroke my hair. I hid my face in the pillow. It felt good to cry this hard. Mother rubbed my back until I'd stopped crying a little. "Is there something wrong at your father's house?" she asked.

I sat up abruptly. "It's Annie!" I yelled. "I hate her! She doesn't belong in our family, barging in here and telling everyone what to do!"

I knew immediately that I'd hurt Mother. Her mouth tightened, and she stared down at the bedspread. I tried to cry some more, but I had no more tears left.

"I'm sorry you feel that way, Ronnie," Mother said

at last. "I love Annie, and she likes you kids so much. You're gone most of the time and I . . . I don't like living alone." She stopped talking, and a tear rolled down the side of her cheek and disappeared into her hair.

"So why not find another *man*!" I yelled. "Then maybe I'd have a chance at living here!" I clenched my hands together in my lap. "I don't understand why you want to be gay!" I muttered. "I just don't get it!"

"I don't *want* to be gay," Mother said quietly. "I *am* gay."

Annie appeared in the doorway. "We'd better go, Maggie," she said. "You know what he's like when you're late."

I stood up. "I'll go change and soak the stupid pants in cold water," I snapped. I grabbed a pair of old jeans from the dresser and stalked past Annie to the bathroom. I turned on the water and began to fill the sink.

"Ronnie, I gotta go to the bathroom!" Katie called, knocking on the door.

"I'm busy!" I yelled.

I heard her jumping up and down in the hall. "But I really have to go!"

I yanked the door open. "So *go*, already."

Katie sat on the toilet, watching me pull off the stained white pants and dunk them into the sink. Cold water sloshed over the sides of the sink onto my bare feet. Katie stood up and zipped her jeans, then flushed the toilet. Instead of leaving the bathroom, she put the toilet seat down and sat on it, still watching me. "Why don't you like Annie?" she demanded.

I stared down at my white pants in the sink. "D'you know what a lesbian is?"

Katie nodded so that her blond ponytails flopped up and down. "It's a woman who has girlfriends instead of boyfriends. Pam and Sage told me. Their mom is one, and so is ours. I think Annie's one, too."

I stared at my little sister. "You mean you've known all this time about Mother?"

Her blond ponytails flopped up and down again.

"Course I knew. Didn't you?"

I frowned and looked away from Katie. "Of course," I said.

Katie shrugged and hopped off the toilet seat. "I gotta go change clothes," she said.

I tugged on my jeans and heard something crinkle inside the pocket. I reached in and pulled out a folded piece of paper— the poem I'd written about Mother that day last spring when Bella threatened to tell everyone about her.

"About My Mother" the title read. Even though I'd written the poem, I'd forgotten a lot of it. Now it seemed almost like someone else had written it. I thought it was a good poem. The rhymes could've been better, but what the poem said about Mother was more important than the writing.

"My mother is kind and smart and funny.
When days get dark, she makes them sunny.
Her laughter is music.
Her smile is warm.
The thought of her comforts me
Through night and through storm."

I looked down at the wrinkled piece of paper. My head ached with thinking so hard. Daniel had asked me why I should stop defending Mother just because she was gay. *Is being gay that bad* — I wondered. And I knew, deep down inside, that I'd be just as angry right now if a man had moved in with Mother.

I wrung out the wet white pants, then dropped them in a plastic bag. I'd make sure Elsa knew that it was my fault I'd stained them. If she tried to accuse my mother of being careless, I'd defend Mother.

I walked into her bedroom and left my poem on her pillow. I tried to imagine myself living in this house with her and Annie— the three of us cooking dinner together, me going to the movies with them sometimes, staying home other times while they went out by themselves. I didn't want to go back to Daddy's house, ever. Three years seemed so far away from now. I wondered how I was going to get through all that time without going crazy.

Everyone was waiting for me in the bus. I nodded toward the plastic bag. "I put the pants in here," I mumbled. "Most of the stain came out."

"Ronnie, look! This is Rowse angry!" Katie grabbed Rowse and tilted the mole down so that its pink head really did look threatening.

Annie laughed and made the mole sit on her lap. It jumped suddenly, then jumped again. "Rowse with the hiccups," she said, and I couldn't help smiling a little.

Tim grabbed the mole. "Rowse is *my* Rowse!" he said.

"Let's sing," Annie suggested. "Ronnie, do you want to start the French Cathedral song?"

"Not right now." I stared out at the neon octopus sign in front of the same fish restaurant we passed every other Friday and Sunday night. Mother, Annie, and Katie began to sing. Annie's clear, deep voice blended with Mother's high voice, smoothing the rough places in my mind.

"Uh oh." Mother put on her brakes as we drove into a traffic jam. The sky was growing dark, and brake lights glowed red ahead of us. Mother and Annie stopped singing. We drove past a mess of ambulances and tow trucks. I tried not to look at the big truck smashed in the middle of the freeway beside a little truck flipped over and crushed like an aluminum can.

Suddenly, I was glad my mother had Annie to drive home with. I pictured them driving together in the dark, singing and talking about the weekend, or whatever it was they talked about, all the way back home. I thought about how long the trip from Torrance to Santa Paula and back seemed to me. I realized that it was twice as long for Mother. And she'd been doing it alone for almost a year until she met Annie.

I was just about to tell Annie that I was ready to sing now when Katie yelled, "Mother! Tim threw Rowse out the window!"

The traffic jam had cleared, and Mother was driving fast to make up for lost time. I looked behind me at all the white, rushing headlights. "Can't we stop?" I cried.

Mother shook her head. "On the freeway?" she said. "I'm afraid he's gone."

Tim sat looking straight ahead of him with no expression at all on his face.

Katie sniffled. "He'll get run over!" she said, tears welling up in her eyes.

I looked out the back window again. When I was younger, I'd loved my stuffed animals. I still thought of them as real, even though I knew better. I imagined Rowse lying out there in the dark, being run over by everyone's tires, and I began to cry. Mother wiped her eyes with one hand and steered with the other. Beside her, Annie sniffed loudly, and I realized that she was crying, too.

No one sang the rest of the way to Torrance. Mother walked us up to the door. Daddy cleared his throat and looked pointedly at his watch. I walked into the hall, which smelled of fresh-baked apple pie, and went into my room.

"Bedtime at nine thirty tonight, Veronica." Elsa walked into my room in her white silk robe and glanced into my closet. "Tomorrow's a school day. We should've gone shopping to get you some new clothes. We'll go next week," she said.

I sat on my bed and hugged my pillow to my chest. I didn't care about the first day of school or new clothes. As soon Elsa left, I reached for my phone and dialed Mother's number. I knew she wouldn't be home yet, but I waited for her answering machine to come on. At the beep, I said, "Hi, Mother, this is Ronnie. I . . . um . . . I just wanted to say that I'm sorry. I love you. And tell Annie . . . tell Annie that I love her, too."

Chapter 11

Even though I'd just spent the weekend with Mother, I couldn't help feeling a little excited about the first day of school when I woke up Monday morning. I didn't feel like dressing up, so I put on a white T-shirt, a pair of jeans and my white Keds with no socks. It was foggy out that morning, but I knew it would be warm later. I went out to the kitchen, where Tim sat at the table half-hidden by a box of Rice Krispies he was pretending to read. Elsa stood at the sink in a peach-colored jogging suit, rinsing Daddy's bowl and plate.

"Good morning, Ronnie. Would you like toast or an English muffin?" she asked.

"Toast, please, but I can make it," I told her.

"It's no problem," she said. "Easier to stand here and do it myself, so that no one bumps into each other."

Katie wandered into the kitchen in her pink quilted robe. My arm brushed her shoulder as I reached into the refrigerator for the milk and she reached up into the cupboard for a bowl. "Watch it," she muttered.

"Girls, the milk and bowls are already on the table," Elsa said. "I really feel that it's easier if I'm the only one in the kitchen in the morning."

I went to the table and poured milk over the Frosted Mini Wheats Elsa had bought as a special treat for the first day of school. I was the only one who liked Frosted Mini Wheats. Katie reached for the Rice Krispies, and Tim grabbed the box. "Iss mine!" he said.

"Tim, you don't own the cereal," Elsa said. She walked over and took the box from him, then handed it to Katie. Tim kicked the table leg and stuck his lower lip out in a pout.

"What's his problem?" Daddy walked in, brushing off the shoulders of his gray suit.

"There's no problem," Elsa said. "Tim didn't want to let Katie have any cereal."

"She only picks that kind on purpose to bug him," Daddy said. Katie poured milk on her cereal and began to eat. "Don't you?" Daddy asked her.

"No," she said, looking straight at him. "I like Rice Krispies."

Daddy's eyes narrowed, and I felt my breath go shallow. "You look just like your mother when you talk that way," he snapped at Katie. My Frosted Mini Wheats became paste in my mouth. "And what's wrong with *you*?"

he asked me.

"Nothing," I said. "I'm just nervous about school starting."

"Damn kids!" he muttered into the depths of the hall closet. "I work all day to put food on the goddamn table . . . " He didn't finish the rest of his sentence— just gave Elsa a quick kiss on the cheek, then walked out the door with his briefcase clutched in white knuckles.

On the way to school, I thought about Katie. She was brave. She'd stand up to Daddy when no one else would. I was more like Elsa. I'd let Daddy yell and be mean, and when he cried and apologized later, I believed him when he said he'd never get angry again.

As I walked around the corner of my street, I saw Bella. I almost didn't recognize her. She'd permed her hair and dyed it blond. In her flowing white dress, she looked like Marilyn Monroe.

"Hi," she said, walking out from under a tree.

I was shocked. She hadn't spoken to me in months. "Hi," I said. "Where's your uniform?"

"I could give a darn about that stupid uniform," Bella said, adjusting the strap of her shiny black leather book bag. "If those nuns want to kick me out, they can kick me out!"

We walked in silence on the railroad tracks for a few minutes. I couldn't help remembering how much fun Bella and I used to have together.

Or did we— I asked myself. Maybe I had been pretending the whole time I was friends with Bella, tricking myself into thinking we were really friends, when all along, she'd known about Mother and planned to tell everyone. Only now, telling everyone about Mother didn't seem like such a horrible thing. I was pretty sure Isabel knew, but she didn't seem to care. Daniel didn't care at all. When I really thought about it, maybe Bella had done me a favor. If everyone at school already knew about Mother being a lesbian, it would save me a lot of explaining at my eighth grade graduation when Mother and Annie showed up together.

I wondered how I should introduce Annie. "This is my mom and her roommate" sounded strange. "My mom and her lover" sounded worse. "My mom and her girlfriend"— I tried in my head. That sounded okay, even if Annie wasn't really a girl.

"I heard you're going out with Daniel Castillo," Bella said at last when we were standing outside my school.

"We're not really 'going out'," I said. I wondered who had been spreading rumors this time. I knew Isabel wouldn't. Would Daniel himself? I knew he hung out with Matt from Bella's school.

Bella ran her hand along the chain-link fence that separated her school from mine. Her white dress billowed out around her in the chilly morning breeze. She reached up and felt her blond curls. "This weather's gonna straighten my hair," she said, turning toward her school.

I shrugged. "Bye," I said and walked away. I was walking across the field to my new homeroom class when I heard her call my name.

"Veronica!" Bella ran across the wet grass in her white sandals. "Matt's mom won't let him go out with me." She laughed hesitantly and tossed her head. "She says I'm not a nice girl."

Then Bella looked at me with something like pleading in her eyes, the same way she'd looked at Elsa the day before the wedding, when she'd hoped people would think she was Elsa's daughter. "Maybe we could all go out sometime. You know? You and Daniel, me and Matt? Ask Daniel if Matt wants to. Maybe his mom will agree to that."

I tried to smile, then gave up and walked away. I knew there'd been a reason she'd walked to school with me.

"I have a new lawyer, Ronnie," Mother told me two weeks later. I'd had cross-country practice on Saturday, so Mother had dropped Tim and Katie off early Sunday afternoon and picked me up in Torrance. "She said I still need to make some changes in order to get custody of you kids. The judge granted your father custody not only because I'm a lesbian, but because Elsa's home every day to take care of you. Maybe the editor of my paper would let me work at home a few days a week . . . "

Mother and I were driving around Los Angeles in her Volkswagen bus, just wandering up and down the streets looking at the people and the tall buildings. On one corner, a man in a wool hat and a long white robe shouted out passages from the Bible. Three black women in bright dresses played bongo drums on the opposite corner. I loved Los Angeles.

"Let's talk to the judge now," I suggested. "Maybe he'll listen to me even though I'm not sixteen."

"Maybe." Mother turned to me as she stopped the bus at a red light. "Remember that group of lesbian mothers I belong to— those women who also lost their kids?"

I nodded and craned my neck to look up at a brick building decorated with stone faces.

"They said you should just ask your father, straight out, if you can come live with me. Of course, I know that's impossible. *He's* impossible." She turned in at a street lined with booths selling clothing and food and brightly-painted masks and instruments. I could hear mariachi music down the street. "This is Olivera Street," Mother said. "It was the first street in Los Angeles."

We got out of the car and wandered through the booths, looking at painted furniture and piñatas and listening to the mariachi band on the round stage. We stopped at a booth that sold tamales, and Mother bought us each one. "These are fantastic!" she said through a mouthful.

I'd never eaten a tamale before. I pulled off the cornhusk wrapping and cut into the outside, which tasted like soft cornbread. It was filled with chicken. "It's good!" I said, surprised.

"I'm going to buy one for Annie before we leave," Mother said. "I think it'll keep a couple of hours."

When Mother mentioned Annie, her whole face lit up, and her blue eyes shone.

"You and Annie are in love, aren't you," I said shyly.

Mother sat down at the side of a turquoise-tiled fountain. "We are," she said. Her cheeks glowed pink. "It's wonderful to have someone care about me, someone I can trust not to hurt me."

I took another bite of my tamale and thought about this. "Do you think she'll mind if I come live with you?"

Mother hugged me to her with one arm. "She'd like nothing better," she said. "She's crazy about you kids."

"Could we still hang out in L.A. if I came to live in Santa Paula?"

"Of course," Mother said. "We'd come down Fridays to pick up Katie and Tim, and drop them off Sundays. We'd have time to visit L.A."

I swallowed the rest of my tamale and looked away. I hadn't really thought about what it would be like living without my brother and sister. Katie and I argued a lot, but whenever I was sad, she could cheer me up just by acting weird. Last weekend, Daddy had yelled at me for changing the channel while Tim was sitting in front of cartoons, and I ran to my room in tears. Katie danced into my room and started clapping her hands and slapping her legs like a German folk dancer to the David Bowie tape I'd bought at a garage sale for a dollar. I couldn't help laughing at her. We'd sat on my carpet and talked for a long time about how Daddy could be so nice one minute, and so mean the next. But Katie liked her school in Torrance, and she and Maria spent every afternoon together playing. She'd never ask Daddy if she could move in with Mother.

And what about Tim— I thought. Elsa let me baby-sit him now when she had to make a quick trip to the store or to the dry cleaners. Tim and I waited for her car to pull out of the driveway, and then we sang our favorite songs as loud as we could and made S'mores in the microwave with chocolate chips and miniature marshmallows on graham crackers. I took him to the park on Saturdays and helped him with his reading flashcards. No matter what I did or said, Tim's slanted blue eyes always looked at me with adoration, and he said, "You the best sister I ever haff."

It would be ten years until Tim was sixteen and old

enough to decide who he wanted to live with. I hoped that the judge would take him seriously if he said that he wanted to live with Mother.

Mother finished her tamale and wandered over to a booth to inspect a rack of red wool ponchos. "We'd better get going," she said when she returned. One of the mariachi players looked up from his silver trumpet and grinned at me as we passed. He looked a little like Daniel, but older, with a dark mustache.

I want to move in with Mother— I thought on the way back to Daddy's house— *but I'll miss so many things.*

Elsa walked into my room the next day after school in a short flowered dress that showed off her tanned legs. "I thought we might go shopping today," she said, "just you and me. I know I'm a few weeks late in buying you school clothes, but you could use a few things, don't you think?"

"I guess," I said. "Just a pair of jeans and maybe some shoes."

"You never wear dresses anymore," Elsa said as she drove to the mall. "You used to wear dresses and the prettiest skirts when I first met you."

"Everyone at school wears shorts and pants now," I said cautiously. I still didn't trust Elsa, but for once, she didn't give me a bad time. She put her Supertramp tape in the tape player and didn't say anything else.

Listening to Supertramp reminded me of when I first met Elsa, and she'd left Mr. Martin for Daddy. I'd been so mixed up then. I'd loved everyone— Daddy, Mother, Elsa— so much. I hadn't wanted to hurt anyone. *I'm still mixed up*— I thought as Elsa pulled into a parking space in the underground parking lot. Only now, I just wanted to keep *myself* from getting hurt. In the parking garage, Elsa's music echoed against the cement walls. "Take the long way home," the man with the high voice sang over and over until Elsa turned off the car.

I was standing in a tiny dressing room falling all over myself trying to pull on a pair of Levis, when Elsa tapped on the door. "I thought you might want to try a few of these on," she said, draping several bras over the door.

I picked them up, surprised. They were white and lacy, cream-colored and satiny, in the smallest sizes. They looked nothing like the cotton training bras I'd been wearing for a year. I took off my clothes and looked at my breasts in the mirror. They were beginning to develop— I'd noticed it at home— but I hadn't thought anyone else noticed. I picked out the laciest white bra and struggled with the straps and hooks until I got it on. It looked nice with my new jeans, sort of sexy. It had just a little padding, which made my breasts look bigger. Not as big as Bella's, but bigger.

I got dressed and stepped out of the dressing room. "Thanks. I'll take these, if it's okay," I said, handing Elsa the jeans with two bras folded under them.

"Lovely," she said.

We walked through the mall and looked in the windows of all the stores, not talking, but comfortable. Elsa stopped at the frozen yogurt shop. "Let's get one," she said. "They're not fattening."

My chest tightened, wondering if she was going to begin another lecture on the dangers of eating fattening food, but she only ordered a single cup of strawberry yogurt and turned to me.

"Chocolate, please," I said.

We sat at a white plastic table and watched the people shopping. A young woman walked by with a little boy. A purple leash stretched from the woman's hand to the boy's belt loop. Elsa shook her head. "I hate it when parents do that," she said. "Why can't they just hold their child's hand?"

I let a spoonful of the smooth, cold chocolate melt on my tongue before I spoke. "Do you ever . . . I mean, d'you miss not being able to have kids?" I asked.

Elsa looked down at her plastic cup of yogurt. Her black hair swung across her shoulders like a curtain, hiding her face. "Of course," she said. "I wanted to experience child birth and take care of a baby, and all that."

"Tim's sort of like a baby, sometimes," I observed.

Elsa looked up and smiled stiffly. "Not really. He's making great progress. And I *do* have kids," she continued. "I have the three of you."

I didn't tell her that it wasn't the same. I was certain that she already knew that. Katie and Tim were still young enough that they went to her with their scraped knees and hurt feelings, but every other weekend, there was Mother on the front porch, waiting to pick us up. I wondered if I should tell Elsa that I wanted to move in with Mother. *She might be more sympathetic than Daddy—* I thought.

"The junior high school in my mother's town is really small," I began, scraping up the last of my chocolate yogurt with the plastic spoon. "They don't even have a cross country team, but there's a special class where the teacher takes kids up in the mountains to learn about nature and camping and stuff. My mother heard about it from a friend she rides bikes with."

"Hm." Elsa nodded briefly and stood up. "Sounds like an odd school," she said with the cold, sharp tone she got in her voice whenever I talked about Mother. I decided that this wasn't a good time to talk about moving to Santa Paula. I carried our Styrofoam bowls over to the trash can.

"Veronica!"

I looked up and saw Daniel walking toward me.

"Hey!" I said, suddenly glad I'd put on my nice green shorts and white T-shirt after school.

"Can you go running later on, maybe after dinner?" he asked me. He waved at a couple of guys from school who were looking at us from the arcade.

"Aren't you supposed to wait at least an hour after you eat to go running?" I asked him. "Coach Lopez says that, anyway."

"So see if you can eat early. Hey, did you read the book I gave you?"

I thought about how I'd read the book about giant cats all in one day, thinking the whole time about how romantic it felt to know that Daniel's eyes had read those same words. "I read it," I said. "I liked it better than I thought I would."

Daniel's brown eyes laughed down at me, then slid up as Elsa came over.

"Ronnie, we've got to go rescue Mrs. DelGrosso from watching Tim," she said. "Or maybe it's the other way around. Well . . . hello," she said to Daniel.

"Um . . . this is Daniel," I said. I hoped she didn't remember him from the night we'd played in the rain together instead of going to the school dance. "Daniel, this is Elsa . . . I mean, my stepmother."

I hated the way the word "stepmother" sounded—cold and wicked, like the word "lesbian."

"It's nice to meet you." Elsa handed me my bag. I held it tightly closed so that Daniel couldn't see the two bras inside.

"I'll see you tonight then, Veronica," Daniel said and walked over to the arcade.

"Where are you going tonight?" Elsa said when we were in the car. "Or hadn't you planned on telling me?"

"We're just going running," I mumbled. "He's on the cross-country team, and he's in my homeroom class."

"You're a little young to be dating, Ronnie." Elsa's red-lipsticked lips compressed into a thin line.

"I'm not dating!" I said. "We're just going running!"

All the comfortable closeness I'd felt with her in the mall vanished. I stared out the window without speaking until we got home. "Thanks for the clothes," I mumbled as we walked up to the porch.

"Don't thank me. Your father paid for them," Elsa said, slamming the front door behind us.

That night, over steak and baked potatoes, Daddy sat at the head of the table and said, "So, Veronica, I heard you're going running after dinner."

"Yeah, just a couple of miles." I almost choked on a bite of baked potato. I sat there trying to swallow it, waiting for Daddy to continue.

"Who's your running partner? Isabel? Bella?" Daddy's smile was easy and friendly.

"No, his name's Daniel," I said. "He's on the cross-country team."

Daddy chewed a bite of steak. Under the table, Katie kicked my leg. Finally, Daddy said, "I don't see a problem with that, as long as you're home before dark."

Elsa got up from the table and went into the kitchen for a glass of water. The cabinet door slammed shut and the glass clattered against the countertop.

Daddy looked at Elsa as she came back to the table. "What the hell's your problem?" he demanded.

"Nothing," Elsa said stiffly, grinding pepper on her potato.

Beside her, Tim struggled to cut his steak. A piece flew across the table and fell on the floor. Katie giggled.

"Stupid!" Tim hissed, trying to cut another piece.

"Tim needs help cutting his steak," Daddy said.

Elsa didn't respond.

Daddy's dark eyebrows lowered. "I said, Tim needs help cutting his steak!"

"Then he can ask for help," Elsa said. "His teacher says he needs to learn to start asking for things."

Daddy scraped his chair sharply over the wood floor until he was beside Tim. He cut Tim's steak into pieces with little, violent jerks. My heart began to race. Katie stared down at her plate, twirling her fork inside her baked potato skin.

"He's *my* son, and I say he still needs some help!" Daddy said, sliding his chair back to his seat.

Elsa looked up from her potato. "Nobody's saying he doesn't need help, Zach," she said calmly. "He just needs to start asking for it."

Daddy's hand flashed out. He snatched the breadbasket, then threw it across the table at the wall. Rolls rolled all over the room. "I don't know what the hell's wrong with you!" Daddy yelled. "You've got a nice house, three kids, plenty of time to water your goddamn plants and play with your goddamn dogs . . . "

Tim shoveled pieces of steak into his mouth. I sneaked a look at Katie. She was staring at Daddy with wide-open eyes.

Elsa stood up and carried her plate to the kitchen.

"Let's discuss this later, Zach," she said. She walked down the hall and into their bedroom. I heard the door shut quietly and lock behind her.

Daddy sat there eating silently, and I thought the worst of the fight might be over. Then he saw Katie staring at him. "What's your problem, sister!" he yelled.

"I don't like it when you talk to her that way!" Katie said. "It's not nice!"

"Oh yeah?" Daddy stood up and leaned across the table. He bent down close to Katie's face and glared at her. She glared back. He raised his hand to slap her.

I pushed out of my chair and ran to my room, grabbed my running shoes, and ran down the hall. As I was halfway out the door, I heard Daddy yelling, "I'd like to see you go to work ten hours a day, then come home to a family that hates you! Let's see how you'd handle it, sister!"

Daniel stood on the lawn outside the house. There was no way he couldn't have heard Daddy's yelling.

"Come on!" I cried. I raced down the street, half-expecting to feel Daddy's hand on the back of my shirt, yanking me back to the dining room table. I raced down the dirt path beside the railroad tracks, ignoring the sharp cramp in my side.

"Jeez, what was that about?" Daniel asked when we got to the high school track.

I sat down on the blacktop, panting hard. "My father," I said. "Sometimes he gets upset."

"I'll say," Daniel said. "You could hear him halfway down the street."

Knowing that didn't make me feel any better. I turned away from Daniel and began to stretch. My calves hurt from running so fast without stretching first. The cramp in my side made it hard to breathe. I breathed deeply, trying to make my pounding heart slow down. The sky above the high school buildings glowed pink and gray. The moon was already out in a dull, pale sliver.

Daniel reached over and touched my shoulder. "I'm sorry, Veronica. It must be awful to have a father like that. If it's any help, mine's not very nice either."

I nodded, fighting back sudden tears.

"Can't your mother move here?" Daniel asked.

"We're not allowed to live with her," I said in a trembling voice. "Anyhow, she hates Torrance. It's really pretty where she lives. She says . . . she says she wants us to be able to spend a couple of weekends a month in the country, away from all the smog and stuff."

Daniel nodded. "Anywhere's gotta be better than Torrance. Can't you go live with her?"

"We've been talking about it," I said, even though I'd promised myself I wouldn't tell Daniel about moving until it was really going to happen. "But I may have to wait three years because the court won't let me live with her right now . . . and besides, there're other problems."

I didn't tell him that he was one of the problems. If I went to live with Mother in Santa Paula, I knew I'd probably never see Daniel again, and he'd find another girl to go running with.

Daniel's forehead wrinkled up in thought. "That's lame that they won't let you live with her because she's a lesbian," he said. He picked a blade of grass and crushed it between his thin, brown fingers. "She's probably a really good mother, while your dad . . . "

He didn't finish. I knew he understood how unfair the situation was. We sat together for a while, listening to the rush of traffic on the freeway nearby and thinking.

"Maybe if you just asked your dad if you could live with her, he'd let you," Daniel suggested.

I nodded. "That's what my mother's friends said. I guess I should do that." My lips trembled, and I hid my face in my hands. "But I'm so scared of him" I whispered.

Daniel patted my shoulder. "It's okay to be scared," he said. "Just don't let it stop you from fighting."

Easy for you to say— I thought miserably— *You're a boy.*

But then I thought about how Katie fought with Daddy— how she stood up to him and challenged him, instead of running away like I had just done. I'd always thought of Katie as just my little sister— someone to play with and tease and argue with. Now, suddenly, I realized that even though she was two years younger than me, in some ways, Katie was a whole lot smarter and braver than I was.

And I knew I had to go back home to help her stand up to Daddy.

I stood up. "Will you walk me back to my house?" I asked Daniel.

He took my hand, and we walked through the streets back to my house. We stood in the front yard for a moment without speaking. Then Daniel's arms were around me, warm and strong. His hug didn't feel like the hugs Mother or Tim gave me — this was completely different. "I'll miss you if you move, Veronica," he said in my ear. "You're . . . you're just great."

I thought he was going to kiss me, but his cheek just brushed against my cheek. "See you at school tomorrow, I hope," he said.

"Bye," I said, watching him jog off down the street.

I walked up to the front door and listened hard to figure out what was going on inside. The house was quiet, so I opened the door and went in. I looked across the living room to the empty kitchen and dining room, then tiptoed to my bedroom. The door was shut. When I opened it, I was shocked to see Daddy sitting on the edge of my bed, crying quietly.

He looked up at me as I opened the door. His chin quivered. "Ronnie, I'm so sorry," he said, holding his arms out to me the way he had the night he found out Grandpa Davis was dying. Always before, when Daddy cried, I would go to him, hug him, and talk to him until he stopped crying. But tonight, I stood in the doorway and folded my arms across my chest.

"I want to move in with Mother," I said.

He kept crying, as if he hadn't heard what I'd said. "There's so much pressure," he said brokenly. "I work all day, then I get home and there're all these women— Elsa, you, Katie . . . and Tim's hardly the son I wanted . . . " He looked up at me. "But I'll try to do better. I'll try to be a better father."

"I want to move in with Mother," I repeated. "Please, Daddy, can I?"

Daddy's face changed abruptly. He stopped crying, and the muscles in his jaw tightened. "Do you know what your mother is?" he demanded.

I took a deep breath. "Yeah," I said. "She's a lesbian."

He winced as if the word hurt him. "And doesn't it bother you that she *sleeps* with other women?"

I shook my head. I knew that by "sleeps with," he meant "has sex with," but I didn't even want to think about myself and sex yet, let alone about my mother and sex. "It's none of my business what she does in her bedroom," I said softly.

Daddy leapt up and grabbed me by the shoulders. He shook me until my head pounded. "How can you say it's none of your business!" he yelled. "It's disgusting and it's wrong!"

"It's not!" I yelled back. "Besides, Mother and Annie have a lot better relationship than you and Elsa. They have fun, and they're nice to each other!"

Daddy slapped me hard across the cheek. My head snapped back from the force. Still, his hand didn't hurt as much as I'd always imagined it would. I put my hand to my cheek and stepped backwards. Daddy glared at me from the middle of my bedroom. The yellow circles in his eyes glittered, but suddenly, I wasn't afraid of him.

"If you won't let me live with Mother now, I'll move in with her when I'm sixteen!" I said. "When I'm sixteen, I can choose!"

"What did you say?" Daddy rushed at me and backed me up against the wall, raising his hand to slap me again. "What did you say to me?"

I blinked up at him, bracing for the slap. I wished there were something I could say to make him understand how I felt. Then I remembered something Daniel had told me the first day we'd gone running together — the day I'd told him about Mother. "There's not a lot of love in the world," I whispered. "If my mother can find love with a woman, what's wrong with that?"

Daddy snorted. "You've been brainwashed, Veronica," he scoffed. "You don't know what you're talking about." But he lowered his hand and walked out my bedroom door, slamming it behind him. After a moment, I heard the front door bang shut, and then his car squealed out of the garage and raced down the street.

I stood against the wall, feeling it solid and strong behind my back. My heart thudded as if it would burst through my ribs and fall, throbbing, onto the carpet. I slid to the floor, crying quietly. I didn't know if Daddy would come back and hit me again that night. I didn't know if he'd already hurt Katie or Elsa or even Tim. I knew he wouldn't let me live with Mother, but at least I'd asked. At least I'd finally stood up to him and asked.

And I realized that I was sobbing with triumph, as much as with pain.

Someone tapped at my door. "Sister?"

Tim opened the door. "I come in?"

"Okay," I said.

He sat next to me on the floor and put his arm around my shoulder. "You cry?"

"Yeah." I wiped my tears away with my hand and patted his bare knee. "I'm okay."

Katie tiptoed to my door. "Ronnie, can I come in?"

"Sure," I told her.

Katie came in and sat down on my bed. One of her cheeks looked redder than the other. I wondered if mine looked like that, too. The three of us just sat there for a while, listening to the quiet and waiting for Daddy to come home to yell at us again. Then Katie whispered, "Remember the time we put salt in Tim's bathwater?"

Tim grinned. "I haff a tail," he said. "Like the mermaid."

"Remember dressing up and eating pancakes?" Katie said, her voice growing stronger. "Those sailors talked to us, remember?"

I began to play the game, too, crowding out this

night, this house. "Remember at Christmas, when Tim pushed you into the ocean?"

Tim laughed his beautiful, bubbling laugh, and I couldn't help laughing along with him. "Katie's all wet!" he said.

"How many more days before we see Mother?" I asked them.

Katie counted on her fingers. "Should I count the Friday after next?" she asked me.

"No, 'cause we'll see her that day."

"Then it's ten days!" Katie held up both her hands, fingers spread.

Tim held up his hands, too. "Ten days!" he repeated.

We fell silent again, thinking about this.

"Know what Mother said, that weekend you had to go to running practice?" Katie said after a while. "She said 'Home is where the heart is.'"

I rolled my eyes. I'd had so many homes in the last year that at first, Mother's words sounded ridiculous. But then I began to think about where my heart was. It was with Mother and Annie and the rabbits and the beautiful purplish-green mountains in Santa Paula, but it was also with Tim and Katie and Daniel, and even Isabel. My heart was in running with the cross-country team and writing poetry in English class.

So maybe it would be three years before I could move in with Mother. Maybe I'd have to stay with Daddy and deal with his yelling and Elsa's meanness until I was old enough to drive up to Santa Paula. But at least I had friends and hobbies and a brother and sister I could laugh with. My heart was in all of these things, and nothing anyone could say would change that.

I clasped my hands against my heart and felt it beating steady and strong. Maybe Mother was right, after all. I'd found my home. Maybe it wasn't the best home in the world, but right now, it was the only home I had. Outside my window, a frog began its steady, musical creak.

"I've never heard frogs in Torrance," I said, walking

over to the window to peer out into the darkness.

Katie ran over to the window. "Last weekend, I caught two in Mother's yard and brought them back in a butter container."

Tim peered up over the windowsill. "I miss my mudder," he said and puffed out his cheeks like a frog.

"She'll be here in ten days." I hugged him tightly and reached out to squeeze Katie's hand. "Ten days is hardly any time at all."

About the Author

Melissa Hart Romero grew up in Southern California. She holds a B.A. degree in literature from the College of Creative Studies at the University of California, Santa Barbara, and an M.F.A. degree in creative writing from Goddard College in Plainfield, Vermont. She teaches literature and writing to high school and community college students. In her free time she runs, bikes, and relaxes with her husband, four cats and two dogs.

And Featuring Bailey Wellcom as the Biscuit

by Peggy Durbin
with artwork by Steve Feldman

When twelve-year-old Bailey Wellcom and her mom move to the sleepy town of Lucien, New Mexico, Bailey is convinced it's going to be Snore City. But soon after, Bailey meets Stevie Z., who quickly becomes her best friend. And her mom meets Melody Callahan, a local rancher.

Confused at first, Bailey, with the help of Stevie Z, Melody and mom, meets the challenges of finding her own special place in the world by confronting misconceptions and ignorance in those around her.

Excerpt from
And Featuring Bailey Wellcom as the Biscuit

Chapter 1. Wide Awake at 3:00 A.M.

I sure as heck didn't get much sleep that night. I kept trying to piece everything together, like it was a giant puzzle. Some things started to make sense to me—like how they looked at each other and how shy they were with each other at first. I started feeling really stupid and naive about it, if you want to know the truth. Why didn't I see it before? The way Melody looked at my mom and how they became friends so fast, the way they held each other after the manure fire, the quiet way they talked together. And now this. Kissing.

If you want to beat up on yourself and come to all kinds of terrible conclusions about yourself and be totally pitiful, do it at three o'clock in the morning. You can come up with a lot of stuff that's not true, but it makes a lot of sense then, and you may even start to believe it. I needed to talk with someone, but who? Stevie Z? I couldn't call without waking up everyone in the Zuñiga house. Melody? Yeah, right. Ordinarily I could call her any time, but this wasn't any old time. My dad?

My dad! He sometimes stayed up late watching an old movie and forgot to go to sleep. Maybe I'd luck out this time. I snuck downstairs and went into the kitchen and dialed his number. The phone rang about twenty times before I heard his voice, all sleepy and muffled. "This better be good."

"Dad? It's me. Bailey."

He seemed more alert. "Good grief, Bailey . . . all right? Are you all right?"

"Yeah. I gotta talk to you."

"What time . . . daylight savings time yet? Is your mother all right?"

"She's fine, Dad." I swallowed. "Dad, you gotta help me."

"Help . . . I need some help . . . light switch." I heard a scuffling sound in the background. "Can't find . . . ."

"DAD!" I said as loudly as I could without waking Mom.

"Are you in trouble? Hurt? Sick?" he asked.

"No, Dad, I'm fine. I just need to talk to you."

"Just a second," he said. "I have to find my glasses . . . can't hear . . . where are my . . . need my specs or I can't hear a thing." I heard some bumping around and rustling, and then he said, "Okay, Bailey. What's up?" He still sounded a little apprehensive, the way Mom did when she answered the phone for a rescue run late at night.

I told him the whole story—what I saw before supper and then backed up and told how Mom and Melody started out as shy friends and then became something more.

He was quiet, so quiet I thought he might have gone back to sleep.

"Dad?"

"Yes, Bailey Baby." He hadn't called me that in years, not since I was a little kid. It made me smile.

"Dad, what do you think?"

"The question is how you feel."

"I feel all confused and happy and scared and creepy."

"Well," he said gently, "go on. Tell me."

"Well, it's weird! Two women kissing. I knew they liked each other a lot, but, Dad, they were kissing!"

"How has your mother treated you in Lucien?" he asked. "Has anything changed?"

I sighed. I didn't seem to be getting anywhere. "No, nothing's changed. She still treats me nice, the way she always did."

"Has she changed?" he continued. "Is she still a good teacher?"

"Yeah."

"Does she do nice things for you, still treat you like an adult?"

"Yeah."

"Does she still do all those slightly goofy things she used to do, like make reservations at McDonald's?"

"Yeah, but now it's the Dairy Dee-Lite in Charleston."

"Well, Bailey, I'd say she hasn't changed. You just know more about her now. Now you know that she's in love with a woman and has told you in a way that she probably hadn't planned that she's a lesbian."

"Um . . . Dad . . . did you know more about her before we left Phoenix?"

There was a short silence on his end. "Yes, Bailey Baby. I did. We talked about it for a couple years before we split up. We thought we could handle it, go on living together, but we knew we couldn't."

Oh, man, I thought. Two years? I didn't know any of this, and they talked about it for two years. I was totally clueless. Where was my mind? Didn't I think or see anything at all. "Bailey? Are you there?" Dad asked.

"Yes, Dad."

"I know how you're feeling right now, Bailey Baby, because I've been there, too. I want you to listen to me. Your mother hasn't changed. She's not a different person. You just know more about her, like I told you. She's still smart and nice, and she loves you with all her heart."

"Dad . . . ."

"Call me a sensitive New Age kind of guy," he laughed. "I'm sorry you found out in such a startling way, and I think she should have told you earlier, but we all make our choices, and we have to live with them."

"So what am I going to do, Dad?" I was starting to cry.

"Well, for starters, you're not going to wipe your nose on the sleeve of your pajamas. We've been through that before." I laughed a little, because I was getting ready to do just that. I wiped my nose on a paper towel. "And second, you're going to be happy for your mom, because she has someone to love. And third, you're going to talk to her about everything that scares you or you wonder about or you think you might need to know. And fourth, you're going to go back to bed, because you can't think clearly if you haven't slept."

I sniffled. "Okay, Dad. Thanks."

"I love you, Bailey Baby."

"I love you, Daddy." I heard a soft click on the other end of the line. As I turned off the kitchen light and started up the stairs, the oddest thought hit me: Dad spoke in complete sentences the whole time, and everything seemed to make sense.I still couldn't sleep, though, and I was getting weird. After thinking about Mom and Melody until about four, I started to think about me and how I was all neglected. I started to feel pathetic and sorry for myself.

It had all seemed so easy. Moving from Phoenix to Lucien, being friends with Stevie Z, being friends with Melody. But it wasn't easy any more. Now I had to figure out what to do. I had loved it here in Lucien, and now I was nowhere. I thought if maybe I remembered everything that had happened, I could piece it all back together and make some sense out of it.

For information on how to order this title, please see the catalogue information on the following pages.

Other Windstorm Creative Titles
You Might Enjoy

And Featuring Bailey Wellcom as the Biscuit by Peggy Durbin. When twelve-year-old Bailey and her mom move to the sleepy town of Lucien, New Mexico, Bailey is sure her life is going to be dull. But then they meet cattlewoman Melody Callahan, and things get really interesting, for Bailey *and* her mom! Illustrated by Steve Feldman.
ISBN: 1-886383-88-X   Price: $12.95

1001 Nights: Exotica by Cris Newport. A multicultural cast highlights this collection of true-life inspired stories of erotic encounters between women. Illustrated with black and white drawings.
ISBN: 1-886383-82-0   Price: $12.95

Roses & Thorns by Chris Anne Wolfe. A beautiful and moving lesbian retelling of *The Beauty and the Beast*. Illustrated in the classic silhouette style.
ISBN: 1886383-64-2   Price: $12.95

Driftwood by Beth Mitchum. A chance encounter on an Oregon beach takes Rita's life in a direction she'd never expected. A classic story of awakening.
ISBN: 1-883573-19-X   Price: $12.95

Annabel and I by Chris Anne Wolfe. Annabel's world is of the 1880s and Jenny-wren's the 1980s. The magic of Lake Chautauqua brings them together, bridging two very different worlds. Illustrated with enchanting pen and ink drawings.
ISBN: 1886383-17-0   Price: $10.95

Keeper of the Piece by Lesley Davis. When Dr. Lorrah Glidden is sent to enlist Tate Bellum's help in finding a rare plant, Tate is less than enthusiastic but reluctantly agrees. As the winter bears down upon, the two women race against time, undergoing a dangerous journey neither might survive.
ISBN 1-886383-70-7   Price: $12.95

Sparks Might Fly by Cris Newport. Classically trained pianist Pip Martin was a child prodigy. But the disastrous ending to a passionate love affair has made Pip unable to play a single note. Canceling a lucrative European tour, Pip returns to Boston, never suspecting that love will find her there.

ISBN: 0-934678-61-8   Price: $9.95

1000 Reasons You Might Think She is My Lover by Angela Costa. One thousand spicy poems to share with someone you love.

ISBN: 1-886383-21-9   Price: $10.95

talking drums by Jan Bevilacqua. A collection of erotic, groundbreaking poems.

ISBN: 1-886383-13-8   Price: $9.95

Signs of Love by Leslea Newman. First released in two volumes, this moving collection of poetry chronicles the author's moving journey from childhood to adulthood.

ISBN: 1-886383-45-6   Price: $12.95

Visit Windstorm Creative Limited's web site for more titles at great prices in all genres.
www.windstormcreative.com
Direct purchases receive an automatic 20% discount.

About this Book

The book you're holding is handmade, something quite rare in this day and age. All of Windstorm Creative Limited's titles are printed, bound and trimmed by hand using an environmental-friendly process. Discrepancies in the depth of margins, even with the book, are quite normal. All our books are made to order.